An Act Quite Easy

By Isabel Herridge

For the two loves in my life

John and Sophie Rose

Table of Contents

Prologue

The boy was caught in the reeds at the edge of the water. There was a large gash on the side of his head, bruises on his thighs and upper arms, and a small bite mark on his left hand. The little girl sat crossed-legged on the ground beside him, staring intently at his face, eerily fascinated as the blood slowly oozed over his left eye from the open wound on his forehead. Smiling, she leaned forward and pushed his head under the water, mesmerized by the bubbles erupting from his final breath. She then stood up and calmly walked out of the woods towards home.

"Murder, in the murderer, is no such ruinous thought as poets and romancers will have it. It does not unsettle him. It is an act quite easy to be contemplated."

Ralph Waldo Emerson.

Part 1

Chapter 1

I stood at the window of my office in chambers sipping my coffee — black, no sugar — while looking out at the courtyard covered in a dusting of snow. It was late afternoon, and the nights were drawing in, but my office felt so cozy. The electric fire at the back of the room emitted a warm glow as I turned on the standard lamp in the corner. All the offices have mahogany bookshelves mainly stacked with legal books, and mine had just enough space for my two lithographs with sketches of these chambers. A very dear friend gave them to me when I started working here many years ago. I don't believe in displaying photographs or knick-knacks that could persuade a possible client I was anything other than a professional barrister. There is nothing in the room that implies I have any personal life. I am well aware it could be used as a way to initiate a friendly conversation, and I never plan on making friends with any of my clients.

My goodness, but it did look cold out there. Could I face freezing to death to have a much-needed cigarette? I have very few bad habits, but smoking is the worst. Shopping is another, particularly shoes. At my age, tottering about in a pair of fuck-me stiletto heels may be ridiculous, but until I fall over and break an ankle, I shall continue to buy them, and I shall continue to totter into court in them. However, I wouldn't have many more opportunities to wear them as I was considering retiring if an interesting case didn't appear on my desk soon.

During my long, and may I say successful career, I'd built a solid reputation for defending some of the most despicable characters from London's underbelly by using my gift for inserting enough doubt of my client's guilt that most juries had no option but to acquit them. But at the same time, I've been lauded for my pro-bono work with the victims of the most egregious human rights violations. So, while the fame and fortune of Chambers were boosted by my work with said unsavoury individuals, my pro-bono work resulted in my taking silk and becoming a Queen's Counsel.

And so, if no other case materialized, I would happily disappear to my house in the country and complete my book — a semi-autobiographical novel based primarily on my life as a barrister. There were so many stories to tell from my years working in the legal profession, and I might add, that there were a few juicy additions from my private life.

I was brought back to earth by a knock on the door.

Amanda, my PA, poked her head in, "Sorry to interrupt Mrs. German-Brown, but a woman on the phone says she would like to speak to Peggy German-Brown. She sounds very agitated."

Ugh, I despise the name 'Peggy.' It's what I was called as a child. As a barrister working in London, I prefer my given name 'Margaret.'

"Did she give a name, Amanda?"

"Yes, Nicola Smith. Apparently, you know her mother."

Indeed, I did know her mother. She and I grew up in a village in the Midlands called Lower Naughton. I asked Amanda to put her through and then picked up my phone.

"Hello, Nicola. What can I do for you?" The call had piqued my interest.

"Hello, Mrs. German-Brown. Thank you for agreeing to speak to me. My mother is Sarah Slater; she said you two know each other. I don't know if you have heard, but Mum has been arrested and accused of the murders of my grandmother and my father." At this, her voice broke, and she sobbed quietly. I remained silent until she had regained her composure and could continue.

"My sister, Jennifer, and I had no idea who to turn to, but Mum suggested I contact you. She is in such a state. I don't know how she'll survive this. Mum is usually such a strong woman. Everyone goes to her for advice and help, but now she's the one in need of help. She said you were highly regarded as a barrister, which she said was quite an achievement, considering where you'd come from."

I frowned. Was that a dig at my past?

Nicola continued, "I did a little research into your background and found that you have defended some quite renowned criminals. I'm not saying Mum's a criminal, absolutely not. She wouldn't hurt a fly. But I read that you have an innate ability to persuade even the most hesitant of juries of your client's innocence or, at the very least, leave the jury with enough doubt that it would be impossible to find them guilty."

I smiled to myself. It sounded as if Nicola was quoting verbatim from my listing on Wikipedia. It was ironic. Nicola's grandmother, Elizabeth Weston, who Sarah was accused of murdering, always thought of me as 'common,' someone not to be trusted, a bit of a ne'er do well. And yet, there I was, possibly about to stand up in court and persuade a jury that Sarah had not killed her mother. Now, I probably shouldn't say this, but if I'm being honest, I really did not like the old woman. But that is what makes this case so interesting: I assume somebody else must not have liked her!

I explained to Nicola that she would have to speak to her mother's solicitor as we would need to work together on the case. Nicola said it was a chap from Burton-upon-Trent, close to Lower Naughton, where Mrs. Weston, her grandmother, lived. His name was James Williamson. I'd never heard of him, so I asked her to give me his contact details. I would talk to him and offer my services. If he agreed for me to take the case to trial — not that he would have much choice — I would do my utmost to prove my old friend's innocence. After hopefully convincing Nicola that all would be well for her mother, we hung up.

So, two of the six children who were my closest friends at primary school have now died, but not from old age — Murdered!

And the mother of another of those friends can also be added to that macabre list.

I put on my coat and went outside for my well-earned cigarette. It looked like my retirement and book would be on hold for a while longer. Not that I minded. The trial should be an exciting conclusion to my career — and it was going to be a *doozy!*

Chapter 2

On the first day of the trial, I woke feeling extremely confident that my courtroom skills would prevail. I was sure my client, Sarah Slater, was innocent of the two murders. Most of the evidence in the trial was circumstantial, so I was optimistic I could prevent Sarah from spending many more days in jail. All I needed to do was present Sarah's side in as sympathetic a manner as possible and to sow sufficient doubt of her guilt in the jury's mind. After all, wasn't I jokingly known in Chambers as 'The Queen of Reasonable Doubt '? Admittedly, an acquittal would raise a disquieting question — If not Sarah, then who?

I made myself a cup of tea and read the headlines from the Times, which had just landed on the mat in the hall with a loud thump. Then, always particular about how I was perceived, I carefully pulled my hair up into a chignon and applied my makeup with my usual finesse, but instead of my normal pale pink lipstick, I chose a dramatic Chanel Rouge Allure red. I dressed in my bog-standard uniform of a crisp white shirt and black knee-length pencil skirt, but as it was going to be my last, and hopefully news-worthy, court case, I had splurged on a pair of black suede Jimmy Choo high-heeled pumps, which I wore with sheer black stockings. Although my barrister's gown would cover most of my clothes, I wanted to look poised and confident and, even if it was only from my knees down, just a little bit sexy. I fed Rocco, my affectionate, although at times, grouchy old black cat, and told him to wish me luck as I headed out the front door to catch the train into London.

Finding a seat in the first-class carriage, I settled down to read the rest of my newspaper, but my mind started wandering and questioning why I enjoyed this job.

A big one for tradition, I had always enjoyed the process at the start of a new case, which usually began when the all-powerful clerk of the chambers assigned the brief. We barristers always hoped to be given a demanding and thought-provoking one. There is something about receiving each legal brief and the act of untying the pink tape with the knowledge that nothing about the process has ever changed. That physical action is a part of history — it has been done that way since the 1780s. No sending over a URL for a website with a list of cases and a memory stick with all the supporting documentation — no, this procedure, this simple routine, is irreplaceable, and long may it continue.

After reading the brief for the first time, the barrister mentally works out how to proceed. In the case of a homicide, there are two critical forensic factors to consider: the last minutes of the victim's life and the first minutes after their death. Most often, this is what the autopsy reveals: how the victim died, and what happened to the body immediately afterward?

It's only after all the detail work is completed: the investigation, the correspondence, the witnesses interviewed, the alibis checked, and with the doubt still lingering, that suddenly a light bulb flashes, and what follows is the certainty that, yes, you've got it nailed. Then comes the anticipation of the trial. This is where the theatre occurs, the most extraordinary theatre in the land, the legal drama. The thrill of the contest between the prosecuting barrister and the defending barrister, each acting their parts, not unlike a Shakespeare play. Who has the edge? Who has that one piece of evidence that will sway the jury? Finally, the satisfaction when, with luck and perseverance and a few prayers from the defendant and their family, the defending barrister, in this case, the illustrious Margaret German-Brown — myself, wins an acquittal.

I still felt butterflies in my stomach whenever I walked up the steps into a courthouse at the beginning of a new trial, and Sarah Slater's trial would be extremely challenging as it involved people I had known almost all my life. I wasn't sure how they would feel after I had forced them to submit to some very awkward questioning, but truth be told, I didn't really care. I would never have to see them again once the trial was over. Without exception, there wasn't one of them I considered a real friend.

After putting on my wig and gown, I spotted Hywell Gryfidd-Jones QC, the barrister for the prosecution, an eminence grise in the profession. He was already robed and prepared for battle as he strode across the lobby, always an impressive figure with his imposing height, barrel chest, and grey flowing hair, displaying, in his inimitable way, an air of confidence and superiority. I caught up with him, and we wished each other well — as always. We have been friends for many years. Hywell's wife Camille and I would sometimes go to the theatre together. Camille, a highly respected clinical psychologist, could often be found seated at the back of the court, viewing the proceedings, ready to critique Hywell's performance later at home.

I told him I'd found a delicious new recipe; scallops and prosciutto, that I wanted to try out, so our regular after-trial, post-mortem dinner would need to be at my house. Then, pleasantries over, it was time to compose ourselves in readiness for Day One of the big event. Hywell confidently expressed his opinion that it was basically an open and shut case and should be over reasonably swiftly, as it was evident that my client was 'guilty as sin.'

"Don't you be so sure," I responded, smiling.

We walked across to the staircase that wound its way up to the courtrooms. It is so impressive with its wide steps, built from Sicilian marble, and its black, wrought iron banister. The walls that curved alongside the staircase contained magnificent stained glass windows. We started to climb, Hywell towards what he saw as an easy win and me towards the potential crowning glory of my career. At the top of the stairs, I entered the courtroom and looked around, absorbing the majestic dignity of the room with its impressive high ceilings with their sturdy wooden beams, and dark oak-panelled walls. On one of the walls hung several large portraits of distinguished men, including the Duke of Wellington — not one woman among them. The raised platform at the front of the courtroom with the judge's bench had the Royal Coat of Arms behind it. The courtroom clock was enclosed in a handsome wooden surround and was purposely positioned to be easily seen by the judge. It was impossible not to appreciate the history of the Court and the many trials that preceded this one. What tales these walls could tell, and now this trial, my swan song, would be absorbed into that history. It suddenly hit me this trial would be the last opportunity I would have to enjoy that magnificent building as a player.

As I sat down, I looked over as Sarah was brought up the narrow, concrete stairs from the cells below with handcuffs on her wrists. She wore a light grey suit with a black crew-neck sweater underneath. The pearls around her neck were a nice touch; they gave a look of confidence, which, unfortunately, she wasn't portraying in any other sense. As the guard escorted her into the dock, I gave her what I hoped was an encouraging smile. She looked forlorn, staring down at her hands, which were shaking with nerves. I suppose I should have felt sorry for her, but sympathy didn't win cases; only my competence could achieve that.

I sincerely intended to do my level best to convince the jury that Sarah was innocent as I knew her to be a devoted wife who had loved her husband and wouldn't have harmed a hair on his head. She also thought the world of her admittedly overbearing mother. All I could do was hope and pray the jury would look on her with compassion and would see that two such savage crimes could not possibly have been perpetrated by someone as thoughtful and caring as Sarah Slater.

The judge, Lord Justice Stanfield, known affectionately in legal circles as 'the mutterer' for his habit of constantly mumbling to himself, made his way to the bench as the courtroom stood. He looked across at Hywell and me, inclining his head to acknowledge our presence, and we both nodded.

Sarah, meanwhile, kept looking down the whole time, almost as if she had already given up. It wasn't a look I wanted the jury to see. I really should have warned her to sit up straight and look confident. I gave a cursory glance around the Court and saw Jennifer, Sarah's older daughter, in a pew near the back of the Court. I nodded to her and tried to look encouraging, but I could see the panic in her eyes despite her half-hearted smile.

The judge spoke directly to the jury, describing the process they were about to undertake.

"There is one basic principle in a court of law, and it is of the utmost importance," he explained,

"And that is the presumption of a person's innocence until proven guilty. It dates back to the Magna Carta and is one of the fundamental tenets of the law. Guilt must be established beyond any reasonable doubt. Jurors must put aside their own prejudices in order to give the defendant a fair trial. The evidence being presented should be listened to and reviewed without bias. Only then can you make an informed decision as to whether the defendant is guilty or not."

The judge emphasized that the jurors must base their decision solely on the evidence provided, not on anything they may have heard elsewhere, nor their own interpretation of the law. He introduced the prosecutor, the Honorable Hywell Gryfidd-Jones QC, and asked him to give his opening statement.

Hywell stood up and walked towards the jury and, in his mellifluous Welsh baritone, said:

"Ladies and gentlemen of the jury, good morning. I would also like to introduce my learned friend Margaret German-Brown QC, who will be acting for the defence throughout this trial. I intend to prove to you, without a shadow of a doubt, that the defendant, Sarah Elizabeth Slater, who stands before you today accused of two brutal murders, is guilty on both counts.

"The first murder was that of her mother, Elizabeth Florence Weston, which occurred twelve months ago. The second murder was that of her husband, Richard Kevin Slater, which happened just six months ago.

"The defendant, Sarah Slater, is the headmistress of the primary school in the village of Lower Naughton in Staffordshire and, to all intents and purposes, a well-respected member of her community. However, I intend to prove that her respectability is a cloak that conceals a heartless, scheming double murderer.

"First, I would like to describe the defendant's relationship with her mother. Mrs. Elizabeth Weston had a reputation in the village for being someone who relished being in charge, whether as the president of the local Women's Institute or as a member of the local parish council. In both instances, she could be relied upon to organize local volunteers with the skill of a drill sergeant; whether it be jumble sales or summer fetes, she would be there as the community liaison.

"This seemingly controlling behaviour was amplified in her treatment of her daughter, the defendant Sarah Slater. As an only child, her parents doted on her, treating her as a precious china doll, and as such, were understandably very protective of her. Unfortunately for the defendant, her mother's attitude toward her changed once she became an adult. Mrs. Weston went from being overly protective of her little girl to trying to dominate her life. Once the defendant was married, Mrs. Weston attempted to be even more manipulative. Now, she had competition for the defendant's time and affection. And instead of taking a backseat to the defendant's husband, as most mothers would, she continued to make more and more demands on her daughter's time and expected those demands to be addressed post haste. For example, the deceased once insisted the defendant return home early from a family holiday because she thought she was having a heart attack. The defendant rushed back to Lower Naughton only to find her mother at the hairdresser! When she asked her mother about the heart attack, she was told, dismissively, that it was nothing, just indigestion.

"Later, when Mrs. Weston was ill with cancer, she insisted that the defendant nurse her. She expected her daughter to take a leave of absence from her position as headmistress at the village school, leave her husband to fend for himself, and move in with her. The defendant's husband, Richard Slater, put his foot down about such a plan, claiming it could hurt his wife's career if not their own relationship. The defendant, in an attempt to mollify both her husband and mother, offered to pay for a carer to go to the house and tend to her mother's needs. To begin with, her mother

18

refused the offer, saying she didn't want strangers in her house, 'and besides, that is what daughters are expected to do.' But in the end, she relented and agreed to a part-time carer."

The prosecutor sounded almost sympathetic towards Sarah when he continued:

"How difficult it must have been for the defendant to run a household, hold down an important job as headmistress, and yet still be expected to drop everything and run after her mother as and when she demanded it. But annoying as that must have been, it was no excuse for what she did." He paused dramatically. "Killing her mother in cold blood."

Those compelling final words removed all vestiges of sympathy from his tone, and it was clear he intended to go hard after my client.

"The prosecution intends to prove that on the fateful day Elizabeth Weston died, the defendant had reached the limit of her patience. That morning, her mother phoned the defendant, insisting that she go to the local shop and buy milk and biscuits for a coffee morning she was hosting for her next-door neighbor. She told her it was urgent as she needed those items by eleven o'clock. It may have seemed urgent to her mother, but that was not how the defendant saw it. She had to prepare for an important School Board meeting that morning and certainly did not have time to leave school, go to the shop, and drop the items off at her mother's house by eleven. However, knowing how upset her mother would be, she said she would try. Phone records show that the phone call came into the defendant's house at 8:30 from the house belonging to her mother, Mrs. Weston. The defendant maintains that her husband, Richard Slater, had already left for work, so she was alone in the house.

"According to her story, she left the house right after that phone call and drove straight to the school, conveniently not seeing anyone on the way there or when she arrived. As she tells it, the teachers were either in the playground supervising the children or in the teacher's lounge. She told the police that she rang her husband on his mobile when she arrived at school, but the phone records confirmed that he did not answer. Fortuitously, for the defendant's story, though, he is also now dead, so we cannot question him about his timeline that morning.

"We do know the defendant went to the board meeting. We also know she had a bandage on her left hand. She said it was caused by slicing bread for toast that morning, but once again, the only witness to her cutting her hand was her husband, who is no longer with us. That morning was especially taxing for the defendant as the reason for the board meeting was to fight for a significant sum of money to build an extension onto the school's auditorium. With the stress of the looming board meeting and her mother demanding she urgently run what, to the defendant, must have appeared to be a pretty minor errand, the defendant was not having a good morning.

"And so I put it to you that in a fit of anger and frustration, she went to her mother's house on the way to school that morning and murdered Mrs. Weston in an indescribably vicious attack, stabbing her repeatedly and accidentally

"Once ensconced at a table, they spent a couple of pleasant hours chatting, enjoying their meals and several alcoholic drinks. After parting ways with their friend, the defendant announced that a bit more shopping might be a good idea, to which Mr. Slater agreed, but only after they had enjoyed another drink in one of the pubs nearby. Unfortunately, as they left the pub, Mr. Slater started to feel unwell, and a decision was made to take a taxi back to their daughter's home. Once he arrived at his daughter's house, Mr. Slater collapsed, and an ambulance was called. He was taken to hospital, where he died later that evening of a presumed heart attack. However, the post-mortem revealed he had been poisoned. The only person with him for every meal he ate and, by implication, with the most opportunities for administering it was his wife, the defendant, Sarah Slater.

"A key issue here, ladies and gentlemen, is that the defendant studied chemistry in college when working toward her teacher training credit. Interestingly, her final term paper was titled 'Poisons in Everyday Life.' I'm sure when Mrs. Slater took that course, she had no idea how advantageous that knowledge would be in her future."

Hywell continued with a final, highly theatrical flourish, "The defendant decided that her marriage to Mr. Slater was no longer what she wanted or needed. Her children were grown, she had rid herself of her demanding mother, and she wished to have the freedom to enjoy the rest of her life on her own terms. To achieve that, she simply needed to dispose of her husband as well. Divorce was out of the question. It was too expensive, and she was looking forward to enjoying the fruits of her inheritance after her mother's death. She had no intention of sharing them with a man she could no longer respect. She saw killing him as the solution to her problem. The question was how to make his death appear to be from natural causes. Utilizing her knowledge of poisons, she chose the one that caused symptoms usually indistinguishable from those of a heart attack: Thallium Sulphate.

"I intend to prove to the court that the defendant is a selfish, manipulative, and greedy woman. She perpetrated these most egregious crimes in order to benefit from the removal of both her husband and mother and, therefore, she must be found guilty on both counts of murder."

Hywell looked across the court in my direction with a hint of a sympathetically wry smile as he walked back to his seat and said in his broad Welsh accent:

"My learned colleague, the Honorable Margaret German-Brown QC, will now present the case for the defence."

It was my turn to lay out the case I had so painstakingly developed. Much of Hywell's opening statement had been pure conjecture. However, I still had to convince the jury that Sarah did not want her mother or husband dead. I intended to begin by building a picture of Sarah's character and close relationships with her mother and Richard. Rising to my feet, I took a deep breath in preparation for the final opening remarks of my career.

"Ladies and gentlemen of the jury, my learned friend has given you his fanciful version of the events that led to the deaths of Elizabeth Weston and Richard Slater. My client, the defendant, Sarah Slater, is accused of murdering both her mother and husband. Now, I would like to share with you the true version. I intend to prove that the defendant was not capable of committing such appalling crimes.

"The defendant and her mother had always had a close relationship. She was, in fact, adamant when she married Richard Slater that they settled in Lower Naughton in order to be near her parents. This became especially important when her father died, and her mother needed her support. The defendant was an only child, and so the responsibility fell on her shoulders to look after her mother during that traumatic time. It was an obligation she willingly took on as their relationship was much more than most mothers and daughters — they were more like the closest friends.

"Mrs. Slater's position as headmistress at the local primary school enabled her to become acquainted with the majority of families in the village as either they or their children attended the school at some point in their lives. She is well thought of and admired and, over the years, has gained their trust. They know she will always take care of their little ones. Does that sound like someone who would murder anyone, especially their own mother? You will hear from friends, colleagues, and acquaintances of the defendant who have known her and her mother for many years and can testify to their affectionate and warm relationship. And you will hear from witnesses who will throw doubt on whether the defendant was anywhere near her mother's house at the time she was murdered.

"As to the murder of her husband, Richard Slater, they were a devoted couple, married for over thirty years. They loved to spend time together hiking in the Dales with their dog Malcolm. Each morning before they went to work, they took turns bringing each other tea in bed before eating breakfast together and sharing a kiss goodbye with a genuine wish that each had a good day. After work, they enjoyed a glass of wine with dinner, during which time they shared stories of their day. Throughout their married life, they supported each other through the ups and downs of their careers. That hardly sounds like a couple who didn't care about each other, does it? Yes, they had some disagreements over the years, but who among us in this room today hasn't had a difference of opinion with our significant other?

"The day Richard Slater died, they spent together in London enjoying a day shopping, having lunch and a few drinks with an old friend on Oxford Street. During the afternoon, Mr. Slater became ill, and the defendant, frightened she was going to lose him, never left his side. He was her rock. He was always there for her, and she was always there for him. I will prove to you that Sarah Slater certainly did not want her husband dead, and I will provide several other explanations for his sad demise. In the interest of full disclosure, My Lord, I need to make it known to the court that many of the individuals involved in this case are known to me personally. Also, you will hear testimony of Mr. and Mrs. Slater having lunch with an old friend on the day of Mr. Slater's death. I was that old friend, My Lord. I have already advised my learned friend, Mr. Gryfidd-Jones, of these issues, and he has no objection.

With that, I wrapped up my opening statement with a warm, friendly smile that I aimed squarely at the jury.

After a brief recess, Hywell launched into the case for the prosecution, starting with the murder of Sarah's mother. His first witness, Mrs. Weston's next-door neighbour, Ethel Woods, was called to the stand. I had previously talked to the old lady myself and found her extremely annoying — she was prone to veer off the subject at hand and start rambling on about something entirely unrelated. She was also hard of hearing, and her hearing aid was far from reliable, which added to her confusion. Apart from that, she was a lovely old lady — if you like that kind of thing.

As she painstakingly made her way to the witness box, pushing her clattering walking frame, her glasses on their gold chain around her neck banging against her bony chest, I noticed a distinct odor of mothballs as she passed me. Her clothes had seen better days, especially the food-stained old woolly cardigan and decidedly wrinkled grey skirt she wore that day. The judge indicated to the security guard to help her and take care of the frame.

Once she was finally installed in the witness box and had sworn to tell the truth, Hywell's voice took on a gently coaxing tone.

"Mrs. Woods, would you please tell the court how you knew the deceased, Elizabeth Weston?

"Yes sir, I lived next door to Elizabeth. I mean, Mrs. Weston. My late husband, Jack, and I lived next door to Mr. and Mrs. Weston for over fifty years. We were married for fifty-five years until his death five years ago. He had a heart attack, you know, very sudden it was. Unfortunately, we could never have children of our own, which is why I felt so close to Sarah, Mrs. Weston's daughter, having watched her grow up. My Jack had been the managing director of a company that manufactured parts for Rover cars, and we had enjoyed a comfortable life, going to Spain for our summer holidays. My husband and Mr. Weston were members of the local Rotary and Masonic lodge, you know." She added proudly.

I had no idea where Mrs. Woods was going with her meandering tale, and, glancing over at the jury box, I saw some jurors smirking while others looked entirely bewildered. Mrs. Woods, oblivious to the reaction from the jury, continued:

"Before my husband died and then Mr. Weston's untimely death in a car accident, the four of us were very close friends for many years. In fact, Elizabeth and I continue to be, I mean were, best friends."

The old lady let out a sob and reached for a distinctly grubby handkerchief, which had been tucked up the sleeve of her cardigan. She blew her nose loudly and wiped her eyes. I feared there was a danger Mrs. Woods could veer further off the question and share her entire life story.

The judge looked down at her. "Would you like to take a moment, Mrs. Woods?" he asked kindly.

She looked up at him. "No, thank you, sir. I'm terribly sorry about that, but sometimes it still affects me. I still miss her, you see. It's quite lonely for me without her, but I'm fine. We can carry on."

As she took a deep breath, Hywell took advantage of the brief pause, and knowing there was a serious possibility of losing the jurors' attention, he leaped in with his next question.

"Mrs. Woods, could you please tell the jury what happened on the morning of Tuesday, April 30th."

"Yes, sir, I was in my kitchen washing up my breakfast things. I knew it was a Tuesday as I always make myself a boiled egg with brown bread toast on Tuesdays, and I was washing up the egg cup. It wasn't worth putting the breakfast things into the dishwasher as there was only a plate, the egg cup, and my cup and saucer."

For God's sake, woman, just answer the bloody question. We don't care about your boiled egg.

"I had just reached for the tea towel when I heard what sounded like a scream. It was quite loud because I had just put my hearing aid in and hadn't adjusted the volume. I finished the drying and was putting everything away when I heard a door slam. I thought I'd better look out the front door and see if anything was going on. It took me quite a long time to walk from the back of the house to the front that day because the arthritis in my knees was playing up, and I needed to use my Zimmer frame to lean on. Once I got to the front door and opened it, I saw a car disappearing down the road."

"Mrs. Woods, would you please describe for the jury what type of car it was?"

"Yes, sir, I'll try, but all I can really remember is the colour. Red."

"And did you recognize the car?"

Mrs. Woods, looking a bit concerned, replied, "Sarah, uh, Mrs. Slater has a red car, and I assumed it must have been her taking her mother out."

"Mrs. Woods, you said you heard screaming. Were you concerned about the screaming? Did you ring anyone else to find out if they had heard it?"

"No, sir, I did think about it, but I decided that, as it had stopped, I had probably misheard and assumed I had heard a cat or some sort of animal. My hearing aid plays up sometimes. If I haven't put it in properly, it can distort some sounds. I remember once hearing a marching band. Quite distinct it was, but when I mentioned it to my late husband, he said I was being ridiculous. Why would there be a marching band outside our house?"

"But Mrs. Woods, what about the door slamming?" Hywell pressed on, ignoring her latest tangent.

"I assumed it was Mrs. Weston leaving the house and the wind blowing the front door shut."

"Mrs. Woods, did Mrs. Weston ever talk about her relationship with her daughter Sarah?"

"Oh yes, sir, she often complained about how ungrateful Sarah was and how she felt abandoned since her daughter married Mr. Slater. Of course, I said, 'Surely not,' as Sarah was always willing to help out, but Elizabeth begged to differ. She always liked to complain about Sarah." Mrs. Woods looked across at Sarah and smiled at her.

"Did you notice if this criticism of the defendant by her mother upset her?"

"Well, I did notice a few times that Sarah, I mean the defendant, would complain to her mother that she wasn't being fair, that she was doing her best, and sometimes she appeared to be quite angry about it."

"I have no further questions of this witness, My Lord." Hywell took his seat, looking confident.

I stood up and walked over to the witness box.

"Mrs. Woods, good morning. Could you please tell the court how often you and Mrs. Weston saw each other?"

"Yes, dear."

How infuriating, so condescending, calling me 'dear,' while good old Hywell warranted a 'sir,'' but I contained my anger and let her continue.

"We saw each other most days. We liked to have our morning coffee together, taking it in turns to be the host. It was nice to chat about what's happening in the world over a cup of coffee and a biscuit. And once a week, we went into Burton to do our shopping. Unfortunately, my eyesight isn't as good as it used to be, so Elizabeth, Mrs. Weston, did the driving, though since she had been ill, Sarah was kind enough to drive us. So yes, we saw each other a lot, although the last two months before she died, it had been less often as Mrs. Weston was so ill with the cancer."

Her voice dropped to a whisper as she said the forbidden C-word as if it were impolite to mention it in public.

"Mrs. Woods, were you intending to see each other the morning she died?"

"Oh yes, we'd planned to have coffee at Elizabeth's house. At eleven o'clock, I pulled on my cardigan and a jacket because, even though it was April and the sun was shining, there was still a bite in the air. I move so slowly these days, so I need a little bit of extra warmth; plus, Elizabeth's house was never very warm. She was very thrifty when it came to the central heating, if you know what I mean."

She glanced over at Sarah, looking a little embarrassed.

"Anyway, I picked up my keys and went out the front door with my frame, down the driveway, through the front gate along the pavement, and up the driveway to Elizabeth's front door. I rang the bell several times, but nobody answered. I thought it very strange she wasn't there because I'd looked at my calendar, I keep it hanging on the wall in the pantry, to check if the coffee was at her place. Then I remembered I'd seen Sarah's car heading off down the road earlier, so I assumed the two of them had gone out and hadn't returned yet. That meant I had to walk all the way back to my house, which may not seem far to you, but with my arthritis so bad and anyway, you'd think she could have rung to apologize."

"Mrs. Woods, did you see any other cars coming and going that day besides the ambulances and police cars?"

"Yes, dear, I did see the red car was back a bit later, just before I heard another scream, so I assumed that Sarah and her mother were home. I don't remember seeing any other

34

cars in Mrs. Weston's driveway, and I remember checking several times to see if they were back. I thought it was too late for coffee, and anyway, I was getting my lunch ready, which was a nice bowl of tomato soup, some crunchy bread, and a glass of lemonade. I was listening to the radio, BBC 2 with Jeremy Vine. I love his programs — such interesting topics, don't you think?"

Oh, for God's sake, woman, focus! I was doing my best to keep Mrs. Woods from going off on a tangent, but my patience was wearing thin. "Mrs. Woods, let's go back to the morning in question. Do you have any idea what time it was when you heard the first scream?"

"Unfortunately, I'm not sure. I have tried to think what time it would have been as I was doing the washing up as I told the nice young man from the police. I can only assume it was sometime around nine o'clock, maybe a bit earlier. In fact, the only thing I remember that day apart from the screams was the sirens blaring as the police cars and the ambulance came flying up the road."

"And do you know what time that was?"

"The policeman arrived at a quarter past twelve. Of that, I am certain because I looked at my watch when I heard the sirens."

"And you said you saw the red car was back outside Mrs. Weston's house?"

"Yes, I went back outside, and I saw Sarah on the front drive. She looked like she was crying. Admittedly, I didn't have my glasses on, but it looked like she had a handkerchief up to her face. I shouted across to her, 'Are you alright, dear,' I said. She shook her head, and at that point, I heard more sirens, and a police car came up the road, its blue lights flashing. I looked across the road and saw Jean Harper in her front garden, and she waved and pointed at the police car. I shouted back that I didn't know what was going on. Anyway, the policeman got out of his car and put on one of those yellow jackets like you see them wearing on the television, so you know he meant business. Then he came up Elizabeth's driveway and walked up to Sarah. She said something I couldn't hear. He pulled those blue paper shoe things out of his pocket and put them on over his shoes and a pair of rubber gloves, and they went inside. I waited a bit longer, and the policeman came out of the house and was sick in the bushes in front of Elizabeth's house. Quite disgusting, really. I shouted to him, but he ignored me and pulled out a phone to make a call, so I gave up and went back inside."

"So, Mrs. Woods, if I may summarize, you have told the jury that you no longer drive because of your poor eyesight, and you depend on your glasses to see clearly. You stated you weren't even positive if Sarah was holding a handkerchief when you saw her on the driveway waiting for the policeman. As for your hearing, it is so impaired that you depend on a not altogether reliable hearing aid, is that correct?"

"Yes, dear." She smiled benignly, seemingly unaware I was tearing holes in her testimony.

"You think you saw Sarah's car outside Mrs. Weston's house sometime around nine o'clock, but all you could really be

36

sure of is that it was a red car. You thought you heard a scream but admitted it could have been a cat. Is there anything else you can think of that could help us establish that it was Sarah that you think you saw that morning?" I leaned confidently on the carved oak balustrade in front of the jury box.

"Um, no, I don't think so, dear."

"Thank you, Mrs. Woods. No further questions, My Lord."

The judge beckoned the guard to bring the walking frame over to the witness box and told Mrs. Woods that she could step down and return to the back of the Court. She was completely oblivious to the enormous assistance she had provided to my argument as I threw a smug nod toward Hywell, whose frown would have intimidated a less experienced opponent.

Hywell then called for Marge Blake, the owner of the village shop.

Mrs. Blake, a middle-aged, overweight matron, stood in the witness box looking serious until Hywell walked up to her and smiled. Mrs. Blake turned a bright shade of beetroot red.

After the usual identification and swearing of the oath, Hywell began.

"Mrs. Blake, would you please tell the court what your business is."

Looking around the courtroom, she proudly answered, "Yes, sir, I'm the proprietor of the village shop and cafe in Lower Naughton."

"Thank you, Mrs. Blake. Now, on the morning of April 30th, do you recall how many customers you had in your shop and if any of them are in this courtroom?" Again, she looked around the courtroom and smiled at a few members of the public she recognized. A number of nosy villagers had apparently made the trip from Lower Naughton to take in the exciting spectacle of one of their own on trial.

"Yes, I had twenty-three customers that morning. And yes, there are five of 'em in here today." She responded with an overpronounced 'H,' which only emphasized that her normal pronunciation would have been 'ere.'

"Would you be so kind as to point them out to the court? You needn't give their names; just point to them."

She pointed to a line of elderly women in the gallery who all sat up straight and smiled at the judge. She then pointed to Sarah.

"For the record, the witness pointed to the defendant," Hywell stated. "When you went to serve the defendant, how did she seem?"

"Well sir, to be honest with you, she looked a bit angry like. She were frowning when she come into the shop, and when she got 'er purse out to pay, 'er hands was shaking. Oh, and she 'ad a bandage on 'er 'and."

"Which hand was the bandage on?"

"'er left hand, sir."

"Did you say anything to her?"

"Well, yes, sir, I did. I says to her was she alright 'cause she don't look so good, and she says yes, she were fine, a bit gruff-like, and could she buy some biscuits, custard creams, I think she said, and a small carton of whole milk."

"Now, Mrs. Blake, would you have any recollection of the time that you served Mrs. Slater?"

"Yes, sir, it were shortly after eleven, and the reason I know is that while I were ringing up 'er groceries, I 'ad to stop to sign for a delivery of wine that was being dropped off. She, I mean the defendant, said that as she'd 'ad a very stressful morning, she could do with a glass of wine 'erself, and we laughed about it. I looked at 'er ' and asked 'er what 'ad 'appened, and she said she'd had a bit of a 'to-do' with 'er mother. And on top of that, she said she'd been slicing a loaf of bread for toast for 'er and 'er 'usband's breakfast and cut 'erself. I told 'er she needed to be more careful."

"Did the defendant say what the 'to-do' with her mother was about?" Hywell asked.

"I did ask 'er, but she said it were nothing; it were all sorted."

"Thank you, Mrs. Blake, for your time. No further questions, My Lord."

I decided not to pursue questioning Marge Blake as I rather hoped the jury would not pick up on the 'to-do' Sarah had mentioned. I didn't want them assuming it was now all sorted because she'd stabbed her mother to death. Letting sleeping dogs lie is sometimes the best way to go.

Hywell's next witness was the local hairdresser, Janet Richards, who had taken over the salon from my Aunty Bridget when she retired. She made her way up to the witness box, her high heels clicking as she walked, her dyed platinum blond hair in an impressive updo. Hywell stood up and walked over to her, smiling in that charming and disarming way he had when he wanted to win over a witness, and asked:

"Mrs. Richards, you own a hairdressing salon in the village of Lower Naughton, do you not?

"Yes, sir, I do," she answered, blushing.

"And you saw Mrs. Elizabeth Weston regularly, is that correct?"

"Yes, sir, she 'ad an appointment for every Friday morning," she confirmed in her strong Midlands drawl.

"Did you ever hear her talk about her daughter, Sarah Slater?"

"Yes, she talked to me other clients while I did 'er 'air. She were always complaining about how mean 'er daughter were 'nthat, and she were always too busy to help 'er. One of me other clients told me that Mrs. Weston told 'er that now she were sick with the cancer, you'd think 'er daughter'd be a bit more thoughtful. I thought she were a bit mean to say that 'cause Mrs. Slater were the headmistress of the school, so of course, she were busy. It's understandable that Mrs. Slater might have reached the end of 'er tether with 'er mum, isn't it?"

I leapt up. "Objection, your honour, much of this witness's testimony is hearsay."

"Sustained," said the judge. I sat back down, pleased with the judge's call but wary that this big-mouthed witness might lead the jury purely based on village gossip.

"Mrs. Richards, was yours the only hairdressing establishment in the village?" continued Hywell, unabashed by my objection.

"Yes, sir. I took it over when the other 'airdresser retired."

"And when was that?"

"Oh, about three years ago, sir."

"Mrs. Richards, can you tell the jury if you saw the defendant on April 30th?"

"Yes, sir, I seen 'er come out of the shop, and I ran over to ask 'er to come in a bit later for 'er 'air appointment that Friday."

"How did she seem to you?"

"Well, sir, I'd say she were a bit shook up, angry like. She weren't 'appy when I asked her."

"Did you, by chance, notice if she had a bandage on her hand?"

Looking very proud at her powers of observation, she responded, "Yes sir, she 'ad a bandage on 'er left 'and."

"Thank you, Mrs. Richards, no further questions, My Lord." Hywell shot me a confident look as he walked past and took his seat.

I had guessed that Hywell would bring up Sarah's bandaged hand as part of his case. Her solicitor had discussed it with her during one of their interviews, but I had asked Sarah about it and was fairly confident it was irrelevant. I also didn't need to hear any more of Janet Richard's unreliable gossip, and for the second time that morning, I was amazed that Hywell had called on such a dubious witness. The judge looked over at me to see if I wished to question Janet Richards, but I shook my head.

The next witness Hywell called was the first policeman on the scene, PC John Winger, a young man who had been on the force for a little over three years. It had been his first murder case. He stood in the witness box, looking a little nervous, but was ready with his small, blue, spiral-bound notebook.

"Officer, would you please tell the court what happened from the time the telephone call came in from Mrs. Slater until the Scene of Crime Officer arrived?"

Flicking back through his notebook, the constable replied, "At exactly 11:58 on the morning of April 30th, the call centre in Burton received an emergency phone call from the home of a Mrs. Elizabeth Weston. The caller was Sarah Slater, the daughter of the homeowner. When the call handler picked up the phone, Mrs. Slater shouted down the phone for help because she said her mother had been stabbed and that she needed the police and an ambulance quickly. The agent asked for the address and told her to stay where she was. He assured her that someone would be right there. He then told me to go straight over while he rang for an ambulance. Once I had surveyed the scene, I was to call straight back. I drove directly to the house as instructed."

"Officer, what time did you arrive on the scene?"

Looking in his notebook, he replied, "I arrived at the house at twelve-fifteen, sir. I had to drive there from the station in Burton."

Gryfidd-Jones then asked, "And who was there when you arrived?"

"A woman was at the front door waiting, looking very distraught." The constable replied. "She said she was the victim's daughter, Sarah Slater. She was crying hysterically, so it was difficult to understand what she said, but apparently, she had arrived at the house to see her mum. She went in the back door as usual and called out to her. When there was no answer, she assumed her mother was taking a nap upstairs. She told me she unpacked some groceries and started to put some things together for her mother's lunch. She then called out again, and still, there was no answer. Apparently, her mother was fighting cancer, so the defendant became concerned that she may have passed out. She said she ran up the stairs to her mother's bedroom and, when she entered the room, found her

43

mother on the floor in a pool of blood. She immediately rang emergency services, telling them she needed the police and an ambulance".

"And what did you do next?".

"After putting on the standard protective coverings, I went upstairs and into the bedroom. The victim was lying on the floor in a pool of blood. Blood was also splattered up the wall behind her. At this point, I ran back downstairs, rang the station, spoke to the sergeant on duty, and told him what I had found. He said an ambulance was on its way, and he would call the SOCO over and ring the coroner."

"Just to clarify, the SOCO, or Scene of Crime Officer, is a forensic specialist. Is that correct, Officer?"

"Yes, Sir."

"And did you have a chance to look around the body? Did you see if there was anything that could have been used as a weapon?"

"No, sir, I decided it would be better to stay out of the room as I didn't want to mess up the crime scene with my footprints or fingerprints, and instead, I secured the scene. I felt it best to wait for the experts."

Of course, he didn't stay to look for a weapon; he was downstairs throwing up in the bushes, according to Mrs. Woods. I smiled to myself.

Hywell continued questioning, "Did the defendant tell you why she was at her mother's house at that time of the day?

It was a school day, was it not, and surely she should have been at the school where she was the headmistress?"

I stood up. "Objection, that is a leading question, My Lord."

"Overruled. Please continue," muttered Justice Stanfield. I sat down, shaking my head.

Again, the constable looked at his notebook.

"Yes, sir; she told me she was there because she had received a phone call in the morning from her mother asking if she would mind going to the village shop near the school to pick up some stuff she needed. Her mother had said it was very urgent."

"One more question, officer, did you notice if the defendant had a bandage on her hand when you arrived?"

"Yes, sir, she had a bandage on her left hand."

"Thank you, officer. No further questions, My Lord."

"Mrs. German-Brown?"

This time, I did want to question the witness. I stood up and strode over to the witness box.

"Officer, did Mrs. Slater tell you anything when you came back downstairs after seeing her mother's body? Had she had an opportunity to check if anything was missing?"

"Yes, ma'am, she did say that Mrs. Weston's handbag, which was usually on her bedside table, wasn't there."

"And officer, did you notice if there were any cars parked on the driveway or on the road in front of the house?"

"Yes, I wrote it down in my notebook. A red Prius was parked in the driveway, but no other cars were parked on the road."

"Thank you, officer. No further questions, My Lord."

The next witness was Chief Inspector Waterstone, and Hywell launched into questioning him with his usual gusto.

"Chief Inspector, you attended at the Weston house, and you were there when the SOCO arrived. Is that correct?"

"Yes, sir."

"So you were there when they examined the room where the murder occurred?"

"Yes, sir."

"Would you describe what was found?"

"When I walked into the bedroom, the first thing I noticed was the large pool of blood on the carpet around the body and the large amount splattered up the wall."

"With that amount of blood, one would assume the perpetrator would have had blood on their clothes, is that correct?"

"Yes. The offender would normally have had blood on their clothes and shoes."

"So, Inspector, with that in mind, did you find any footprints or handprints?" asked Hywell.

"Yes, sir. We found one set of footprints in the bedroom."

"Only one set of footprints surely, with that quantity of blood, there would have been some sort of handprints or marks that the murderer left behind. Would that not normally have been the case?"

"Normally, yes, but all's that was found were the one set of footprints in the bedroom, and they were identified as belonging to the defendant. They matched the shoes she was wearing. Every inch of the bedroom was gone over, but there was no second set of footprints, handprints, bloody marks, nothing. Whoever did this must have been diligent in their efforts to leave no trace of themselves. There was no sign of blood being carried away from the bedroom on any other shoes or items."

"Can you explain the lack of blood on the defendant?"

"Well, sir, she might have changed her clothes, and the original clothes she wore when she killed her mother were discarded," Waterstone claimed.

I stood up again, "Objection, my Lord, that is a presumption."

"Sustained." Justice Stanfield looked at Hywell.

Hywell continued, "So, assuming you are correct, and Sarah Slater changed her clothes, did you look for any items of clothing in the dustbin at Mrs. Weston's house or the defendant's house?"

"Yes, sir, we looked all around the house, in the garden, and the dustbin but didn't find anything. We also went to the defendant's own house but didn't find any items of clothing or shoes with blood on them. "

"What other conclusions did you arrive at that suggested the possible identity of the attacker?" Hywell was pushing for something tangible to convince the jury.

"Well, sir, although we didn't find any clothes with blood on them, we did find a discarded latex glove with some spots of blood buried at the bottom of Mrs. Weston's dustbin under her regular rubbish. The blood matched Mrs. Weston's blood. Although we never found any other items of clothing, we assumed she had abandoned said items in the bins either at the school or maybe at the shop she went to after the school meeting. We didn't have an opportunity to examine those bins as they were emptied the following morning, the normal pickup day in the village, unfortunately."

"And was there any sign of the weapon that was used? Did you check if any knives were missing from the victim's kitchen?"

"No, sir, we never found anything that could have been used as a weapon. We asked the defendant to check on the knives in the kitchen. She said her mother was meticulous about how her kitchen was kept, 'a place for everything and everything in its place' was how she put it, and she confirmed that nothing was missing."

"As you had your suspicions about who the murderer could be, did you accompany the defendant when she checked the knife drawer? She could have said everything was there if she had gone downstairs by herself, couldn't she?"

I smiled to myself; this was standard procedure, but talk about jumping to conclusions.

"Yes, of course I did, SIR! I had a constable go with her." Chief Inspector Waterstone was clearly not impressed at the implication his team had not done their job properly. The tone of his response was laced with sarcasm.

"No further questions, My Lord." Hywell thought it best to wrap up his interrogation before he completely lost the favour of the Chief Inspector.

Looking at me, the judge asked if I would like to cross-examine.

"I would, yes, please, My Lord." I approached the witness box.

"Chief Inspector, you stated that whoever killed Mrs. Weston must have had blood on their clothes, yet the defendant did not have any blood on her clothes. Is that correct?"

"Yes, that is correct. There was no blood on the clothes the defendant was wearing when we arrived at the crime scene, but she would have had plenty of time to discard anything that had blood on it before we arrived."

"And yet she did have blood on the soles of the shoes she was wearing. Why would she have blood on her shoes, do you think?"

"If she were the attacker, the original pair of shoes would certainly have been covered in blood, so she could have discarded those shoes and the clothes she wore when she killed her mother. However, the pair of shoes she was wearing when we arrived would have blood just on the soles and heels if she had just gone into the bedroom and found her mother's body."

"Was there not a second pair of footprints from the constable who had accompanied the defendant upstairs to view the body?"

"No, ma'am. The constable only got as far as the door to the bedroom when he spotted the body, and he immediately, and I should add, correctly, ran downstairs and rang the station in order to alert them to send help."

"I would like to go back to the rather fanciful idea that the clothes the defendant wore when she allegedly committed the murder were dumped somewhere else later." Margaret continued, "How do you suppose she achieved all this in just forty-five minutes? According to the Prosecution's fanciful timeline, she left her home at eight-thirty, drove to her mother's house, killed her in a fit of rage, went home again, changed, dumped the bloody clothes somewhere else, and still arrived at the school appearing unflustered, in time for the board meeting at nine-fifteen?"

"Well, ma'am, she could have abandoned the clothes after the board meeting."

"Yes, that is possible, but what about the car? Did you check the car to see if there was any blood or other evidence from the crime scene? Surely, there should have been something?"

"We did go over the car, and no, we did not find anything."

"And what about the missing handbag? Did you find that anywhere?"

"No, Ma'am, we searched for the bag but didn't find that either."

"So, are you implying this was pre-meditated? The defendant had planned the whole thing. Meaning the sudden 'fit of rage' argument collapses. The phone call she received from her mother at eight-thirty that morning had infuriated her so much that she grabbed a sheet, a set of clothes and shoes, and a knife and drove over to her mother's house. She laid the sheet or some plastic covering over the inside of the car to protect it from any blood that was on her clothes, then she stabbed her mother, stripped off her bloody clothes, changed into clean clothes, threw the bloodied clothes into the car with the bloodied knife, and wrapped them up in the sheet ready to abandon them somewhere the police would not think of checking. Then, she drove to the school and calmly walked into the meeting as if nothing had happened. Is that what you are saying, Chief Inspector?"

"No, ma'am. All's I was saying was if she had blood on her clothes, she had time to change out of them and abandon them after the meeting."

"Chief Inspector, am I correct in thinking that all you have is an assumption that the bloodied clothing the defendant wore when she supposedly murdered her mother had been dumped somewhere, but you haven't found them? The one set of footprints from the crime scene matched the shoes the defendant was wearing *after* the murder had been committed when she found her mother's body. And, by the way, which she didn't need to do as, according to you, she knew her mother was already dead. Finally, a latex glove with blood spatters that was discovered at the bottom of the victim's dustbin could have been dropped in there by a nurse or doctor who had been tending to Mrs. Weston for her cancer. And yet you concluded Sarah Slater had to be your main suspect? Is that correct, Chief Inspector?"

Blushing and looking extremely embarrassed, he responded, "Well, basically yes, ma'am."

"No more questions for this witness, thank you, My Lord." I was well pleased with how the questioning had gone. The Chief Inspector had given no firm evidence that Sarah was the one who killed her mother, and so reasonable doubt still stood. The Chief Inspector left the Court, looking a bit deflated.

Gryfidd-Jones immediately moved on to his next witness, the pathologist.

Dr. Rajiv Gupta marched swiftly up to the witness box. He was a small, compact man, slightly balding, a very serious bureaucrat, meticulous in his descriptions of a crime scene. He'd grown up in a family of Indian civil servants who moved to England in the sixties. I had seen him on several occasions over the years and found him to be highly competent and very thorough, a lover of routine and order but with the most delightful sense of humour.

"Doctor Gupta, would you please tell the court what you found when you arrived at the deceased's house?" Hywell began his questioning.

"The body was lying on the floor of the main bedroom. The throat had been slashed from ear to ear, and there were over twenty random stab wounds to the chest and stomach areas. Blood was splattered up the wall, and a considerable volume of blood had pooled on the carpet around the deceased's body. As I saw it, the wound to the neck was undoubtedly the cause of death. The subsequent chest wounds appeared to have been inflicted thereafter, out of sheer rage."

I stood up, "Objection, My Lord, the attacker's state of mind is pure conjecture."

The judge looked across at the jury as he said, "Sustained, the jury should disregard the last comment."

"Doctor Gupta, were you able to identify the type of weapon used to kill Mrs. Weston?" Hywell continued.

"Yes, by the shape of the wounds and the depth of the injuries to the body, I would say that a professional butcher knife was used. The wounds had clean edges, which indicates the knife must have sliced through the body very easily."

"Doctor Gupta, would you show the jury how you arrived at your findings?"

Dr. Gupta walked across to a television that had been set up in front of the jury. He retrieved a telescopic pointer from his top pocket, which he extended and clicked the remote in his left hand. On the screen appeared a set of gruesome-looking, close-up photographs of the upper body of an elderly woman. Dr. Gupta clicked the remote and pointed to the screen. An audible gasp came from a woman on the jury. I looked over at Sarah; she wasn't looking at the television. To be honest, I didn't blame her. It was not pretty, and knowing it was her mother would have made it doubly unpleasant for her.

"If you could please look at the screen, you can see the amount of damage sustained. The victim had initially been sliced across the neck. The cut was so deep that it severed the carotid artery and the jugular vein, which explained the distance the blood splatters had reached on the wall behind her."

He clicked the remote again, and a close-up of the wound on the neck was displayed.

"The larynx was also cut through, and if you look here," he pointed to a spot on the screen. "Here, you can see how deep the wound is. This is the spinal cord. The victim was almost decapitated — and very effectively."

A groan came from another member of the jury. I looked over and saw one of the women with her head in her hands. Dr. Gupta clicked the remote once more, and this time, the whole body was displayed. He waved the pointer around the screen.

"The remainder of the blood, which you can see splashed around the body, was due to the large number of stab wounds that appear to have been executed in what could only be described as a frenzied attack."

"Thank you, Doctor, for that very thorough description. Just one more question, Dr. Gupta, do you have an estimation of the time of death?"

"I examined the deceased at thirteen hundred hours, and I would say, by the state of the body, that she had been dead for between three and five hours."

"So somewhere between eight and ten that morning? Thank you, Doctor. No further questions."

"Mrs. German-Brown, do you have any questions for the coroner?" Mr. Justice Stanfield asked, looking at me.

"No, thank you, My Lord."

Dr. Gupta clicked the remote, and the screen went blank, much to the relief of several ashen-faced members of the jury who were sitting closest to the television.

Looking at the jury, the judge wisely decided it might be a good time to take a fifteen-minute break. The evidence had obviously affected a couple of them who looked like a glass of water might be in order. In fact, one poor woman looked so pale after seeing the gruesome crime scene photos that a stiff brandy would probably have been more appropriate.

I grabbed my bag and walked out of the courtroom. After a quick trip to the toilet and a few puffs on my cigarette outside, in the fresh air, the fifteen-minute recess was over, and I headed back inside.

Hywell and I had agreed beforehand that he would call Sarah to the stand. Sarah thought she stood a better chance of persuading the jury of her innocence if they could actually hear her answering questions rather than simply relying on someone else giving their opinions of her character. And I felt it was in Sarah's best interests to let him question her as we had exhaustively reviewed the types of questions I believed he would ask. So Sarah was invited to the stand and took her seat, flattening her skirt nervously.

As Sarah would be his key witness, Hywell went in with all guns blazing. He strode across the courtroom, but this time, there was no disarming smile and no warmth in his voice, and I watched Sarah wither under his steely gaze as he began his questioning.

"Mrs. Slater, I will not ask the obvious question of whether you killed your mother. We must leave that up to the jury to decide based on all the evidence. However, we must consider where that evidence takes us.

"Now, your position as headmistress of the local primary school is quite demanding, is that correct?"

"Yes, sir, it keeps me busy, but I enjoy it — I love children."
Sarah's mouth was dry, and her voice cracked as she spoke.

"It must have been quite a balancing act working full-time,
running a household, and being on-call for your mother,
knowing how dependent she was on you."

"I was lucky. Richard, my husband, was very understanding
and happy to run errands for her if I was busy with school
matters."

I was well pleased with her response, but Hywell brushed
over it and continued.

"But even so, this must have been difficult for you, having to
rely on your husband to run around after your mother. We
have heard from other witnesses how your mother could be
very demanding?"

"Oh, she wasn't that bad. And as I just said, Richard would
help out. She was my mum, and she was very ill. I was
happy to be able to do things for her while I could, to make
her more comfortable."

Well done, Sarah. She was nailing it just as we had
rehearsed.

"Let us go back to the morning when your mother was
killed. Did you speak to your mother that morning?" Hywell
continued his interrogation dryly.

"Yes, sir, she telephoned me before I left for school."

"And what time was that phone call, and could you please
tell the court why she phoned you?"

"She rang me at half-past eight, just before I left for school. She wanted me to go to the shop for some milk and biscuits, as her neighbour was coming for coffee. She said it was urgent as she needed them by eleven o'clock."

"And what did you tell her?"

"I told her I would do my best, but I had an important school board meeting to attend."

"And what did your mother say to that?"

"She told me I would surely have time for a quick trip to the shop and to drop the items off at her house before the meeting."

"And how did you feel about having to do such a trivial errand when you had other more urgent matters to deal with?"

I knew Hywell was pushing Sarah to show some annoyance at her mother's request, so I jumped up.

"Objection feelings are superfluous to the trial. We just need facts."

Hywell looked at the judge, "My Lord, in this instance, the defendant's state of mind is critical to the case."

The judge nodded, "Overruled. You may continue with your questioning, Mr. Gryfidd-Jones."

Sarah had admitted to me how irritated she was about her mother's unreasonable demands, so I was willing for her to stay calm.

"Um, I remember trying to work out how I could fit the errand into my schedule. I was quite concerned as I didn't like to put any undue stress on my mother." Perfect, good answer.

"So when did you decide you had the time to fit in the errand?"

"Well, the meeting was supposed to end at half-past ten, so I figured I had time to go to the shop and back to Mum's house by eleven or maybe a few minutes later."

"Mrs. Slater, what time did you arrive at school that morning?"

"Just before nine."

"Did anyone see you arrive?"

"No, I parked in the car park at the side of the building and walked round to the main entrance at the front of the school. My office is opposite the front door. I didn't see anyone until the board meeting at nine-fifteen."

"How long did the meeting last?"

"Nearly two hours — it ran longer than was scheduled. It ended just after eleven o'clock."

"And where did you go after the meeting?"

"I drove straight to the village shop." Sarah was clutching her hands so tightly her knuckles were turning white.

"Mrs. Slater, to reach the village shop from the school, don't you have to pass the end of the road that your mother lived on?"

"Yes, sir."

"Did you drive up to your mother's house to see her?"

"No, I did not."

"But you were so close; you could have stopped in to warn her you would be late and maybe find out if she needed anything else from the shop."

"Yes, I could have, but I decided it would be more efficient to go straight to the shop. I was concerned that my mother would be upset and worried if I didn't arrive at her house by eleven o'clock. She was very sick, and my being late might agitate her."

Hywell strode right up to Sarah and glared down at her in a blatant attempt to intimidate her. "So why didn't you ring and warn her you would be late? Was it because there was no point as you knew she was already dead?" he said loudly and accusingly. Sarah looked up at him, shaking her head furiously.

"Mrs. Slater, we have heard you told the shopkeeper, Mrs. Blake, you had a bit of a 'to-do' with your mother that morning but that you had 'sorted it out.' How did you sort it out? Did you, in fact, kill her to shut her up and 'sort her out'?"

Sarah looked down, visibly upset, and shook her head as Hywell continued.

60

"When Mrs. Blake asked what you'd done to your hand, you said you'd cut it slicing bread, a rather convenient excuse, don't you think? Are you sure that's what happened?"

She looked across at me; panic was written all over her face as she nodded anxiously. Her eyes were welling up with tears. "Yes, sir, I was cutting the bread for toast, and I wasn't looking at what I was doing. I didn't kill my mother. I just meant that I was a bit frantic about the meeting and that her phone call was a bit upsetting."

Hywell looked down at Sarah and, trying to intimidate her, said, "Wasn't it much more likely you cut your hand as you were stabbing your mother?"

Sarah looked horrified at what he said. She shook her head and shouted, "NO!"

I leapt up at the same time, "OBJECTION."

The judge immediately looked over at Hywell, "Sustained. That was uncalled for, Mr. Gryfidd-Jones."

Hywell started to walk away, a look of triumph on his face, and then stopped and turned back.

"Oh, just one more question, Mrs. Slater. Did your mother ever say anything to you about a child in the village looking a lot like your husband, Richard?"

What the fuck? Where did that come from? What was Hywell playing at? Hopefully, I succeeded in not looking concerned. That was all Sarah needed was to see me panicking.

61

Sarah looked at him with a blank look on her face. "No, sir."

"Thank you, Mrs. Slater. No further questions, My Lord."

I looked over at the jury, who were all furiously writing down what they had just heard. I needed the questioning back on track quickly. I stood up as the judge looked over to see if I wanted to question Sarah. Too bloody right, I did.

I smiled at Sarah reassuringly, trying to convey to her that everything would be fine, willing her not to panic.

As calmly as I could, I began to question Sarah, "Mrs. Slater, your mother was very ill with lung cancer; is that correct?"

"Yes." She answered quietly, sniffing and trying to compose herself after Hywell's dramatic interrogation.

"Did she take frequent naps during the day?"

"Yes, her medication made her very drowsy."

"So, can we assume she would usually take a nap in the morning after her breakfast and another in the afternoon after her lunch? And can we also assume she may be a bit confused if she were woken up during one of her naps?"

"Objection, My Lord, counsel, is leading the witness."

Oh, shut up, Hywell! I turned and glared at him.

The judge looked at me over the top of his glasses, "Objection overruled, but do be careful, Mrs. German-Brown."

I attempted to look contrite while inside I was delighted. I'd managed to express my point to the jury.

"Yes, My Lord." I nodded serenely.

"Mrs. Slater, why didn't you ring your mother to say you would be late?"

"I didn't ring her because the medication made her sleepy, and she could be confused about where she was and what time it was until she was properly awake. I decided to do her shopping and then go to her house and make her some lunch during my lunch hour. I figured I could pop in to see Mrs. Woods and apologize about Mum missing the coffee morning."

"Mrs. Slater, before your mother became ill, you saw quite a lot of each other socially; is that correct?"

"Yes, ma'am. I would take her and her neighbour, Mrs. Woods, to do their grocery shopping in Burton each Saturday. And every Sunday, I would take Mum to church with me. After the service, I would bring her back to our house for Sunday lunch."

"One more question: did you see the postman that morning?"

"No ma'am. He usually delivers the post earlier in the day, around nine o'clock, I think my Mum told me."

"So nobody waved to you when you arrived at your mother's house that morning?"

"No, I didn't see anybody except Mrs. Woods, but that was after I'd found my Mum."

"Thank you, Mrs. Slater. No further questions, My Lord."

I noticed the judge looking at Sarah as she left the witness box. She was looking down at her feet as she was escorted back and up to the Dock. Once there, she looked across at me with a slight shake of her head and a questioning look on her face. I smiled and gave her a brief nod of encouragement. She had responded to the questioning perfectly. The members of the jury were impressed with her. I saw several of them looking in her direction, and a couple were smiling sympathetically. Hopefully, that was a good sign.

The judge asked the prosecutor if he had any more witnesses he needed to call, and Hywell shook his head, "No, thank you, My Lord. The prosecution rests its case."

Now, it was my turn to present the case for the defense and, at the very least, sow as much doubt as possible in the jury's minds. I had decided, when planning my defence strategy, to provide some insight into Sarah's character to the jury, and indeed, after Hywell's questioning, it became even more crucial. I needed the jury to like Sarah, to see she was a kind and gentle person and not quick-tempered and violent. So, I opened my arguments with a character analysis strategy.

"My Lord, I would like to call my first witness, Mrs. Nicola Smith."

Nicola walked confidently to the witness box as I smiled at her encouragingly.

"Mrs. Smith, would you be so kind as to explain to the court your relationship with the defendant?"

Nicola looked over at her mother and smiled.

"My name is Nicola Smith, and I am Mrs. Slater's younger daughter." She spoke confidently.

"Mrs. Smith, do you still live at home?"

"No, ma'am, I moved away to London after graduating from university eight years ago."

"So, you weren't living at home in Lower Naughton when your grandmother was killed?"

"No, ma'am, I left home when I was eighteen to go to university and never moved back, although I speak to my mother regularly on Skype, and we text each other most days."

"And you and your sister are both schoolteachers, is that correct?"

"Yes, ma'am. Like our mother, we both love children and growing up watching how the kids react when they are around her, we both decided we would follow in her footsteps. She is an awesome teacher; everybody in the village loves her." She smiled proudly.

"It's a wonderful compliment to your mother that you have followed in her footsteps. Now, I have a couple of questions about your grandmother, Mrs. Elizabeth Weston. What was she like as a grandmother? Were you close to her?"

"To be honest, I didn't really have much to do with her once I left home. I do recall going to her house a few times for Christmas and that kind of thing when I was younger. She was nice enough. She and my grandfather were very generous, always buying Jennifer, my sister, and me presents. When we visited her, our mum would warn us that we had to be on our best behaviour. She would warn us to keep our elbows off the table as Grandma was very strict about table manners. She was also very houseproud, so we weren't allowed to make a mess or anything, but I don't remember her ever being angry with Jennifer or me."

There was a slight murmur from the courtroom and a nodding of heads as recollections of such family occasions resonated with everyone.

"Do you recall your mother ever talking to you about her? Maybe to your father or anyone else? Were you aware of any ill feelings between them?"

"Not really. My mum would sometimes tell me on the phone that Grandma had been a bit confused and insisted that she do something when she'd already done it, but Mum would laugh about it and blame it on Grandma's cancer medication. I can tell Mum misses her terribly. It was especially hard for her on what would have been Grandma's birthday. She called me in tears, saying she couldn't believe she was gone. Mum said she was looking at the photograph of Grandma she kept on her dressing table. In it, my sister and I are sitting on either side of her, and we all look so happy together."

I was delighted with how Nicola was responding to the questions. I could feel the jury's hearts softening from metres away.

"So you don't remember your mother ever being angry or frustrated with her mother?"

"No, ma'am. As I said, Grandma would sometimes be upset, which was understandable when she became ill, but Mum just took it in her stride. To be honest, I thought Mum had the patience of a saint. I did ask her if she ever got annoyed with Grandma, always wanting her to do stuff, but she said I should be nicer, that Grandma couldn't help it, she was very ill, and the medication made her confused."

"Thank you very much, Mrs. Smith. No further questions, My Lord".

The Judge asked if Hywell would like to cross-examine the witness.

"No, thank you, My Lord, not at this time." He saw no benefit in questioning a witness so clearly prepared to stand up for her mother.

My next witness was the Reverend Trevor Owen, the local vicar. He walked slowly to the witness box, smiling beatifically to the public gallery as he passed by as if they were members of his congregation. His bald pate was shining from the lights in the courtroom, and a veritable forest of white hair sprouted from his ears.

"Good morning, Reverend. Would you be so kind as to tell the court who you are and where your parish is?" I began.

"My name is Trevor Owen, and I'm the vicar of St. Gregory's church in Lower Naughton."

"Thank you. And how do you know the defendant?"

"Mrs. Slater is one of my parishioners, as was her late mother, Mrs. Elizabeth Weston, a lovely lady she was too. I've known them both for over twenty years, from when I first came to the parish."

"Does the defendant attend church? Is she an active member of your congregation?"

"Oh yes. Mrs. Slater and her mother were regular churchgoers. Every Sunday, they could be found in their usual spot in the second pew. They were the most enthusiastic of singers, Mrs. Weston, with her contralto voice contrasting with Mrs. Slater's more timid, but nonetheless, beautiful soprano voice. The choirmaster tried in vain to entice them to join the choir, but they refused as they had so many other commitments. Mrs. Weston was on the parish council, you see, and was very involved with the church, and Mrs. Slater, being the headmistress at the local school, was very busy, but she was always willing to volunteer her spare time. She arranged the flowers each week in the church, and you should see the spectacular way she displayed the gifts in front of the altar for the Harvest Festival. Afterward, Mrs. Slater would help organize the distribution of the bounty to the almshouses. Honestly, I don't know how she found the time to do so much, what with her job and lately looking after her mother. Such a kind and gracious lady."

Okay, slightly over the top. One would think we were putting her up for sainthood. However, I wasn't about to complain as the kindly old man's testimony played right into my plan to emphasize Sarah's compassionate character.

"Thank you so much, Reverend. No further questions."

Hywell shook his head when asked if he wanted to question the vicar, who then stepped down and smiled as he walked past Sarah. She smiled back at him and mouthed, "Thank you."

The judge checked his watch and then looked up at the courtroom clock. "I think it would be most practical if we adjourn for lunch. We will reconvene at, shall we say, one o'clock?" muttered Justice Stanfield.

With an encouraging glance over at Sarah, I scooped up my papers and walked out of the courtroom with Toby, a junior barrister. Toby was a tall young man with a shock of ginger hair and a thick but perfectly groomed beard. No matter the weather, he always wore a three-piece suit with a pocket watch, something I admired immensely. Rain, shine, or snow, Toby was consistent in his dress and his demeanor. He had a calm manner and a strong work ethic. I believed the standard of work in the younger generation was dire, so I was thrilled when I came across Toby when he was just starting out. His role was essentially to do all the crucial donkey work that could make or break a case, drafting pleadings, reviewing witness statements, and the like. I had great hopes for Toby's future. He had all the skills necessary to be a brilliant barrister. His insightfulness meant he could contribute to discussions about any part of a case with wisdom beyond his years, and his recollection of facts made him invaluable.

"Toby, are you free for lunch? I'd like to discuss how you think it's going so far?" I asked.

"Absolutely."

We headed off to the local Pret-A-Manger, and after picking up sandwiches and coffee from the self-service counter, we found a table by the window. As we ate our lunch, we discussed the witnesses, laughing as we recalled the testimony of Reverend Owen.

"I loved how determined he was to show the court what a wonderful woman Sarah is," laughed Toby, "almost saint-like. Still, that probably wasn't a bad thing to have a witness like that."

"I agree, but I was concerned when Hywell kept asking Sarah how she managed to juggle all those responsibilities and still care for her mother. I think he was implying that the strain of it all caused her to snap and that, in a fit of rage, she killed her mum. I did figure he would take that stance. A bit of a weak argument if you ask me, with absolutely no supporting evidence, but it may work with the jury." I was anxious about Hywell's argument.

But Toby responded positively, "I thought she handled herself well. I watched the jury's reaction to those questions, and nobody seemed too concerned. A couple of them made some notes, and one chap shook his head, but I don't think we need to worry. My biggest concern is the lack of witnesses who saw Sarah at school early that morning."

"I couldn't agree more. The prosecution wouldn't have a case if just one person had seen her at school before the board meeting."

We ate our sandwiches in silence for a few minutes while we pondered the morning's proceedings.

"Knowing Hywell as well as I do, I'm surprised by the flimsy case he's built. He seems to be relying on tricks that I thought were beneath him. What do you think he was playing at when he brought up Sarah cutting her hand when she was stabbing her mother? He must have known the judge wouldn't let that pass. It's up to the jury to establish whether Sarah stabbed her mother and not for him to plant the idea in their heads."

Toby shook his head, "It was a bit brutal. All we can hope is that the jury sees Hywell being overly dramatic and over-acting. Hopefully, Rev. Trev will have persuaded them of her true character," he said, smiling at the clever nickname they'd cooked up for the kindly old vicar.

After we'd finished eating, I asked Toby if he would mind if we went for a walk — I badly needed a cigarette. He shook his head disapprovingly.

"I know I shouldn't smoke, but now is not the time to give it up. I'll give it up once I'm retired."

After throwing the remains of our lunch in the bin, we walked out into the cool London air.

We walked along the side of the Thames, me enjoying my cigarette, trying to blow the smoke away from Toby. I knew it was ridiculous, as London pollution was nearly as harmful as smoking a pack a day, but I knew Toby didn't approve of smoking, so I did my best to keep the smoke away from him.

After a few minutes, we stopped and leaned against the wall of the Embankment. The river was at high tide, and we watched the muddy brown water as it flowed under Blackfriars Bridge. Barges loaded with gravel, timber, and the inevitable trash chugged past on their way east toward the docks. There was a gentle hum from the engines of the ferries and tour boats crammed with tourists, mobile phones up to their faces, trying to capture the thrill as they passed under Tower Bridge and headed downstream toward Greenwich. As the boats glided along, small wakes appeared after them as they pushed through the water. Tiny swells and ripples drifted up the banks of the Thames and splashed gently against the grey stone wall beneath us. How reassuring it was to know that no matter how many wars, how many pandemics, and how cruel, how vicious, even how violent, people are to each other, the river will absorb it all, wash it away, and continue its endless movement drifting in and out to sea long after we're gone.

We walked back in quiet contemplation, preparing ourselves for the afternoon's inevitable intensity.

Back in court, we took our seats in readiness for Justice Stanfield to appear and the afternoon session to begin.

My next witness was Bill Turner, the postman.

He walked shyly up to the witness box as I smiled encouragingly at him.

"Mr. Turner, would you please tell the court your occupation?"

"P-Postman," he stuttered nervously, his head down as if directly addressing his feet.

The judge looked over at him and, with a kindly smile, asked, "Would you please speak up, Mr. Turner, so that the court can hear you?"

He looked up and repeated, "Sorry, your honour, I'm a postman," a little more loudly.

"Mr. Turner, how long have you been the postman for the village of Lower Naughton?" I asked.

"Ooh, let me think. I should say about fifteen years, miss."

"So, you know most of the people who live on Mrs. Weston's road?"

"Yes, miss, all the old-timers. There's a few new'uns, but I know most of 'em."

"Mr. Turner, would you please tell the court what happened the morning of Tuesday, April 30th?"

"Yes, miss, I were doing me rounds like I always do. I'd just put the post through the letterbox of the house opposite Mrs. Weston's when a red car backed out of her drive, and so I waved at the driver."

"Did you recognize the car? Who did you think was driving?"

"Well, it were a red car like what Mrs. Slater drives, so I thought it were her, but she ignored me. In fact, she speeded up, driving the car down the road like it were the Grand Prix, which I thought were a bit odd cos she, um, Mrs. Slater, is usually a very slow and careful driver. Anyways, she always waves to me. She don't live there no more, but she's always friendly-like. I assumed she were late for school or summat since she didn't wave or nothing." His Midland accent was far stronger than the other witnesses thus far.

"Mr. Turner, do you remember if anyone else was in the car? Maybe Mrs. Weston?"

"Not sure, miss. I didn't see no-one else, but the car were going so fast I didn't get much of a chance to see if anyone else were in there."

"Mr. Turner, are you absolutely sure the car you saw was Mrs. Slater's car? Did you actually see or recognize Mrs. Slater herself?"

"I think so, miss. It looked like her car; it were red, and Mrs. Slater drives a red Prius, and I think that's what it were, but it were going so fast."

"Mr. Turner, remember you are under oath when you answer this. Could you swear that without a doubt it was Mrs. Slater driving the car and that it was definitely Mrs. Slater's car, one hundred percent?"

"Um, well, not one hundred percent, cos it were going so fast so I couldn't swear it were her, and I don't know her

74

number plate or nothing, but the car looked like a red Prius, and Mrs. Slater's got a red Prius, so I suppose I just assumed, like."

Yes! That was all I needed.

"No further questions, My Lord."

Looking over at Hywell, the judge asked if he would like to cross-examine, but he declined.

Meanwhile, I had a couple of other witnesses I hoped might help my case.

I called for Douglas Lloyd, the chairman of the school board. With an air of self-importance, he strode up to the witness box. His smart grey trousers had a perfect crease, and his navy blazer had a regimental badge prominently sewn onto the breast pocket. Slightly balding and wearing gold-rimmed spectacles, he was quite an imposing figure.

"Mr. Lloyd, would you be so kind as to explain to the jury how you know the defendant?"

"Yes, ma'am. I know Mrs. Slater because I am the Chairman of the School Board, and she is the Headmistress."

" And how long have you known her?"

"I've been a board member for about ten years, five of which I've been the chairman. I also have four children who are or who have been at the school, so yes, I've known her for a long time."

"And how would you describe the defendant's performance in her role at the school?"

"Mrs. Slater has my, and the rest of the board members, complete confidence as headmistress. She has always been committed to doing her best for the school. She loves the children and has the trust and loyalty of the teachers."

"Mr. Lloyd, have you ever heard of any complaints regarding the defendant losing her temper and shouting at anyone? Pupils or teachers?"

"Absolutely not. The board members have always been impressed with how calm and controlled she is, no matter the circumstances. She has always put the school's reputation above all else."

"And would you please explain to the court where the defendant was on the morning of Tuesday, April 30th?"

"The morning of April 30th, we had a board meeting at the school to discuss the forthcoming expansion of the school hall."

"And would you please tell the court the length of time of the meeting?"

"As the minutes will confirm, we convened the meeting at precisely 9:15 am and concluded at 11:00 am. It should have ended at 10:30, but unfortunately, it ran over as such meetings tend to do."

"My final question for you, Mr. Lloyd. On the morning of April 30th, did Sarah Slater appear to be her normal, calm, professional self?"

"Absolutely. As always, she conducted herself with the utmost professionalism." As I'd hoped, Douglas Lloyd was the perfect character witness, concise and convincing in his answers.

"Thank you, Mr. Lloyd. No further questions, My Lord."

"Mr. Gryfidd-Jones, would you like to question this witness?"

Hywell stood up.

"Just one question, Mr. Lloyd, perchance, did you notice if Mrs. Slater had a bandage on her hand at the meeting?"

"Yes, she did. Her left hand was bandaged."

"Thank you. No further questions, My Lord."

I then called for Mrs. Weston's oncologist, Dr. Jocelyn Grey, a small woman in her late fifties; what she lacked in stature, she made up for in energy as she bustled up to the witness box. Dr. Grey was well known for her lung cancer expertise, and Mrs. Weston had been seeing her for the last six months of her life since she was first diagnosed.

"Dr. Grey, I understand that normally you would not be able to discuss your patient's condition due to confidentiality and privacy laws, however, in these extenuating circumstances, I wonder if you could tell the court approximately how long Mrs. Weston would have survived her terminal lung cancer diagnosis?"

"Mrs. Weston's metastatic lung cancer had progressed to stage four. She most probably would have survived three more months at the most."

"And were Mrs. Weston and her daughter, the defendant Sarah Slater, aware of that prognosis?"

"They certainly were."

"Thank you, Dr. Grey, for your time. You have been most helpful."

Mr. Gryfidd-Jones was asked if he would like to question Dr. Grey, but again, he declined.

The doctor stepped down from the witness box and left the courtroom.

I stood up, "My Lord, I would like to recall the defendant, Sarah Slater."

Sarah walked over to the witness box. We had rehearsed this so there would be no surprises in my questioning, but I needed to have Sarah explain how she had cut her hand. It was infuriating that Hywell's entire case seemed to revolve around this fucking 'bandaged hand.'

"Mrs. Slater, on the morning of Tuesday, April 30th, could you please tell the jury what happened to your hand?"

"Richard, my husband, and I had breakfast together as we always did. I was slicing a loaf of bread for toast when the knife slipped, and I cut into the palm of my hand. It was bleeding profusely. Thank goodness Rich had taken a first aid class at the brewery, and he bandaged it up for me. I probably should have gone to A and E to have stitches as it was quite deep, but I didn't have the time, what with the board meeting."

"And remind me again, you said earlier that you didn't see anyone at the school until the meeting; is that correct?"

"Yes, that is correct."

"Thank you. No further questions, My Lord."

"Mr. Gryfidd-Jones, do you need to cross-examine?" The Judge asked.

He shook his head, "No, no questions at this time. Thank you, My Lord."

"In that case, and considering the time," Justice Stanfield mumbled, " I think we can conclude today's session. We will reconvene tomorrow morning."

So that was it for the case against Sarah for her mother's murder. I didn't think the prosecution's case had enough substance to persuade the jury she was guilty. She had an alibi for most of the morning, and hopefully, the problem with the bandage on her hand had been explained. Surely, the lack of concrete evidence would make it impossible for the jury to find her guilty, at least 'beyond reasonable doubt.'

The next day, the trial against Sarah for the murder of her husband would begin. Hopefully, there wouldn't be any surprises there, either.

After removing my wig and gown and hanging them in the fusty-smelling wardrobe, I headed out, lighting a cigarette as I walked towards Blackfriars Underground Station for the tube across to Victoria Station. My mind was focused on the upcoming segment of the trial. The prosecution's case relied mainly on the relationship between Sarah and Richard and the pathologist's report. Hywell surely would do his best to project an unhappy marriage. But I had a few surprises of my own in store.

Chapter 3

The following day, I woke feeling optimistic that I would successfully put the case to bed. This could even be my last day in court, and I was excited about what was to follow. Once this was over, what would my new life have to offer? I went through my usual early morning routine, a cup of tea and a cigarette, as I read the headlines from the newspaper. After showering, I put my hair into a chignon, applied my makeup, and dressed. Again, I wore black stockings and my now hopefully 'lucky' Jimmy Choo black suede pumps. I fed Rocco and asked him to wish me good luck. As usual, I was rebuffed as he haughtily turned tail and returned to his basket.

With my usual impeccable timing, I stepped onto the platform as the train arrived and sat in the first-class carriage. I attempted to read the rest of my newspaper, but my mind was going in so many directions I barely made it past the front page. It would have to wait until the evening commute.

It was a poignant moment as I dressed in my wig and gown for this one last case. I walked into the courtroom, sat behind the defence counsel's desk, and looked across at Sarah, who appeared even paler than the previous day. She'd not worn any makeup or jewellery, and her clothes, a plain navy blue dress, hung on her now diminished frame, giving the impression that she had given up. 'Come on, Sarah, we can do this,' I mentally chided her. 'You will not spend another night in that cell if I can help it. Today, we will prove that you did not murder your husband.'

Gryfidd-Jones and I nodded to the judge when he entered, and the courtroom sat down, ready to begin what could well be the last day of arguments.

Hywell stood up, clearing his throat dramatically to obtain everyone's attention.

"Ladies and gentlemen of the jury, I would like to call my first witness for the case against the defendant, Sarah Slater, for the murder of her husband, Richard Kevin Slater, Detective Inspector Tony Graham of the Metropolitan police."

A nondescript man of about fifty strolled up to the witness box, looking a little surly. His grey suit, judging by the shine on the trousers, had definitely seen better days. The detective likely dragged it out of his wardrobe for just such occasions. He wore a brown tie that absurdly depicted several miniature dachshunds appearing to run up to the knot at his neck, ready to pounce on his white shirt with their dirty paws.

Hywell opened his questioning:

"Inspector, would you explain your role with the Metropolitan Police?"

"Yes sir, I am a detective currently assigned to the Murder Squad."

"Could you tell the court how you came to be involved with the death of Richard Slater?"

82

"We received a phone call from the pathologist's office informing us they had a man's body in the morgue, and they were convinced he had been poisoned as they had found Thallium Sulphate in the contents of his stomach. They passed on details of the deceased and his next of kin, and we began our investigation."

"Would you tell the court what your next steps were?"

"Yes, sir, my team interviewed his wife, the defendant Sarah Slater, and she informed us that she had spent the whole day with him on the day of his death. She gave us the names of everyone they had contact with that day, the meals he had eaten, and with whom. We interviewed those contacts and also spoke with friends, family, and neighbours of the Slaters."

"And what led you to conclude that Sarah Slater was responsible for her husband's death?"

"Well, sir, through our rigorous questioning, we discovered that Sarah Slater met all three requirements of a textbook murder scenario: she had the means, the motive, and the opportunity."

He continued matter-of-factly, "We heard from several sources that the victim and his wife had marital issues, providing Mrs. Slater with a motive. Interestingly, our investigation also uncovered the fact that the defendant had quite a detailed knowledge of poisons. Finally, by her own admission, she was the only person to have shared every meal with the deceased in the twenty-four hours up until he died. With all that in mind, we concluded that Sarah Slater must be the murderer."

"Thank you, Inspector. No more questions, My Lord."

Judge Stanfield looked at me. "Do you have any questions for the Inspector, Mrs. German-Brown?"

I nodded. "Thank you, My Lord, yes I do." I walked across to the witness box.

"Inspector Graham, thank you for your detailed account of the rigorous investigation you and your team undertook," I said with just a hint of sarcasm. "I'm sure the jury was impressed with your explanation of means, motive, and opportunity, but I fear you failed to mention a crucial element of proving guilt — any convincing physical evidence," I said pointedly. "So apart from Mrs. Slater having the odd fight with her husband and her being the only person with the victim over the entire day, what other evidence do you have, or did you just leap to your conclusion?"

If the Inspector had looked surly before, he now looked positively hostile.

"The evidence we uncovered was irrefutable, and we stand by our decision — Mrs. Slater murdered her husband."

"Very well. Perhaps we can review your evidence. Did you find any trace of Thallium Sulphate that Mrs. Slater could have used to administer to her husband as poison?"

"Well, not exactly. We searched her handbag and the suitcases she and her husband had left at her daughter's house but found nothing. She had probably dumped any remaining poison. She could have flushed it down a toilet somewhere."

"So you went over her clothing in case any of the poison had spilled onto her person?"

"Yes, we tested the clothes she was wearing, but she must have been vigilant when she used it, as we didn't find any."

"Do you know where she might have obtained this banned substance?"

"I do not, no."

"You suggested their marital situation as a motive. Indeed, you said you interviewed some of Mrs. Slater's friends and family, who all attested to the Slaters having an unhappy marriage; is that correct?"

"Yes, ma'am. We spoke to their neighbours, who said they had heard them quarrelling on a couple of occasions. And her daughter, who she was staying with, also said her mum and dad sometimes argued when Mr. Slater came home drunk from the pub."

"Well, Inspector, I don't know if you are married or in a relationship, but I would be astonished if there were any couples who've been together for over thirty years who have not had at least one disagreement. These neighbours who've heard a couple of raised voices over the years, and Mrs. Slater's daughter, who stated her parents had the odd domestic, is hardly a reason for Mrs. Slater to have administered a large amount of poison to kill her husband."

A slight mumble from the court and nodding heads as folk acknowledged they too had the odd argument with their other half.

"And yet, Inspector, you are adamant that the defendant was the only person who could have committed this crime. Slightly presumptuous, don't you think?" Inspector Graham shifted uneasily in his seat.

"Just one more question, Inspector. You implied that the other people Mr. Slater saw during that twenty-four hours could not or would not have had cause to kill him, and if Mrs. Slater didn't kill him, did you ever consider the possibility of Mr. Slater having committed suicide?"

"SUICIDE!" He exploded, his face turning purple with anger. "Certainly not."

"What makes you say that, Inspector, and with such certainty?" I pressed him.

"Well, for a start, no one in their right mind would choose Thallium Sulphate to commit suicide. It would be an extremely unpleasant death."

Smiling benignly, I calmly responded, "Thank you so much for clarifying that for the jury, Inspector. I'm sure they, like me, had no idea that the Metropolitan Police viewed most suicides as pleasant. No further questions, My Lord."

Mumbling to himself, Inspector Graham glared at me as he walked past and out of the courtroom while I sat down, trying hard not to smile.

"I would like to call my next witness, Doctor James Foinette, the forensic examiner."

Foinette was a tall, athletic-looking man in his mid-forties. His short black hair was gelled to withstand hurricane-force winds, which suited his chiseled, tanned face. His suit, a royal blue, was cut to show off his toned body. He made quite an entrance as he swaggered up to the witness box.

After the usual preliminaries, Hywell began his questioning.

"Doctor Foinette, would you please tell the court your findings on examining the body of Richard Slater."

"Certainly, the initial cause of death was assumed to be cardiac arrest. After examining the body during the routine postmortem and finding no other physical cause for the victim's demise, I examined the stomach contents. After an extensive review, however, I found that a poison had been ingested, Thallium Sulphate."

"Could you please tell the court how this particular poison works?"

"Thallium Sulphate is slow-acting. It is colourless and tasteless and easily dissolves in water."

"What would be the victim's reaction to the poison?"

"Once it starts to work, the victim will act as if they are drunk with stomach pains, nausea, and vomiting, eventually exhibiting symptoms similar to that of a heart attack."

"So, Dr. Foinette, does this mean the victim could have had a meal containing the poison several hours before it took effect?"

"Yes, although, when we re-examined the stomach's contents, there was nothing to suggest which of the meals he'd consumed had contained the poison. It could have been mixed with anything the victim had eaten or drunk within the previous twenty-four hours."

"Thank you, doctor. No further questions, My Lord."

Hywell looked confident, knowing that Sarah had spent most of that twenty-four hours with her husband.

The judge looked across at me, "Mrs. German-Brown, do you have any questions for the witness?"

I stood up, "Dr. Foinette, isn't Thallium Sulphate banned in this country?"

"Yes, ma'am."

"And yet you are absolutely certain it was Thallium Sulphate that you discovered among the contents of Mr. Slater's stomach?"

"Yes, absolutely certain. Although it is banned here, it is possible to obtain it in other parts of the world."

"No further questions for this witness, thank you, My Lord."

"Thank you, doctor." I smiled at Doctor Foinette, hopefully not too pruriently. I wished I could have thought of something else to ask him, just to keep him on the stand a while longer. He was most certainly a much-needed dose of eye candy on this dreary morning, especially compared to some of the bleak array of witnesses — eye candy they definitely were not.

Gryfidd-Jones then called Professor Jonathan Williams. There was no mistaking the man's profession — he looked exactly like someone who had spent his long career in the hallowed halls of academia. He was what you would describe as roly-poly, due probably to too many college dining hall steamed puddings. His ample belly hung over his brown, corduroy trousers that were held up with braces. His well-worn grey cardigan had leather patches on the elbows, ubiquitous within the realm of tenured education professors. He peered at Gryfidd-Jones over his Coke bottle reading glasses. Professor Williams was the epitome of a shambling professor straight out of Central Casting.

"Professor, would you please tell the court your area of expertise?" Hywell began.

"Certainly, I am a Professor of Chemistry."

"And how do you know the defendant Sarah Slater, or Weston as she was before her marriage?"

"Sarah Weston was a student of mine for a term at the college where I was teaching. And a very astute and keen student, may I add." His eyes twinkled as he looked over at her.

"Would you say that she was well versed in the use of poisons?"

"Oh yes, she passed my class with flying colours by producing a final paper titled 'Poisons in Everyday Life.' She was really interested in the subject."

"Professor, can you tell the court a little about Thallium Sulphate?"

"Well, basically, it was used as a rat poison years ago, but in small doses it could be used to treat other things, such as syphilis, gout, or dysentery. Hence, Miss Weston's paper referring to the common uses of poisons. However, I should have prefaced the discussion with a warning that Thallium Sulphate is very dangerous. It has the appearance of just being a powder, meaning it could be confused with other more innocuous chemicals. It can be easily administered and absorbed into the system."

"Professor, can you be absolutely certain that you reviewed thallium sulphate with the class the defendant took?"

"Well, it is one of the poisons I talk about in my class as it is so interesting. I cannot be one hundred percent sure as it was so many years ago, but I'm fairly sure it would have been discussed."

"Professor, am I correct in thinking that Thallium Sulphate is banned in the United Kingdom? Wouldn't it have been almost impossible for the defendant in her capacity as a schoolteacher to obtain any?"

"It is indeed banned here now. But it would certainly be possible to obtain it from other parts of the world. In fact, even here, there would be a possibility. I would hazard a guess that most farmyard barns and garden sheds have a shelf at the back with forgotten jars and tins that have been there for donkey's years, and it's possible Thallium Sulphate could be found in one of them."

"Thank you, Professor. No further questions, My Lord." Hywell wore a smug expression as he walked back to his seat.

The judge looked across at me to see if I wanted to cross-examine.

" No, thank you. I have no questions for this witness, My Lord." I wasn't about to touch that witness and his testimony with a ten-foot barge pole.

Hywell's next witness was Colleen Ryan, Sarah and my former schoolmate, and Sarah's current housekeeper. Although she was now in her late fifties, Colleen was still an attractive woman. Her hair, an auburn colour, was down past her shoulders, and although she was small in stature, she was well-endowed, as the bodice of her dress revealed an ample chest and deep cleavage. I could see how she would appeal to most men. However, today, she appeared quite timid as she slowly walked to the witness box, her head down, looking at the floor. Hywell approached her with a disarming smile, but she shyly kept staring down as she waited for him to ask his first question.

"Mrs. Ryan, how do you know the defendant, Sarah Slater?"

"I does 'er cleanin', sir."

"I believe you and your husband have been married for quite a long time. How old were you when you married him?"

"Eighteen."

"You have five children, correct? And you also had another little girl, Tiffany, who died, is that right?"

She nodded. Hywell looked at the clerk of the court, "For the court, the witness nodded to agree that she does indeed have five children plus one who died."

"Mrs. Ryan, your little girl Tiffany died in a car accident several years ago. Is that correct?"

She nodded, "Yes."

"But could you tell the Court what happened? I understand how difficult this must be for you."

"I picked 'er up from playschool; she were only three years old and such a little thing. Anyway, I 'ad to go to the Post Office on the way 'ome, and while I were in there cashing me child benefits cheque, she ran outside and into the road. This car come out of nowhere and slammed into her, and then just drove off."

Her voice broke, and she wiped her eyes on the sleeve of her jumper. The judge leaned across and handed her a box of tissues and, after muttering to himself for what seemed an eternity, said to the court, "Let us take a fifteen-minute break while this witness composes herself."

I immediately walked outside for a cigarette and felt someone coming up behind me. It was Colleen Ryan looking furious and upset.

"Peg, can I bum a fag off you?" Much as I dislike being called Peg, I needed to keep her on my side, so I gave her a cigarette and lit it for her. She took a hefty drag. "How could he ask me something like that? It's not fair. I agreed to be a witness, but he should've warned me what he were going to make me say."

"I'm really sorry, Colleen. You're right; he should have warned you. I didn't expect it, either. I'm not sure where he's going with this, but hopefully, it will be all over soon. Before we go back into court, can I ask you a question about the car accident? Did the police ever find out who did it?"

"No, someone who saw it happen said they saw a big black car, an SUV, or summat, and they thought the number plate had a 22 in it. They weren't sure of the make of the car, but they said it looked expensive, maybe a BMW. There must've been some damage to the front of the car, you'd think, but the police never found it or the owner. They reckon it were out-of-towners."

I nodded sympathetically as I took a final drag of my cigarette and then gently guided Colleen back inside.

I went back to my seat in the courtroom, and Colleen went back into the witness box.

Hywell then continued with his questioning, "Mrs. Ryan, did you know Mr. Slater before he died?"

"Yeah, I told you, I clean their 'house."

"Yes, but how *well* did you know Mr. Slater?"

"I just told you."

"Did you ever see Mr. Slater away from the house? Please remember that you are under oath."

She looked down at her hands, and her cheeks turned pink.

"Well, he drove me 'ome sometimes after I done me cleaning."

"Did Mr. Slater ever stop the car when he was driving you home?"

"Maybe." She mumbled.

"Mrs. Ryan, Tiffany was a very pretty little girl from the photographs in the newspapers. She had long black hair that was tied up in a ponytail. By any chance, did any of her brothers and sisters ever say anything about her hair?"

"Not to me, no. Why would they?"

"Well, they, like you and your husband, are redheads. I assume that was because you and he are of Irish heritage, so a little girl with black hair would rather stand out in your family. Were you aware that your husband was quite concerned about it? In fact, he was so concerned that he had a paternity test taken to see if he was Tiffany's father?"

Colleen moaned as she grabbed the edge of the witness box, looking like she might faint. She obviously had no idea

94

about Kevin taking a paternity test. She shook her head, "No."

"Mrs. Ryan, I'm sure you would like to know the result. In the interest of justice, your husband, Kevin Ryan, has agreed that I may divulge the result of that test. He was not, in fact, her father."

There was an audible gasp from the courtroom; the judge looked up and banged his gavel on his desk. Hywell was on a roll, his voice becoming louder, all the better to achieve a good reaction from the court.

He continued: "Mrs. Ryan, there was someone else in the village, though, with the same hair colour as Tiffany, wasn't there, someone who used to take you home after you had finished cleaning his house?"

Colleen let out a sob.

I looked across to Sarah, who looked stunned.

So this was Hywell's piece-de-resistance. He was going to try and convince the court that Sarah had murdered her husband because she found out he'd had an affair with Colleen, and he was, in fact, Tiffany's father.

More gasps and mutterings could be heard from the public gallery. The judge banged his gavel a couple more times before he gained their attention.

"Ladies and Gentlemen, may I remind you that you are in a courtroom, and as such, you are required to remain silent. Any further outbursts, and I shall have to clear the court. Thank you."

Hywell pressed on with his questioning.

"Mrs. Ryan, did anyone else ever comment about Tiffany's hair colour?"

Colleen took a deep breath, wiped her tears with a tissue, and responded uncomfortably: "Um, well, yes, sir. One time, I were in the shop, and Mrs. Weston come in and looked at Tiffany, and she said what a pretty little girl she were and were I babysitting her. I said no, that she were my daughter. Then she said, 'Oh well, she don't look nothing like your husband, does she?' I'm afraid I lost it and told her to mind her own business."

"Do you know if Mrs. Weston said anything to her daughter, the defendant, about Tiffany?"

"I dunno about that." She looked over at Sarah, her eyes pleading for forgiveness.

"No further questions, My Lord," Hywell concluded confidently.

It finally became clear how Hywell was attempting to manipulate the jury's thinking. Much as I felt sorry for Colleen, I needed to convince the jury that Sarah was unaware of this sordid affair and the resulting child. I stood up and walked across to Colleen.

"Mrs. Ryan, did Mr. Slater know he was Tiffany's father?"

"Well, I never told 'im, and 'e never asked, so I don't think 'e knew."

"Did Mrs. Slater say anything to you about Tiffany? Do you think she may have guessed that her husband was Tiffany's father?"

"No, I don't think she knew. She were always very nice to me when I cleaned 'er house, and she always had gifts for me kids, for their birthdays and Christmas and stuff, and she always included Tiff right up till she died. She treated 'em all the same. I don't think she suspected anything were goin' on, thank goodness."

"Thank you, Mrs. Ryan. No further questions, My Lord."

If Hywell had been trying to establish Sarah's anger as a motive, hopefully, Colleen's testimony would help convince the jury that Sarah knew nothing about this turn of events.

The judge asked Hywell if he had any more witnesses, but with his last bombshell, he was done. That was his case for the prosecution.

It was my turn, and I needed to pull out all the stops to obtain that acquittal.

I recalled Nicola again to the stand — this time for her knowledge of her parent's relationship.

"Thank you again, Nicola, for your time. Would you please describe to the Court the relationship you had with your father?"

"We had a great relationship. We both liked sports and whenever I was at home, he and I would watch football or cricket together. Sometimes, we would go into Burton to watch Burton Albion play. My sister and my mum were more into tennis, which I like too, but I prefer football and played on the team at school. My dad actually coached the team for a couple of years."

"And how was your mother and father's relationship with each other?"

"My mother thought the world of my father. They were married for over thirty years. She was absolutely devastated when he died. All she kept saying was, 'Who would do this to Rich because he's such a lovely man.'"

"Was your father a drinker?"

"My dad used to like a drink but had stopped drinking just after he and my mum were married. He had started again a few years ago, but as far as I know, he never drank to excess."

"Do you know the trigger that started him drinking again?"

"Jennifer, that's my sister, and I think it may have been our fault, actually. We married a year after each other, which may have caused some financial problems for Mum and Dad."

"But as far as you know, the drinking never became a serious problem?"

"If you mean was he ever so drunk that he would physically hurt Mum, not as far as I know. They would have the occasional argument mostly over money, but nothing really serious."

"Thank you, Nicola. No further questions, My Lord."

Hywell was on his feet already as the judge looked across to see if he wanted to cross-examine Nicola.

"Yes, My Lord, I do. Mrs. Smith, you said that your parents didn't really argue except over money. Could you explain to the court what you know of these money problems?"

"Well, that was a few years ago now. My sister and I were married within a year of each other, and I think that may have caused some financial problems. I know they had to cancel a holiday in the south of France the year after my wedding, and Dad had talked about buying a new car, but that never happened. But as I said, that was a few years ago. So far as I know, they haven't had any money problems recently."

"Going back to the weddings, was this when your father started drinking again?"

"Um, thinking back, I don't remember him ever drinking when I was living at home, but I do remember him having a drink at my wedding reception. I don't recall him being drunk; he told me he just needed something to calm his nerves before giving his speech, you know, a bit of Dutch courage."

"So, between the drinking and the financial problems, do you know if all this stress could have caused your father to blame your mother? Was it possible that he could have physically abused her?"

I jumped up. "Objection, My Lord, we have already established that they never hit each other."

"Objection overruled; continue with your line of questioning. I'm interested to see where you are going with this," muttered Stanfield.

"Thank you, My Lord. Mrs. Smith, I know you said that your parents, as far as you know, had never hit each other, but was there anything else that could be construed as being physical?"

"Well, sir, Mum did call me one time just a couple of months before Dad died. She told me he had come home from playing darts in the pub and was a bit tipsy after having a few beers with his mates. He'd got a bit physical, was how she put it; he staggered into her, pushing her up against the wall when she asked him how many beers he'd had. I asked if she was alright, and she said absolutely. She just hit him with her handbag and pushed him away. She said she probably shouldn't have even mentioned it to me and was sure it was an accident. Dad was quite a large, imposing man who didn't know his own strength, and he could be quite clumsy. She laughed and said that he did have a black eye from where the bag hit him, so she must have hit him pretty hard."

"No further questions, My Lord."

Shit, how did he manage to find out about that? Nicola had not mentioned it to me. I have minimal tolerance for ambush, and Hywell was a master of the art.

My next witness was an old friend of Sarah's, Catherine Stratton. She was known as the clever girl from primary school and was now a medical director at one of the large teaching hospitals in London.

"Doctor Stratton, would you tell the court how you know the defendant?"

"I have known Mrs. Slater since we were children back in Lower Naughton in the Nineteen Fifties. She and I were best friends, you could say, in primary school."

"So, you have remained friends, is that correct?"

"Yes, we are. I was recently remarried, and Mrs. Slater was a witness at my wedding".

"So you knew the defendant well? Could you tell the court why your friendship has lasted all these years?"

"Of course. Mrs. Slater is someone I knew I could trust. She was the first person I went to when anything bad happened. She helped me through my divorce. I stayed with her and Richard for several months as it was a particularly acrimonious time, and it affected me very badly, but she helped me through the whole episode. I could call on her anytime to chat about any troubles I was having with work, and she knew she could come to me if she had any problems. She was that type of friend."

"You also knew the victim, her husband, Richard Slater, is that correct? From your observations, when you were all together, how would you describe their relationship?"

"I've known Richard as long as I have known Sarah — we all went to the same primary school. Whenever I saw them together, they acted very naturally, just like any couple

101

married for a long time. There was a bit of joking, some banter back and forth, and occasionally some mild bickering, but nothing serious. Mr. Slater would tease his wife probably more than she did him, but she would laugh it off; it was never to the point of being embarrassing or awkward."

"Throughout your friendship, did you ever witness any displays of a violent temper from your friend Sarah?"

"Never." She sounded adamant, "She was always the most even-tempered and gentle person I knew."

"Thank you, Doctor Stratton. No further questions, My Lord."

The judge looked over at Gryfidd-Jones to see if he would like to cross-examine, but he shook his head.

My next witness was Kevin Ryan. He ambled over to the witness box and stared at me expectantly.

"Mr. Ryan, good morning. Would you please tell the court how you know the defendant, Sarah Slater?"

"She married me mate, Dick."

"By Dick, do you mean the victim, Richard Slater?"

"Yeah."

"How long have you known Mr. and Mrs. Slater?"

"Since we was kids at school. Dick, sorry, Richard, lived just up the road from me. You lived there too, didn't ya?"

I felt the jury and the public in the gallery looking at me, but I ignored him and carried on with my questions.

"Mr. Ryan, are you married?"

"Yeah"

"How long have you been married?"

"I dunno, around forty years."

"And to whom are you married?"

"Colleen O'Brien, as she were."

"And how did you meet her?"

"We've known each other since we was kids. She went to the same school as me, but she were a couple of years younger."

"Mr. Ryan, do you have any children?"

"Yeah, I got five kiddies. Actually, I did have six, but me littlest, Tiffany, died in a car accident."

"I am very sorry." And I truly meant it.

"Mr. Ryan, you and Mr. Slater had a falling out in the past, correct?"

"Yeah, we had a fight about summat, but that were years ago."

"Wasn't the fight over whether the victim, Richard Slater, had an affair with your wife?" There was an intake of breath from Sarah.

"Yeah, but it's all sorted. A big misunderstanding it were."

"How long ago did this all take place? Wasn't it just before your daughter Tiffany was born?"

"Yeah, but I told ya it's all sorted."

"Mr. Ryan, your daughter Tiffany was not your daughter, is that correct?"

"Yeah, she were," he answered indignantly.

"I'm sorry. I will re-phrase my question. Tiffany was not your biological daughter, was she? Yes, for all intents and purposes, you brought her up as your own, but she had a different father to your other children. Is that correct?"

"Yeah, but I loved her just as much as me other kids. She were a lovely little thing."

"Do you know who her actual father was?"

"Yeah, I'm pretty sure I know who it was, but I'd rather not say."

"I understand. When did you last see Richard Slater?" Kevin looked up at me, taken aback.

"Uh, I think it were a coupla days before he died. We used to go down the Falconer's Arms for a coupla pints. We was on the darts team, and we'd just beaten the crap outta the Cooper's Tavern and was celebrating."

"How did Mr. Slater seem?"

"He were ok, a bit quiet when we first met up, but after we won the darts, he were his old self."

"Mr. Ryan, are you sure that was the last time? You didn't see him again after that?"

"Oh yeah, I forgot. I met him for a quick one 'cos he wanted to tell me he couldn't play the next week as he would be in London with his daughter."

"Do you remember when that was exactly?"

"Yeah, it were the day before he died. We had a drink up at the pub that evening. He said they was leaving first thing the next morning."

"To make sure I've understood, you said you met him for a drink in the pub the night *before* he died. Is that correct?"

"Yeah, that's right."

"Do you remember whether he had anything to eat?"

"Yeah, we had some chips 'cause we was hungry on account of going there straight from work."

"Mr. Ryan, what do you do for a living?"

"I'm the foreman at a farm in the next village over from Lower Naughton."

"Could you explain to the court what it is exactly that you do at the farm?"

"I'm the manager. I oversees all the areas of the farm, from making sure the cows is looked after, their barns is clean, that they's milking equipment is sterilized, and I supervise the lads lookin' after the pigs and sheep. All stuff to do with the animals."

"Mr. Ryan, does the farm have any problems with vermin — rats and mice, for example?"

"Yeah, same as all farms. We got a coupla cats that's supposed to take care of that, but to be honest, there's too many of them buggers, so we have to sometimes put out rat poison in the fields just to keep 'em down. We don't want rats anywhere near the milking sheds."

"What sort of rat poison do you use?"

"These days, we use any product that's approved for farming. Years ago, we'd sometimes use thallium, but since it's now banned we can't get it. Shame, really; it were very effective on them buggers."

Bingo! I didn't even have to ask him. He provided that piece of crucial information all by himself. 'Thank you, Kevin.'

"No further questions, My Lord."

As I sat down, I saw Gryfidd-Jones looking at me with a 'where did that come from and what's it all about' look on his face. I don't know why he was looking at me like that. He knew I would question Kevin as I'd put his name on my list of witnesses. I guess he hadn't done his homework when he reviewed the list. I smiled to myself.

"Mr. Gryfidd-Jones, do you have any questions of this witness?" He shook his head. Of course, he didn't. He was just as baffled as the rest of the courtroom.

Kevin, being the last witness, the judge asked Gryfidd-Jones to give his closing speech. Confidently, he rose to his feet and approached the jury.

"Ladies and Gentlemen of the jury, over the course of this trial, you have heard how Elizabeth Weston, a defenseless and very sick old lady, was murdered in the most vicious and brutal manner at the hand of a calculating and devious person, her daughter. The defendant had grown impatient with the demands made by her mother, who, because of her illness, was depending on her daughter more and more.

"That particular morning, the defendant was due to make a presentation to the School Board about her plans for the school's future. Concerned about how the meeting would go and with ideas on how to present her arguments still buzzing around in her head, she was preparing to leave her house when her mother phoned. Mrs. Weston told the defendant she needed her to perform what she felt was an essential errand, namely grocery shopping. In the defendant's mind, this was hardly essential. Running errands was the last thing the defendant needed to be doing with the vital meeting coming up. It just added to her stress. How could her mother be so selfish? Surely, she knew the meeting was important, but as usual, her mother's needs came ahead of everyone else's. Sarah Slater had had enough — it couldn't go on that way. She looked at her watch; she had forty-five minutes before the meeting, which she realized was enough time to go to her mother's house on the way to school and give her a piece of her mind.

"The more she thought about it, the defendant became more and more incensed. How dare her mother expect her to drop everything just because she needed a stupid errand run? She arrived at the house and let herself in. By that time, she was beside herself and had reached boiling point; she was at her wit's end, completely insane. The anger she felt towards her poor mother had caused her to lose all sense of reason. She went into the kitchen, grabbed a butcher's knife from the drawer, and ran up the stairs, where she found her mother in her bedroom. On seeing the fury in her daughter's eyes and the knife in her hand, Mrs. Weston immediately started screaming, making the defendant even more angry. She grabbed her mother's hair, pulled her head back, and slit her throat. Still enraged, she stabbed her repeatedly in the chest and abdomen to make sure her mother was dead. She then went back downstairs, washed the knife and put it back in the drawer. Unfortunately, in her frenzy, the defendant had sliced her left hand; this meant spending time finding a bandage, dressing the cut, and cleaning up the blood. Time was not on her side; she ran out of the house, slamming the front door, drove to her home, changed her clothes, and drove to school, arriving just in time for the meeting. In retrospect, she was hoping it would give her an alibi for around the time the murder was committed.

"To cover her tracks, after the board meeting ended, she went to the shop and then drove to Mrs. Weston's house, pretending to find her mother in her bedroom bleeding, although she knew she was already dead. She then rang the police station to report the murder. With her mother out of the way and no longer having to comply with her unreasonable demands, she had her freedom and the added bonus of collecting a sizable inheritance. Unfortunately for the defendant, her red Prius had been spotted in her mother's driveway at roughly the time her mother was killed.

"As to the second charge facing the defendant, the murder of her husband, Richard Slater, let me review the facts. The defendant painted him as a physically and mentally abusive drunk to her daughters, telling them he had come home from drinking at the local pub the worse for wear and had taunted her until she couldn't take it anymore and would attack him. More important than the drinking was the knowledge that he had fathered a child by their cleaning woman. We heard that the defendant's mother suspected this, so wouldn't she have discussed it with her daughter? And knowing her husband had an affair that had resulted in a child and with the added embarrassment of knowing that her mother knew all about it, would it not have been too much for the defendant to bear?

"The day Mr. Slater died, the defendant and the victim ate breakfast on the train, had coffee with their daughter in London, and lunch with an old friend in the West End. At any point, the defendant could easily have surreptitiously sprinkled the poison onto his food or drink without it looking suspicious. Due to her extensive knowledge of poisons, she knew which one, in particular, to use as it could take up to twenty-four hours to work. She hoped it meant she could kill him without anyone questioning his death, as it would look like a heart attack. She chose the day he died deliberately as she had arranged it so that they ate every meal with other people. She was confident that whichever meal the poison was added to, someone else would be there who could potentially be blamed for his death.

"She had her future planned out, and it did not include either her demanding, selfish mother or her drunken, unfaithful husband.

"Ladies and gentlemen of the jury, you have no other option but to find the defendant, Sarah Elizabeth Slater, guilty of premeditated murder for these deliberate and psychopathic acts committed on these two innocent people."

With that verbal flourish, he sat down, giving me a rueful smile as if to commiserate on my loss of both cases. Don't hold your breath on that thought, matey.

The judge looked across at me, "Mrs. German-Brown, would you now give your closing remarks?"

I stood and walked across to face the jury, genuinely expressing concern for my client. I deliberately spoke with a quiet confidence that I hoped was in contrast to Gryfidd-Jones' loud and aggressive diatribe.

"Ladies and Gentlemen, it is actually your clear duty to find the defendant, Sarah Slater, innocent of these baseless charges of murdering her mother, Elizabeth Weston, and her husband, Richard Slater. The case for the prosecution simply does not hold water. After extensive reviews of the witnesses' testimony, one can see that it consists purely of circumstantial evidence that barely qualifies as evidence — nothing more than spurious assumptions and unreliable accounts. Now, let's review the true facts as we know them.

110

"At 8:30 on the morning of April 30th, the defendant received a telephone call from her mother requesting that she purchase items for a coffee morning she was hosting for her next-door neighbour, Ethel Woods. Somewhere around nine o'clock, Mrs. Woods thought she heard a scream but, when giving her evidence, admitted she had a problem with her hearing aid. It had not been inserted correctly and needed adjusting. She was, therefore, unable to differentiate between the sound of someone screaming and the sound of a bird or animal. Around the same time, Mrs. Woods looked out of her window and saw a car speeding down the road. Her vision, which is also unreliable, meant she could not guarantee that the car she saw was actually the defendant's car; all she was sure of was that it was red, nor could she categorically state how many people were in the car, let alone who.

"Coincidentally, at the same time, the postman, Bill Turner, also saw a car on the road. He, too, could not be one hundred percent certain that the vehicle being driven away from Mrs. Weston's house belonged to the defendant or how many people were in the car. He admitted that the speed it was going was totally out of character for the way the defendant typically drives. Therefore, he could not reliably state it was the defendant driving the car. Nor did the driver acknowledge the postman, as she usually did. All we know is that both witnesses saw a red car being driven fast.

"We also know from one of the other witnesses, Mr. Douglas Lloyd, that Mrs. Slater had that morning been at a meeting of the School Board that lasted around two hours

— a meeting where she behaved with her usual calm, professional demeanor. I ask you, ladies and gentlemen of the jury, how could anyone who had just murdered their mother in such a violent manner act with such composure? And how could such behavior fit with Mr. Gryfidd-Jones' fanciful tale of someone being driven into such a violent rage over a bottle of milk and a packet of custard creams?

"So, let us review the murder as fancifully detailed by my learned friend for the prosecution. At eight-thirty on the morning of April 30th, it was established that the defendant received a phone call from her mother asking her to go shopping for her. Mr. Gryfidd-Jones would have you believe the defendant hung up the phone from her mother and, in a fit of anger, drove to her house. She grabbed a knife from the kitchen, ran up the stairs, slit her mother's throat, and stabbed her multiple times, out of control with rage, accidentally cutting her hand in the process. Then, somehow, she managed to bandage her hand, remove any evidence of her presence, then clean herself up or change into a second outfit she conveniently had with her, as she must surely have been covered in blood. She made sure there were no bloody footprints, then she washed the knife and put it back in its place in the kitchen. She ran out of the house, slamming the door shut, and drove back down the road. Ignoring the postman and Mrs. Woods, she went straight to school for the board meeting, where we heard she acted perfectly normally. After the meeting concluded, the defendant went straight to the village shop to purchase the promised items for her mother. Mrs. Blake, the owner of the shop, verified that the defendant was indeed in the shop sometime after eleven that morning. Now, ask yourself this: if she had killed her mother, would she have bothered buying milk and biscuits and then gone back to her mother's house, knowing the old lady was lying upstairs in a pool of blood? And then calmly rung the police?

"And just one more thing. We know that Mrs. Weston had lung cancer. Her oncologist stated that due to the late stage of the disease, she had only a matter of months left to live. If, as the prosecution suggested, the defendant was desperate to collect on her inheritance, would she have murdered her mother at this time and risked spending the rest of her life in prison? She only had to wait a little longer, and it would all be taken care of. We heard from several witnesses that the defendant was very close to her mother. The two of them regularly spent time together. They attended church every week, following which Mrs. Weston would be invited back to the defendant's house for Sunday lunch. The defendant enjoyed spending time with her mother, even doing their weekly grocery shopping together. There is a distinct lack of evidence of any deep malice shown by the defendant toward her mother.

"And so, in summing up, the evidence that Sarah Slater murdered her mother as presented by the prosecution is based on second-hand gossip and unreliable witnesses and is circumstantial at best. The suggestion that she was so desperate to have her hands on her inheritance that she murdered her mother when she only had a short time to wait as her mother was dying is absurd and devoid of any credible supporting evidence.

"The prosecution has not produced any concrete or forensic evidence to link the defendant with the crime scene, any weapon, any bloody clothes, or even the mysterious red car. Everything is simply coincidence and conjecture. And so, based on the so-called 'evidence' presented by the prosecution, you must find the defendant not guilty of the murder of Mrs. Weston.

"Now, turning our attention to the death of Richard Slater, we heard from various witnesses that the defendant and her husband enjoyed a warm and affectionate relationship over many decades. Yes, like any couple who've been married for a number of years, they had their ups and downs, but from the evidence given by their daughter, they had a good, stable marriage. Richard Slater was known on occasion to have a pint or two at the pub with his friends. On the night before he died, he had a drink with a member of the darts team, Kevin Ryan. Now, here was a man who had an excellent reason to feel vindictive towards Richard Slater as he suspected that the victim had had a relationship with his wife that had resulted in the birth of a child. Far from accusing Kevin Ryan of anything, as this is not his trial, it does introduce a new component to the equation as maybe he had more of a reason for the murder than the defendant. Not one witness has given the slightest hint of a justifiable cause for Sarah Slater to have killed her husband. After all, she knew nothing of the affair or the resulting child's birth until it was mentioned during the trial.

"So, ladies and gentlemen, we have discovered a plausible alternative that also fits the means, motive, and opportunity criteria valued so highly by the police. An alternative those same police failed to investigate. Another scenario the police ignored was the potential of Richard Slater having

114

taken his own life. We have no idea of the deceased's state of mind, but could he have been concerned his relationship with Mrs. Ryan might be discovered? I am not saying that Kevin Ryan is responsible for the murder or that Richard Slater committed suicide. What I am saying is that the police, in their eagerness to solve the crimes, chose the easy way out, relying on circumstantial evidence rather than investigating thoroughly and proving solid facts.

"The prosecution made much of the fact that the defendant has some knowledge of various poisons. Thallium Sulphate, used to kill Richard Slater, was known to treat ringworm on the scalp, as anyone who has read an Agatha Christie novel would know — it being a particularly favourite poison in her books. We also know that the defendant was not the only person who knew about poisons, particularly rat poison. In the twenty-four hours prior to his death, we know Mr. Slater saw other people besides his wife; therefore, the poison could have been administered in anything he ate or drank by anyone who had a grudge against him. They would have had plenty of opportunity to kill him. Having said that, Thallium Sulphate has been banned in England for many years, and so it would have been challenging to obtain any. Maybe it can be found for industrial or agricultural purposes but certainly not for use by the general public."

Again, I let the implication of Kevin's job on the farm register in the jury's minds.

"The defendant, Sarah Slater, was one of the most trusted and admired residents of the village. She was generous to a fault with her time, the Headteacher of the village school and president of the local branch of the Women's Institute,

115

just as her mother had been. She was a loving wife, mother, and devoted daughter.

"I put it to you, ladies and gentlemen of the jury, that my learned friend has hardly provided the staggering weight of evidence that would prove the prosecution's case beyond a reasonable doubt. The evidence that has been provided has been purely circumstantial in nature and leaned precariously toward the flimsy, the fanciful, and implausible. Quite apart from the absence of solid evidence, there is plenty of scope for doubt in almost every aspect of both these tragic deaths. We still have no real idea who may have committed these dreadful crimes. But it is patently clear from the so-called circumstantial evidence presented by the prosecution that, in either case, they were not perpetrated by the defendant here before you. Therefore, you must find the defendant not guilty of the murders of her husband and mother."

It was done, and with a sigh of relief and an encouraging smile at Sarah, I took my seat in anticipation of "the mutterer's" summation.

The judge neatly summed up the evidence and told the jury what was expected of them.

"Ladies and gentlemen of the jury, you have seen and heard all the evidence, and it is now your responsibility to decide whether the prosecution has proven, without a shadow of a doubt, that the defendant, Sarah Elizabeth Slater, is guilty of one or both of these murders. Should you have any doubt about the burden of proof, then you must find the defendant not guilty."

The judge leaned forward and added, "Please remember, when deliberating over the defendant's guilt or innocence, your decision should not be based on emotion or sympathy but purely on the specific facts that have been presented to you. Thank you."

The judge left, the jurors were led from the courtroom, and everyone else filed out to await the verdict.

Chapter 4

Once outside the courtroom, I swapped my heels for a pair of flat shoes, popped the pumps into my bag, along with my wig, and headed down the street to find something to eat. I needed to stay reasonably close to the court in case we were called back to hear the verdict. I had no idea how long the jury would take to reach a decision, especially as they had to deliberate on two murders. Still, I couldn't imagine it would take less than a couple of hours to return a verdict, and they would undoubtedly be provided lunch before settling into their deliberations.

With that in mind, I made my way to my usual sandwich shop. How could I go anywhere else? It was the last time I would have to suffer the agonizing wait for a verdict, and although I told myself I wasn't superstitious, I felt I couldn't change the habit of a lifetime. After ordering my usual sandwich, I walked over to an empty table by the wall where I could see anyone coming in. I wasn't feeling particularly social, so I could hide behind my newspaper if anyone I knew wandered in. I fumbled around in my handbag for my mobile, changed the setting to vibrate, and put it on the table so I could grab it if anyone tried to contact me with the news that a verdict was imminent.

I sat there for at least an hour before texting my team to see if they had heard anything. They replied that the jury had finished lunch and begun their deliberation and had already sent for clarification on a couple of the conversations with the coroner, Dr. Gupta. His accent had caused a little confusion. Dr. Gupta had impeccable English, having been born here, but being from 'up north,' the Staffordshire accent can sometimes be challenging for inhabitants of the more 'genteel' southeast of the country. Seeking some fresh air, I left the familiar shop, perhaps for the last time, and walked down to the Embankment. Finding an empty bench, I sat down and rummaged around in my bag for a much-needed cigarette, which I then inhaled deeply, savoring that first blissfully calming sensation as the smoke traveled down to my lungs.

A benefit to taking this one final case was having the opportunity to enjoy London for a bit longer. My emotions were torn. Much as I was looking forward to retirement and living in the country, I had always loved working in one of the most fascinating, vibrant, and exciting cities in the World. I was lucky that Lindford Court, where my chambers were situated, was in such a superb location. Stepping out of my office and being able to walk around this beautiful city had always made me feel a small part of it. Much as pushing my way through the throng of commuters exiting the trains each morning and rushing down the escalators into the underbelly of the city to reach the Tube could be somewhat overwhelming at times, I suspected one lost that wonderfully intimate feeling of ownership, of being a part of something special that, coming up to London only for the odd visit a couple of times a year, one could no longer claim.

Ridiculous as it may sound, I actually enjoyed taking the Tube. The number of times I'd stood on the platform at Victoria waiting for the train to arrive, wishing it would hurry up as I had a meeting fast approaching and regretting not taking a taxi. Ears cocked toward the dark, hoping to hear the rumbling further down the track and feeling the vibration as it moved closer. The whoosh of warm air swirling tiny flakes of dust around the platform, and finally, the deafening roar as it rushed out of the tunnel and pulled to a squealing halt. The doors opening with that unique hiss, and crowds of people pour onto the platform while I pushed forward, everyone crushing each other in their eagerness to find that elusive seat ready for, in my case, a six-minute ride to Blackfriars. Strangely, I would miss the stress-inducing challenges of that commute.

On some occasions, when I wanted to make an impression for one of the more prominent, splashier cases, I would have one of the Clerks of Chambers organize a car and driver, preferably an E350 Mercedes Benz. All the clerks knew that if they could score my favourite driver, Max, there would likely be a bottle of wine in it for their efforts. I do wonder, though, if this need to impress was insecurity raising its ugly head.

Anyone would think I didn't want to retire, but that wasn't the case. I was looking forward to the freedom of not having schedules to keep to and not having to pretend to care about the gruesome crimes of some degenerate felon just because it was my job. Of course, I would miss the thrill of defending said reprobate — an almost undoubtedly guilty member of either a well-known family, or a notorious gang member, or maybe a shifty executive of a financial company. Only after defending someone in a court of law does one have any idea of the power one holds over them. Their fate was in my hands. Defendants, who were in control of every aspect of their own lives on a daily basis, were now dependent on me to find some way out of their mess. Finally, after I had, hopefully, obtained that all-important acquittal, there was the rush of adrenaline as I led them out of the court to their limousines, cameras flashing, microphones thrust into their faces for comments.

Then, the excitement of knowing that the following day, I would almost certainly be on the front page of the daily broadsheets: 'Margaret German-Brown QC prevails again.' But I could guarantee one thing: although retirement may lack that exhilaration, I wouldn't miss the hours of preparation to achieve that goal. But, having said all that, I most certainly would not be turning into another member of the beige anorak brigade, shuffling around the stately homes of the National Trust with more interest in the gift shop than in the history of the place. There was absolutely no way I would be seen shopping in Marks and Spencer for that anorak any time soon.

Lost in my reverie, as I sat by the river, I pulled my Kindle out from my bag and settled down to read. A while later, and feeling a little chilly, I checked my watch to find over two hours had passed, and I had heard nothing. Rifling through my bag, looking for my phone in case I'd missed a message about the verdict, I realized I'd left it on the table in the café. I grabbed my bag and, walking as fast as I could, headed back to the cafe in hopes of retrieving it. Fortunately, the staff knew me, so if it had been found, I was pretty sure they would have held it for me. Sure enough, as I walked in the door, Sue, the manager, waved and signaled that they had the phone. After thanking her profusely, I checked for messages to find that, indeed, Toby had been trying to contact me for the last fifteen minutes to let me know the jury had reached a verdict. Shit, I needed to hurry back.

I ran back to Court, indecorously pulling my gown out of my bag. Deciding the lift was probably quicker than the stairs, I stepped in and pressed the button. At least that would give me a few seconds to pull on my wig and gown and change my shoes. The lift hadn't moved when the door re-opened, and in walked Hywell. Thank goodness, at least I wouldn't be the last one back into Court. We chatted about where we'd had lunch. Hywell's wife, Camille, had joined him, and they had chosen much heartier fare, having gone to a pub around the corner where he'd enjoyed sausage and mash and a half-pint of bitter. Before entering the courtroom and in recognition of the closeness of our friendship, we wished each other good luck.

"May the best man or woman win," Hywell said with a wry smile. Of course, neither of us meant it as we both wanted to win — but it is the polite thing to do, after all.

And in we went. Scanning the courtroom, I saw Nicola and her sister Jennifer looking worried. Looking up at Sarah, I gave her a 'fingers crossed' sign, and she offered a watery smile.

"Be upstanding," instructed the Clerk of the Court as Lord Justice Stanfield entered the courtroom. He looked at Hywell and me, and we nodded. Disconcertingly, Lord Justice Stanfield looked rather sternly across at Sarah.

"Would the defendant please stand?" Sarah stood up, shaking as she held onto the front of the dock for support.

The foreman of the jury stood up, and the Clerk of the Court, in his most formal voice, asked him:

"Members of the jury, have you reached the verdicts upon which you are all agreed?"

"We have," responded the jury's foreman as he handed the written verdict to the bailiff to pass to the judge.

The Clerk of the Court continued:

"Concerning the first count of murder in the first degree of Elizabeth Florence Weston, do you find the defendant guilty or not guilty?"

I held my breath, and my chest tightened in anticipation.

"Not guilty."

I hope my huge sigh of relief was not too loud. The butterflies of nervous excitement began flitting through my stomach again.

"In relation to the second count of murder in the first degree of Richard Kevin Slater, do you find the defendant guilty or not guilty?"

I took another deep breath.

"Not guilty."

I heard a sob come from the dock. Sarah had collapsed onto her chair and understandably burst into tears.

"Mrs. Slater, you have been found not guilty on both counts, and you are free to go." The judge smiled warmly and directed the security officer to release her.

Hywell walked across, and we shook hands as he graciously said, "Congratulations, Margaret." We then agreed on a day for dinner the following week to discuss the trial's outcome. Camille, Hywell's wife, loved participating in these discussions as she would attend some of the more exciting trials that Hywell and I worked on together. It was always interesting to have a third opinion, although sometimes it could lead to a few expletives, as Hywell or I would realize we'd overlooked some obscure fact that may have helped our case. Camille's position as a highly regarded criminal psychologist made her an ideal observer at spotting those minute details that we'd missed. Fortunately, those details were never earth-shattering enough to change the outcome.

I then walked across to Sarah, who was hugging her daughters. She turned and hugged me, thanking me over and over for all my work on her behalf. Excusing myself, I wished them a good evening and went to pick up my bags, feeling well pleased with my swan-song performance.

On the way back to Chambers, I stopped off at an off-license to pick up a couple of bottles of champagne. I decided that a well-deserved glass or two of bubbly was the least I could do for Toby and the team. They had been phenomenal in helping me with the case, putting in long hours to obtain DNA results, research poisons, and accumulate all the witness details.

Toby alone had achieved a minor miracle with a magnificent bit of investigating, having discovered the DNA paternity test Kevin Ryan had taken years earlier to determine if he was Tiffany's dad. I owed Toby and the other 'devils' so much, not just for Sarah's case, but for all the years we had worked together and the support they'd given me. A few other members of Chambers who were not in Court joined in the farewell gathering. And as I walked into the office, they all cheered and clapped. I actually felt quite sentimental, which was not an emotion I usually felt. In fact, I don't usually feel much about anything these days. Champagne corks popped, and glasses clinked as we toasted the victory — two acquittals. We wished each other all the best for the future, and that was that.

And suddenly, it was all over. A long and illustrious career had come to a positive end. Uncharacteristically, emotion took over again; I felt a lump in my throat knowing it was the last time I would be in those Chambers, at least on business. The inevitable doubts over my decision to retire flooded my mind.

Sneaking away from the celebrations, I went into my office, picked up my handbag and briefcase, put the remaining few items on my desk into my case, and had a last look around. There was something symbolic about turning off the standard lamp in the corner, and I was just about to leave when I spotted the two lithographs on the bookshelves; they were much too important to leave, and I added them to my bag. My dear friend Harry bought them to congratulate me and wish me success when I started my job there all those years ago. Harry had meant so much to me, and those two small items were the only meaningful things I had any desire to take with me. I waved at Toby as I opened the door and walked out onto the street. I couldn't understand why I was feeling so much emotion. It wasn't like me at all, but I suppose leaving somewhere that was all I had known, retiring from doing something I had loved for so many years, I should have expected to feel something — maybe I was human after all.

Part 2

Chapter 5

It was bittersweet leaving Chambers and everything that had been my life for so many years — the end of my career and the end of an era. But now, I could look forward to retirement, which sounded pretty dull after all the years of thrills from the numerous high-profile trials I had been involved in. However, if all went to plan, I still had one more exciting project to look forward to, which, if successful, would give me the climax for the semi-autobiographical novel I'm writing. Like most people, my life seemed to have been made up of a series of events that had culminated in that final day in court. We're born, obtain some sort of education, find a job we hope we enjoy, maybe marry and raise a family, and finally retire to a bungalow overlooking the sea and fade away. That's it, our allotted three score years and ten — if we're lucky.

I had moved to a village near Reigate in Surrey nearly twenty years previously. While I had loved working in London, I craved the peace and quiet of the countryside, so I'd sold my flat in Marylebone, bought a house with a large garden, and adopted a cat. That first cat had long since died, but I loved cats and was now on my third — Rocco, my handsome and affectionate black cat. He was a blessing to have around. After a bad day in court, I knew that, even though I was feeling grouchy, Rocco would greet me as soon as I opened the front door. And every evening, he would curl up beside me on the sofa while I worked late into the night.

The house, which is Grade II listed, has a red brick exterior and was built in 1898. I thought it would be perfect for my retirement, which started when Sarah's trial finished. The house has four bedrooms, one of which I use as a study and where I am writing my book. My bedroom is painted the palest shade of grey with a similar shade of bed linen. I have a matching pair of slipper chairs in a soft, dusky pink beside a small table under the window, and covering one wall is a large built-in wardrobe in dark walnut. Thinking about it, I suppose I should clear out my work clothes, my uniform of a white shirt and black pencil skirt, and take them to the charity shop in town. The third room is the guest bedroom with matching bed linen and towels. The fourth room has some basic gym equipment I'd bought with the best intentions but hardly ever use — probably another candidate for the charity shop.

Downstairs there are three reception rooms. The drawing room, which I rarely use, has a bay window overlooking the front garden. I'd bought the furniture with some interior design input from my old friend Harry. On the coffee table is a beautiful Asian wooden bowl made from bamboo and painted a vibrant garnet red with a thin black stripe across the center. The bowl has sentimental value as Harry and his partner, Michael, brought it back from the last trip they had taken together to Bali.

The sitting room, where I spend most of my time, has a large and extremely comfortable sofa and two matching armchairs, one with an ottoman. In the centre of the room is a rectangular, Asian-inspired coffee table. The white marble fireplace has an imposing mantlepiece, which provides the perfect spot for the two lithographs I had brought back from my office in chambers — they deserved pride of place because they reminded me of Harry. The television is attached to the wall above the fireplace, not that I watch it very much. I only turn it on to watch the news as I sip my nightly gin and tonic.

In the formal dining room, there's an old oak table with eight matching chairs I'd found at an antique shop in Guildford. The large farmhouse-style kitchen is at the back of the house, with a door opening onto the kitchen garden. In the door is a conveniently placed cat flap for Rocco to come and go as he pleases. I love to cook, and the built-in bookshelves overflow with more recipe books than I could ever use. The old, well-used kitchen table is from my grandparent's house. Finally, the breakfast nook, where I enjoy my first cup of coffee each day, has a window seat piled high with cushions, with a view of the kitchen garden.

The benefit of no longer working means I can spend more time in the garden, which is almost an acre in size. I have a gardener who takes care of all the big jobs I can't manage anymore, but there's still plenty of work for me to do. Rocco loves to spend time out there. He usually finds a sunny spot to lie and be quite content napping while I potter about deadheading roses or pulling up a few weeds.

As we had arranged earlier, Hywell and Camille arrived at my house for dinner the week after the trial. I'd been baking most of the day and was ready for a cocktail when they knocked on the door. After the initial welcome hugs and exclamations over the bottles of wine they had brought with them, which were deposited in the kitchen, we went into the sitting room. Hywell, who had been to the house many times and knew his way around, set to making pre-dinner drinks.

The conversation veered naturally to the trial. Hywell, who all the way through had stuck to his convictions that Sarah was guilty, now surprised me by saying, "I have to admit I didn't really believe Sarah had murdered either her mother or Richard."

Camille, with her reputation and expertise in criminal psychology, had sat in on parts of the trial, and Hywell had naturally discussed how he would present his side of the story with her. She now shocked us both.

"Surely, you don't really think Sarah is innocent. Good heavens, if Elizabeth Weston had been my mother, I'd have been sorely tempted to bump her off."

"Seriously, Camille, you'd have thought about killing your own mother?" asked a somewhat stunned Hywell.

"Absolutely, if what you said was correct, the woman was an absolute horror. Her treatment of Sarah was despicable. You know, mothers and their little boys have this, um, I don't know what you'd call it, but it's a bond. Little boys are perfect in their mother's eyes, whereas daughters are put on this earth to look after them. We've seen it in many cultures; the sons are the heirs to the kingdom, whether it is literally a kingdom or a shop or factory, you know it's always called So and So and Son, never So and So and Daughter. So yes, if she treated me as her servant and tried to control me, I'd be very tempted. Don't look at me like that, Hywell. Of course, I wouldn't actually do it. I'm too nice, but in the back of my mind, well, who knows."

"Darling, why didn't you say this before? You're so good at reading people's minds?"

Camille looked at him. "I could hardly have given you my opinion when the trial was ongoing, could I? But now, well, there it is."

Trying to calm the slightly tense situation, I suggested we move into the dining room and eat. Once seated and food and drinks were on the table, I asked Camille about Richard.

"So if you think Sarah could have killed her mother, what about Richard, her husband? Do you think she killed him too?"

Camille took a sip of wine, "There was a good enough reason for her to have done it. And she had the opportunity, but I'm not sure. She was obviously in love with him, and although she may have been furious about the affair and subsequent child, I just don't think she would have killed him. He was, after all, the father of her children. So, no, I don't think so. To be honest, she would have had to have been one heck of an actress, as it certainly seemed to me that she didn't have a clue about him fathering a child. The news seemed to hit her like a bombshell in court."

"Ok, so although Sarah is still a possibility as her mother's murderer, let's for a moment assume she's innocent of both murders. Now, if it's not her, then what other suspects do we have?" I asked them.

"We only know what the Police and lawyers have dug up, and it sounds as if the cops were happy to jump to first conclusions and build whatever case they could around that without looking too hard for other possibilities," ventured Camille.

Hywell, looking pensive, said, "That said, there's Kevin, Colleen's husband, who gallantly brought up the bastard child as his own. He had motive and opportunity. It's doubtful, but there is Nicola, Richard's daughter. She had the opportunity, but we don't have a motive."

I jumped into the conversation: "I still wonder about suicide. Could the guilt about what Richard had done have needled at his conscience? He must have been worried that he would be found out after having an affair with his best friend's wife, but why now?

"I have also had this idea at the back of my mind: what if Richard had killed Elizabeth? What if she had found out about the affair and was going to tell Sarah? Could he have been driven to kill her? And later, suffering remorse, killed himself?"

Hywell, who had finished eating, helped himself to a whiskey and looked first at me and then at Camille.

"That is certainly a reasonable hypothesis. Margaret, I have a suggestion, now that you've officially retired and Camille, darling, you keep saying you'd like to take a break to refresh the grey matter. What if you two play detective and find the real killers, whether that turns out to be Sarah Slater or someone else. Camille, your background in neural mechanisms and how they affect human behaviour should stand you in good stead. And as you and I know, Margaret, being a barrister requires us to scrutinize and investigate the evidence we've been given to put a case together for the crimes our clients have supposedly committed. So I think you two would make a great team. Don't Elizabeth Weston and Richard Slater deserve to have the real killers exposed?"

Camille and I looked at each other. Camille spoke first: "Well, I admit, I am a little intrigued by the whole thing." She smiled to herself as she considered her husband's proposal.

"Yes, I suppose I am, too," I agreed. "But Hywell, please don't think that just because I'm retired, I'm sitting here watching soap operas all day. Well, okay, I admit it, but only in the afternoons. Anyway, how do you suggest we go about this detective thing?"

"What if we meet, say for an hour or so over tea or coffee, a couple of times a month, more if we've found some good stuff," Camille replied.

"Great idea. What about coffee on Thursday morning at Starbucks in Guildford, and we can develop a plan of campaign?" I suggested.

I paused for a moment, then wondered aloud: "But what if our investigations point to the fact it was Sarah who did both?" Camille looked at Hywell, who shrugged his shoulders and pushed himself out of his chair.

"Now that would be something, wouldn't it? Anyway, we really should be off, darling. It's getting quite late."

As Hywell and Camille headed home, I cleared up the remains of the meal while thinking about how Camille and I could begin our pursuit of the guilty party.

Chapter 6

Thursday arrived, and I drove to Guildford and luckily found a parking spot not too far from Starbucks. I walked in and ordered a coffee. A table was vacant in a quiet spot in a corner nook, and I immediately commandeered it just as Camille arrived. She was unmistakable in her eclectic outfit. Camille was one of the most eccentric people I knew, and it was evident by her dress sense. On this particular day, she was dressed in a royal blue frock that looked suspiciously like a retro Vivienne Westwood, as there were more ruffles, buttons, and bows than I'd seen in a haberdasher. It wasn't to my taste, but I had to admit that Camille always looked fabulous. She waved at me as she picked up her drink and walked over. After putting down her cup and hugging me, she sat down. Opening her Tumi tote, she pulled out a fresh notebook, a ballpoint pen, and some coloured markers — she meant business. My first thought was that she must have high hopes we would come up with some serious suspects.

After the usual discussion about what we'd been up to since the dinner, Camille gave me a brief update on Hywell's latest court case. For a few seconds, I felt a wee bit envious, but I soon shrugged it off. Camille then asked if I'd mind describing Lower Naughton, the village where the first murder had occurred, and what it was like to live there as a child. She wanted to know about the characters from the trial and what they were like as children. What were their backgrounds? How did they relate to each other? And finally, where did I fit into all this? Knowing her area of expertise, I could understand why she would want to learn as much as possible about the personalities, behavioural characteristics, and interrelationships of all the main players. So, most of that first meeting was spent chatting about growing up there, providing as much background detail as I could remember.

"Let me introduce you to Lower Naughton, the setting for poor Sarah's tribulations. Well, it has all the required elements one would expect of a bucolic idyll. It sits in a valley with a shallow brook meandering through the center, drifting off toward the river Trent to the south. Rolling green hills on one side gently slope down onto fields that are ablaze with bright yellow rapeseed flowers in the spring. A road snakes through the centre and heads off to a new dual carriageway a couple of miles away that takes the villagers into the town of Burton-upon-Trent. Farmland stretches out from the village — cows and sheep peacefully scattered in the fields — a delightful pastoral scene.

"Like most villages in Britain, Lower Naughton functions on a clearly defined structural hierarchy based entirely on the noxious British class system. When I lived there as a child, there were minor members of the aristocracy at the top of the pecking order — Lord Percival German-Brown and his wife, Lady Celia. The pair of them veered erratically between merely eccentric and certifiably deranged. They occupied Nawerton Manor, named in the Olde-English spelling of the village and known locally as 'the Big House.' Below them came the upper middle classes led by Sarah Slater's father, Charles Weston, who was a Member of Parliament until he died, and the now-deceased Elizabeth

Weston. And then on down to the council estate where I lived as a child."

Camille, looking at me, asked, "This is the first time you have mentioned where you grew up. German-Brown, that's your last name. Are you related to this Lord and Lady German-Brown?"

"Well, living in a council house is not something I'm going to boast about, and I'm only telling you this as the village dynamics could be relevant as we investigate further. As for the German-Brown last name, I'll explain later how I married into the family, but for now, let me tell you about the darker side of the village.

"On the face of it, Lower Naughton is a peaceful and idyllic place to live, but hovering beneath the surface is a degree of mendacity and cruelty that belies its serene image," I deliberately said spookily. "Adding to the two recent, gruesome murders that you know about was the murder of a child around fifty years ago, for which the father was accused, convicted, and eventually sent to prison based on a flimsy piece of evidence. And as if that wasn't enough, there was the supposedly accidental death of the toddler, Tiffany, Colleen's little girl. If you remember, Tiffany was mentioned in the trial when Kevin was questioned about the result of the DNA test that was taken to determine who her father was. For a small village, Lower Naughton has certainly experienced more than its fair share of violence."

Camille was fascinated and started writing. I noticed she had made columns on the page and asked her to explain what she was doing.

"Well, to keep it simple, I have titled the columns VICTIM, SUSPECT, DATE OF MURDER, and MOTIVE. So we have three victims if we include the boy whose father supposedly murdered him, as you implied it might have been a wrongful conviction, and we have Elizabeth Weston and Richard Slater. We have the actual dates of their murders. As we go through this process, we can fill in the other columns. I was assuming these were the only victims, but with your suspicion about the 'supposedly accidental' death of Tiffany, I'm considering adding her to the victim column; what do you think?"

"Yes, I agree. We should add Tiffany because I'm not convinced it was an accident." I stated matter-of-factly.

"Perfect. Now Margaret, back to Lower Naughton."

"Right, so there used to be a small, wooded area that extended alongside the brook and was a favourite place for the local children to play hide-and-seek and chase rabbits. The older kids used to hide amongst the trees, sneaking a quick cigarette or an equally furtive snog and grope of the latest girlfriend or boyfriend. The brook that runs through the centre of the village looked relatively shallow but very clear — reeds grew along the banks, and you could see smooth stones and gravel at the bottom. I would paddle in it in my wellington boots, scooping up a few tiddlers and sticklebacks that swam around among the rocks in the deeper areas. Overlooking the brook was a row of almshouses; all well looked after; the front doors freshly painted and framed by colourful hanging baskets; the front steps gleaming from a weekly polish with Brasso."

Camille was trying hard to suppress a grin at my over-the-top description, but I carried on nonetheless.

"Margaret, if, as the jury seemed to believe, Sarah really was innocent of the murders of her mother and husband, it seems logical to assume that somewhere within this picturesque village, some other malevolent force must be lurking. Maybe it was the work of outsiders, with mysterious motives as yet unknown. But let's start with the obvious local possibilities. Everyone at the trial, from the unfortunate victims, the so-called innocent defendant, and the witnesses, lived in the village at one time or another, right?"

"Yes, most have stayed there. A bit more information about the village may help you visualize some of the scenarios from the trial. Along with the usual components of any village: the church, the school, and the pub, there was a hairdresser, the village shop, a Post Office, a garage, and a blacksmith. There was a well-supported cricket team, and as we know from the trial, there was a darts team.

"The parish church, St. Gregory's, is a rather majestic, grey sandstone Norman building from the twelfth century. It is beloved by the villagers, most of whom would have been christened there, married there, and eventually, will be buried in its graveyard. When I was a child, I used to wander around the cemetery after Sunday School. It was so quiet and peaceful, the smell of the newly mown grass between the graves, the occasional rustle of dead flowers on abandoned wreaths after a long-forgotten funeral. On some of the gravestones, the words had worn away with the passage of time and were barely visible through the lichen

139

and moss. Yew trees with their red berries and an old stone wall dotted with moss surrounded the graveyard as if guarding its precious occupants."

I noticed Camille smiling to herself again at what I considered another very eloquent description.

"The primary school dates back to the end of the Nineteenth Century, and just about everyone in the village went there. At least three generations of my family went to the school.

"And lastly, probably the most significant and socially important part of the village is the pub, the Falconer's Arms. It sits between the church and the bridge that spans the brook. Anything important in the village happens there, from wedding receptions to darts and quiz nights to jumble sales. I cannot imagine anyone in the vicinity who hasn't been there at least once during their lifetime. I'd bet quite a few of the men, at some point in their lives, have staggered home from there in a sorry state, supported by a couple of their best mates. All of them drunkenly pledging their undying love for each other, pretty sure they were in for a rollicking when they eventually arrived home."

Now Camille was laughing, but this time she was nodding in agreement.

"As a child, I would go to the Falconer's Arms with my parents on a summer evening. Of course, I'd have to stay in the garden with the other children as you probably remember, back then, children weren't allowed in the pub. I never minded being dumped outside as my dad would bribe me with a bottle of Tizer and a packet of Smith's crisps. Do you remember them? The best part was delving into the bag to find the screwed-up piece of blue, waxy paper that contained the unfailingly damp salt to shake over the crisps."

Camille grinned, "Yes, and when you shook the salt, it came out in a lump. So annoying."

"Exactly! Once I had my crisps and bottle of pop, I would commandeer one of the swings and be quite content watching the other children. Even then, I was more of an observer than a joiner. Occasionally, I would see Sarah Slater or Weston as she was then. I assume that would have been on the odd occasion when her dad came to socialize with his constituents in an effort to be seen as a 'man of the people.' I told you he was a Member of Parliament."

Camille nodded while making a note of this piece of information.

"Anyway, when she was there, she and I would gravitate to the seesaw, trying to ignore the boys who were usually showing off. I remember one time, Alan, who was the blacksmith's son and could be a bit of a bully when his dad wasn't around, dared, or more likely threatened, Kevin Ryan to sit on one of the swings and make it swing high enough that it would go over the top of the bar. Alan started pushing the swing harder and harder as it went higher and higher, Kevin pleading with him to stop, but Alan pushed all the harder, and eventually, poor Kevin did go over the top. He came crashing down on his side and started screaming. I saw Alan run off and hide as everyone in the pub rushed out. The next day at school, Kevin came swaggering into class with his arm in plaster. He was considered something of a hero, being the only kid we knew who'd managed to swing high enough to go over the bar, albeit with a lot of help from Alan and a broken arm to show for it."

Camille stopped me, "This Alan, he wasn't mentioned in Court. What happened to him?"

"He's the child who was murdered. You've added him to your spreadsheet." Camille made a note about him being a bully, and I continued.

"Colin Brown was Alan's dad; he was the village blacksmith and a regular in the Falconers. Most evenings, he'd be in there propping up the bar, drinking heavily amidst clouds of smoke from his ever-present pipe, his dog, Blackie, at his feet. Occasionally, he would bring his timid-looking wife and Alan with him. I assume Alan had inherited his thuggish attitude from his father, who was known to have a vicious temper. I'm sure it was made worse by the drinking.

"One of the errands I'd run for my mother was to go to the blacksmith for paraffin. I've no idea what she used it for, but I never minded going as Mr. Brown was always nice to me and let me watch him shoe the horses. Walking in off the road, you found yourself in this vast barn-like structure, the walls black from all the smoke that had built up over time. Lying on a dirty blanket in the corner was Blackie, his black Labrador. Mr. Brown never went anywhere without that dog by his side. He would grunt 'hello' and ask if I wanted 'the usual' taking the can from me to fill it up.

142

"Watching him work with the horses was fascinating; he became a different person. You could tell he had a connection with animals; he loved being around them. He was kind and gentle and would speak softly to them, stroking their muzzle to calm them down before he started working on them. In all the times I went there, I never saw a horse upset, raise its head in fear, snort, or back away trying to escape. I'm pretty sure he preferred animals to people."

Again, Camille stopped me, "Ah, so this Mr. Brown, Colin, right? He was the chap who was accused of murdering his son?"

"Yes, that's right. It was so long ago I'd forgotten. Thinking about it, he must have been released by now."

Camille, writing furiously, exclaimed excitedly, "Could he be a suspect? Maybe, for Richard's murder. We should find out when he was released and where he is now."

"Yes, but just a small detail. Do we have a motive?"

"Well, maybe not yet, but give us a chance; we've only just started," Camille responded.

This time, it was my turn to smile at her enthusiasm. I nodded, then continued with my village update,

"Back in those days, we were a scruffy bunch of kids. A few of us were from the council houses. Kevin Ryan, Richard Slater, and I lived next door to each other. Colleen O'Brien and her brother Harry, who I'll tell you about later, lived on the road behind us. Colleen and I were pretty close back in those days, even though I was a year or so older. Our mothers were quite good friends, so we used to play together. Colleen's dad drove the delivery van for the local baker, and he used to let Colleen and me sit in the front passenger seat as he delivered the bread around the village. As for Sarah, when she was a child, she lived at the north end in a nice upper-middle-class enclave of large, detached houses built just before the second world war. Her mother continued to live in that house until she died.

"Actually, just a minute." I reached into my bag and pulled out a rolled-up school photograph taken when I was a child. I unrolled it onto the table, using the coffee mugs to hold the edges down.

"Just after my parents died, I had to clear out their house. Going through one of the cupboards, I spotted this. It's a school photograph taken at the village primary school. I thought it might be useful to show you who everyone was back then. You know, put a face to a name."

I pointed to the front row of the photograph, where I was sitting cross-legged on the playground.

"That's me. That's Sarah in the middle, with Catherine Stratton next to her. If you remember, she was one of the character witnesses at the trial." Then I pointed to a boy sitting on the other side of Sarah and said, probably a bit unkindly:

"That's Richard, Sarah's future dead husband, and that's Colleen next to him, his future mistress and mother of his child. It all sounds rather sordid, doesn't it? Ironically, on Colleen's other side is her future husband, Kevin, wearing his characteristically cheeky grin. And there we have it, a murder victim surrounded by possible suspects — no idea what the future would hold. Such innocents. We must only have been around six or seven."

Looking at the row behind, I pointed to a couple of other boys:

"Ah, standing in the back row is Alan Brown. He was the lad supposedly murdered by his father. And that is Chris, my future husband. Oh, and that's Harry, Colleen's brother, who years later became my closest and dearest friend. Who would have dreamed back then how we would all interact as our lives unfolded."

Looking over at Camille's notebook, I saw she'd drawn a rough diagram of the photo with the children's names, presumably so she could identify them. Then she pulled out her phone and asked if she could take a picture of the photograph, "Absolutely, that's a great idea," I said as I continued my story:

"Now you have an idea of who we all were back then. In those days, the traffic was so sparse that the boys could play cricket in the street in the summer. Despite the clear disadvantage of my gender, I was allowed to join in — basically, because they were short a fast runner in the outfield. Believe it or not, back then, I was a scrawny little kid, but I was a really fast runner, so I was always pressed into service when the ball was either hit for a six into the field opposite or it had rolled down the hill."

Camille looked me up and down and, laughing, said, "Well, you're not exactly obese now, are you? And from this picture, I could see you would be quite the little sprinter."

Ignoring her, I continued, "Listen to this! One particular time I was playing cricket with the boys, Richard, Kevin, and Alan, when Kevin asked us if we would like to see his chickens. He lived two doors down from me, so I thought it would be okay. Anyway, I followed the boys as they headed up Kevin's back garden path. My father worked very hard on our garden. He grew most of our vegetables, and he was very particular about keeping the lawn mown regularly, the stripes in immaculate parallel lines, the edges neatly clipped. I expect you have a gardener for that, right?" Camille nodded.

"Anyway, Kevin's back garden was quite the opposite; it was an absolute tip. I can still see it in my mind's eye; it was such a mess. What should have been the lawn was a veritable orgy of weeds, and what looked like fruit bushes had been left in a vast tangle of thorns and dead wood. In the midst of this overgrown mess were a couple of rusty old bikes that had been abandoned, probably because they were missing their tires. The body of a pram with the hood all torn sat on what should have been the path. A couple of dolls lay inside, their heads ripped off, looking like something from a horror movie. I assume they belonged to Kevin's sister. The undercarriage and wheels were up by the chicken coop, and someone had put a piece of plywood on top, maybe in the false hope of turning it into a go-cart. I clearly remember some grubby-looking washing hanging on the line — a couple of sheets which at one time were white and were

146

now a delicate smokey grey with several holes. A couple of pairs of knickers also hung on the line; the elastic in the waistbands looked like they would never again hold anything up."

I seriously doubted Camille could even visualize this scene. I'm sure there wasn't a washing line within sight of the house where she'd lived as a child, and even if there was one, the sheets would be spotlessly white, and the underwear would be immaculate and very fancy.

"Kevin unlatched the gate to the chicken coop, and the four of us went inside. The stink was so bad, Camille. It literally made my eyes water. I'd never smelled anything like it. I shouldn't think the Ryans ever cleaned it out. There were about half a dozen scrawny chickens, looking uncared for, pecking around in the dirt and chicken shit, looking for food. I can't imagine they were capable of producing any eggs, so goodness knows why they even kept them.

"I remember looking down the garden path and realizing you couldn't see the house from in there, and the boys immediately took advantage of the fact. You have a brother, but I had no idea what was considered fun for boys, so I was taken aback when they decided to compete to see who could pee the furthest and highest up the wall at the back of the coop. I think Alan won, but he was about three years older than the other two, so he had an unfair advantage — well, as far as I could tell. It was the first time I'd ever seen a penis, and the boys were very keen to show me. I was only around seven at the time, so I was still quite naïve."

147

Camille, laughing, said, "Okay, I have to admit I did once catch my little brother peeing up the back wall of the kitchen garden, seeing how high he could make it go. He was about the same age."

"What is it with little boys? They do seem inordinately proud of their strange little appendages. Anyway, I felt very awkward and uncomfortable and backed away from them. But then things worsened when they decided that as I'd seen theirs, it would only be fair if I showed them my 'stuff,' as they called it. Alan gleefully boasted that one time he'd seen his dad on top of his mum, and they hadn't any clothes on: 'My dad was putting his willy into my mum,' he bragged gleefully. And then, he came up with what he thought was a brilliant idea. What if he and I had a go at what his mum and dad had done? The three boys turned and looked at me enthusiastically. Jesus Christ, not bloody likely. I was in a complete state of panic — frightened to death. I told them I needed to leave, that I could hear my mum calling. I fumbled around, trying to unlatch the gate to the chicken coop, and ran down the path back to my house; my heart was pounding as if it would burst out of my chest. Thank goodness I could run fast because I could hear them coming after me. As you said, I was quite the little sprinter."

Camille looked horror-struck. "Good heavens, that must have been terrifying. Are you sure Alan is dead? He sounds like an absolute arse. If he hadn't been murdered so long ago, he would undoubtedly be at the top of the list of suspects. I bet he would have been a very unpleasant character had he grown up. But what about his father? Didn't you say you thought he'd be out of prison by now?"

148

"If I remember correctly, he was put away for at least forty years. Let me do some research and see if I can find out what happened to him. And, come to think of it, I wonder what happened to his wife. Oh goodness, I just remembered something. I looked up the court case a few years ago, and I remember reading that Richard Slater had testified at the trial. He was only a young boy, but he said he'd seen Colin Brown on the road beside the brook walking towards the woods around the time Alan was killed."

"Now that's interesting, Margaret. Do you suppose this Colin Brown could have blamed Richard for his being found guilty? Do you remember anything else that was used as evidence?"

"Yes, Richard said Colin Brown was smoking his pipe, and one of the pieces of evidence the police found was pipe tobacco near where Alan's body was found."

Camille was busy writing on her notepad, "How did Alan die?"

"His father, supposedly in a fit of temper, hit him on the head with a rock or something, then dragged him to the brook and pushed him in, holding his head under the water until he drowned."

"Now I feel we're getting somewhere. I didn't expect to uncover anything new this early in our investigation. But we have someone who could have been holding a grudge against Richard, blaming him for what happened, and it has been festering in his mind for what, over forty years." Camille said excitedly.

Continuing, I said, "So besides Kevin and obviously Sarah, we may have a third suspect for Richard's murder. Now we need to find a culprit for Mrs. Weston's." Camille nodded enthusiastically at our progress.

"If you're sure I'm not boring you, I'll carry on, and hopefully, we'll find something. You know my mother would have been furious if she'd ever found out about the chicken coop saga. Her feeling was we might live in a council house, but goodness me, we certainly did not have to act as if we belonged there. Every Sunday morning, dressed in my best clothes, I was sent to Sunday School as I wasn't allowed to play with anyone on Sundays. In 'polite society,' children didn't play on Sundays, or so my mother thought."

Camille snickered at that comment.

"Come on, Camille, you're from 'polite society.' I'm sure you never played on Sundays either, right?" I said a tad sarcastically. Camille now burst out laughing. "Where on earth did your mother come up with that idea?"

Looking a bit put out, I said, "Mum said the Queen had said it, so it must be true!" then I burst out laughing, "Anyway, after Sunday School, I was expected to go straight home for my dinner. In those days further north, lunch was called 'dinner.' It was a delicious meal, though, consisting of the tiniest joint of over-cooked roasted meat, boiled potatoes, boiled cabbage, boiled carrots, and something she called gravy, an insipid, watery, brown-coloured liquid. Bless her heart — my mother was no cook."

"To be honest, Margaret, my mother was no Nigella Lawson either. If our cook had the day off, my mother's idea of making a meal was to make reservations, which was a relief to my brother, my father, and me. Anyway, tell me more about the village."

"Okay, well, across the road from my house was a farmhouse. It was built from grey stone and was covered in ivy with a generous coating of spider's webs. It was the creepiest place. Should you happen to be in the farmyard when it was dark, the owls and bats would come swooping down from the barns, scaring you half to death. The gate at the entryway to the farm was permanently stuck open as the hinges were all rusty. This was lucky for me as whenever I was late home for my tea and needed a shortcut. I would run from the wood by the brook, cross the road, run around the back of Catherine's house, over the field, and through the farmyard. The cobblestones leading from the farmhouse to the road were uneven; some were missing, and some were covered in moss, making it quite challenging to run on, especially when they were wet and slippery from the rain. My heart would be pounding when I took that shortcut, hoping against hope that the farmer wouldn't see me as he was a mean-spirited old bugger. I have no idea how old he was — to a six-year-old, he could easily have been the twin brother of Methuselah."

Camille started laughing again as I continued with my description.

"He had long, straggly grey hair surrounding a sallow, wrinkled face. His eyes were deep-set with furrowed eyebrows that made him look permanently angry, and his

151

voice was deep and hoarse, probably from all the cigarettes he smoked. There was always a half-smoked cigarette dangling from the corner of his mouth. God help you if he found you on his land, he would chase you, shouting menacingly for you to get off his property as he raised his shotgun and let off a shot in your direction. However, I was more afraid of my mother than him, so I continued to use the farmyard as a shortcut."

Another interesting facet of life in Lower Naughton suddenly occurred to me:

"One of the year's highlights was when the Statutes came to town each autumn."

"What's a statute?"

"Oh, it's just a fancy name for a fair in those parts: coconut shys and candy floss booths, the usual rides: the helter-skelter and roundabouts. But what fascinated me were the freak shows, you know, the bearded lady and so on, not that they are called that anymore. They were deemed too scary for young children, so we weren't allowed in, which made me all the more determined to have a look.

"One year, my parents took Sarah and Richard with us. I think they felt a bit sorry for Richard. His dad had died when he was a baby, and his mum was bringing him and his sister up by herself. I don't think there was much money for extras as his mum took in laundry. Poor woman, her hands were all red, and the skin looked like lizard skin, dry and cracked, and she always looked worn out. They lived next door to us, and my mother would be so annoyed with her because she'd come around to our back door, a quick knock, then open the door and come in calling out, 'Cooee, just me, is it time for elevenses love?' Mum was such a snob, and she thought this was just not done."

Camille smiled to herself, thinking she'd probably heard that from the Queen, too.

"Anyway, I remember thinking it would be a great idea to find a way for Sarah, Richard, and me to sneak in to see the freak show; the question was how to do it. After walking around the outside of the tents, I realized you could crawl under the flaps at one corner. While my parents were busy at the coconut shy, I asked Richard to come with me, but he would have nothing to do with it. He was always very well-behaved around my parents. So I asked Sarah. To start with, being a bit of a goody-goody, she refused, but with a little gentle persuasion and, I think, curiosity on her part, she agreed. I asked Richard to keep watch, which he was useless at, and then Sarah and I took turns sneaking under the tent flaps. I'm still not sure it was worth the risk as the 'bearded lady' and the so-called 'tallest man' weren't particularly scary. I thought we were safe, but, as adults are wont to do, my dad spotted us. He was livid, and I knew I was in for a beating once we were home. I could turn on the waterworks if I thought it would gain some sympathy, but I also knew when to suppress the tears. My dad's mantra was that if you didn't stop crying after he smacked you, he'd give you something to cry for, which meant smacking you again but harder. So, I would try desperately hard not to cry in the first place. My dad had a mean hand, and you felt it when he hit you. I'd bite my lip, trying not to cry when I was a little girl."

"Good grief, were you really smacked as a child?" Camille looked quite stunned.

"Oh yes, you felt it when he hit you, but it's all fine; it's in the past. Anyway, this is an interesting bit that might be relevant. One year, we were at the Statutes when I saw Alan with his parents. I remember it distinctly because Colin Brown had his wife's arm in a vice-like grip as he marched her through the crowds. Tears were streaming down her face, and she appeared to have a black eye. He looked furious. Alan was running behind, sobbing, trying to keep up with them, and looking frightened. At school, Alan was a bully, and in the chicken coop I'd been frightened senseless about his threats to reenact his parents' naked maneuvers, but among the flashing lights and hurdy-gurdy music, I could only feel sorry for him. In the shadow of his violent father, the boy had become a sniveling child. It was well known in the village that Mr. Brown had a temper, and after a night at the pub, he would go home drunk and beat up his wife and then take his belt off and whip Alan."

Camille was making more notes, "I think it's looking more and more possible that Colin Brown is a viable suspect, as long as he was out of prison by the time Richard was murdered. I can imagine him sitting in his cell, anger simmering, then once he was released, finding out that Richard liked to go to the Falconer's Arms and hanging out there until that evening, Richard met Kevin and slipping something into his drink. I bet he knew all about catching rats and mice. He probably kept some poison at his blacksmith place."

"I suppose it's possible," I was starting to feel a bit weary from my travels down memory lane. "Right, I think we've done enough damage for one day. How about meeting again in two weeks?"

"That sounds like a great idea. Why don't you come to my house for lunch?" Camille offered.

"Fabulous. This has been lovely and quite productive. See you in two weeks." We packed up our things and walked outside to our cars. I waved to Camille as she drove away. It was starting to sprinkle, and I was looking forward to getting home out of the rain.

Chapter 7

Two weeks later, I drove to Weybridge to Camille and Hywell's house. The standing joke about Weybridge is that it is so posh that even the staff has staff. I drove up their tree-lined drive to a beautiful limestone two-story house that shone gold in the midday sunshine. I pulled around the twinkling fountain and parked just outside the front door.

Before I could knock on the brass lion knocker, Camille swung the door open and whisked me inside. We walked through to the kitchen, where Camille had a cafetière ready to go, and she pushed down the plunger. Once the coffee was poured into her shabby-chic mismatched Wedgewood porcelain mugs, we sat at the marble-topped kitchen island to resume our investigations.

"Last time we met, you mentioned that your family left the village, but before that happened, were there any further interactions you had with our motley cast of characters?" chuckled Camille. "Tell me a bit more about your background."

"I can't remember anything else that happened. We moved to Luton when I was around nine. Mum and Dad bought a house there — no more council houses for us — we were going up in the world. The new house had hot and cold running water and an inside lavatory — heaven."

Camille, looking a little stunned, choked on her coffee. Laughing, I explained:

"Oh, didn't I tell you we had no running hot water or an inside lavatory in the Lower Naughton council house? Poor as church mice, that was us back then." I admit I did make it sound a lot worse than it actually was, but a good story needs a bit of embellishment, doesn't it! Besides, we didn't have an inside toilet.

"Anyway, after passing the eleven-plus, I went to the girls' high school in Luton. It was so different from the Primary School in Lower Naughton. Gone was the petty provincialism to be replaced by an egalitarianism that I never dreamed could exist. The high school had over a thousand pupils and was more concerned with how well you performed academically than where you lived. Everyone wore a uniform, so to the outside world, we all looked the same."

Camille looked a little uncomfortable as I commented on the class system — she was undoubtedly Upper Class and had never been confronted with the inherent contrasts of other segments of society. I've never minded commenting on class disparity, and I believe this current case involved several layers of the class system, from the 'haves' to the 'have-nots.' Richard, Colleen, Kevin, and I were all brought up in council houses. Then there was Sarah, whose parents were middle-class. Finally, Chris, my future husband, was the son of a Lord, but more about that later.

"At my new school, I joined the drama club; sometimes, I was lucky and would snag the lead, unlike in Lower Naughton, where Sarah always had the starring role. I was a decent all-around athlete and represented the school at some of the inter-school athletic meets. But more importantly, I was determined to do well academically. I'd had a rough start at Lower Naughton — mocked for my second-hand clothes and my accent — constantly feeling that I was never good enough or clever enough. But at the new school, things were different. The teachers encouraged everyone to do well, not just the girls whose parents were Members of Parliament. It was there I finally realized I could be anything I wanted to be — it had nothing to do with who my parents were or where we lived. I decided I would never return to the life I'd endured in Lower Naughton. I had spent my life up to that point feeling like a second-class citizen. I was determined to become somebody."

Camille winced but nodded encouragingly as I continued:

"I remember being so thrilled when I received the letter telling me I had been accepted to read law at Oxford University. I passed it across the dining table for my mother to read, expecting her to be pleased. Disappointingly, though, her response was less than enthusiastic. Frowning, she asked how much it would cost, suggesting I consider a local university that would be cheaper. She commented that Oxford seemed a bit over the top, 'So who are you trying to impress?' My mother was a complete contradiction in terms. She had spent half her life worrying about what the neighbours would think and trying to impress them, yet when I achieved something I thought would make her proud, she did nothing but belittle me. To be honest, it was a bit overwhelming the idea that I, a kid from such a lowly background, was about to take my place at Oxford University, among the higher echelons of society."

I stopped talking as I finished my coffee, lost in thought as I contemplated my relationship with my mother. I'd never told anyone, but I'd always tried to please her, tried to make her proud of me. Unfortunately, the only sentiment she ever showed me was her lack of interest or her disappointment. I could never do anything right in her eyes. Water under the bridge now.

"At the time, I was convinced the other students would look down on me. I had nightmares that I wouldn't fit in. My clothes would be old-fashioned, and my broad Midlands accent would show me up. Even worse, I'd come across as common. My mother was right; I shouldn't be there. And here's an admission: I was so determined to fit in that I took a few elocution lessons to lose my accent. I spent all my savings on a new wardrobe that I hoped would make me look at least halfway decent. I didn't want to stand out. I was much too shy for that, but the last thing I wanted was to be sneered at for sounding or looking different from everyone else. Mum should have been proud of how much I had achieved academically, but sadly, in Mum's eyes, none of that counted. Her narrowly defined idea of success was quite simply — who I married."

Camille gave my arm a consoling squeeze. "Let's stop there and put the lunch together." I nodded in acquiescence, grateful for the break.

Camille had laid the table in the conservatory as it wasn't warm enough yet to eat outside. As she put together a salad, she updated me on Hywell's latest case. Again, I felt a slight pang of jealousy, not for the hard work involved, but I envied the excitement of it. We sat down and helped

159

ourselves to quiche and salad. Camille poured two glasses of Evian (a glass of something stronger was what I needed at this point), and I continued my story.

"At the end of that summer, I nervously packed my bags. Dad, who was feeling charitable for once and, I suspect and hope, quite proud of me, drove me across to Oxford. I went to Magdalen College. I said I'd been nervous, but once I settled in, I thoroughly enjoyed my time at uni, and although I worked extremely hard, I still made time to sign up for some of the activities on campus. I joined the debating society, a handy skill to have, as you know from watching Hywell. And, of course, I joined the Dramatic Society, which was great fun."

I paused and took a few bites of my food. Camille had always been an excellent cook, and the quiche was delicious.

"I must say, Margaret, you amaze me with your confidence and knowledge in court. No one would have any idea about your humble start in life. I admit I was fortunate. The saying 'there but for the grace of God go I' is so apt. I was born into a wealthy family. We had a townhouse in London and a stately pile in Buckinghamshire, and we took it all for granted. I went to Marlborough College and Cambridge, while my brother went to Harrow and then on to Cambridge. Not once did we stop to think how lucky we were. We just assumed that was what everyone did. This is a real eye-opener for me. Thank you so much for sharing it in such intimate detail."

"Thank you for letting me rattle on like this! It's quite cathartic, actually," I admitted.

"So, you asked about my further contact with the old gang from the village. During the summer holiday, at the end of my first year at university, I arranged to spend a week in Lower Naughton with Sarah. Mrs. Weston must have been impressed with my going to Oxford as she had agreed to my staying at her house. Sarah met me off the train in Burton, and we drove to her parent's house in the little Mini they'd bought her for passing her 'A' levels. We had many things planned for the week, but on the first day, we decided to hang out at her home, catching up on everything that had happened since we'd last seen each other. We spent the better part of the day in her bedroom, trying to outdo each other with our stories. I started by telling her about one of my boyfriends when I still lived at home in Luton and how it turned out:

"I was fifteen, and at that age, you go for looks, right? Well, Peter was pretty hot, and that's why I went out with him. We'd had a couple of dates, you know, the usual cinema outings. We saw West Side Story and Dr. Zhivago. At least I tried to watch the films while he tried to work out how to undo my bra. On date number three, he said he would take me out for dinner. He came to my house, and my mother was very impressed to discover that he was the head boy at the grammar school. Anyway, he picked me up in his dad's Morris Minor, and after announcing his plan to take me to experience a highlight of culinary excellence, we sped off, at forty-five miles an hour, for a romantic meal in Forté's restaurant on the M1 motorway. Oddly, he thought I'd be impressed at having a meal at a service area on the M1! I'm sure he thought I'd be equally impressed with the romantic soundtrack coming up from the lorries thundering past and that I'd be so overwhelmed with the deliciousness of my food that he'd convince me to let him finally undo my bra. And if I were really bowled over, he'd find out what was under my skirt. Whereas I was thinking that it would take a hell of a lot more than a cup of tea and greasy egg and chips before I let his grubby hands anywhere near my knickers. Needless to say, I was unceremoniously dumped shortly afterward for not showing my appreciation for our romantic evening."

Camille burst out laughing. "Yes, I've had a few of those dates myself."

"The thing was, once I told Sarah my story, she then told me of an incident from her life. And this is where it becomes quite interesting as I'm going to introduce you to a new character who could potentially have a connection with Mrs. Weston's murder."

Camille put her cutlery down on her plate and leaned forward in anticipation.

"Apparently, before she started dating Richard, Sarah had a date with the son of a friend of her mother's. Sarah said that her mother had always been very secretive about friends from her past, but there was this one woman she used to go down to London to meet for lunch two or three times a year. Anyway, this one particular time, Mrs. Weston took Sarah with her. I think she said she was sixteen at the time. They were going shopping and then meeting this

162

woman for lunch. If I remember correctly, the woman's name was Barbara Russo. I remembered the name because I've represented a number of gangsters from the East End over the years, and the name 'Russo' was vaguely familiar. Anyway, they were eating lunch and chatting when Barbara said Sarah should meet her son, Paul. She said he was very handsome, and she thought they'd make a lovely couple. Sarah said she thought her mother was going to have a heart attack; she started choking on her sandwich. Talk about going into a state of panic. She thought of every reason under the sun for Sarah not to meet this chap, but Barbara insisted that Paul would drive up to Lower Naughton and take her out for a meal, not, I hasten to add, at a motorway café. So, about a week later, Paul showed up in a fancy sports car with the top down. He was very polite and introduced himself to Sarah's mother and father. She said she was impressed because he shook her dad's hand. Remember that because there is some irony to that gesture."

Camille had her notebook beside her and started writing on a new page. She wrote down the two names and the hand-shaking and underlined them.

"Sarah said that Barbara Russo was right; this Paul was very good-looking, But, and again, you should underline this, she remembered him having a cockney accent. Anyway, they drove into Burton to a restaurant, Italian, I think she said, not that it matters, and she remembered him trying to make her drink red wine, which she wasn't keen on. They chatted about what music they liked and what films they'd seen, you know, just general stuff like that. I asked Sarah if he'd said where he lived in London, and she said it was somewhere near the docks in the East End, Whitechapel, I think she said, which explains the Cockney accent."

Camille continued writing, trying to keep up with my story.

"When they returned to the car after dinner, Paul put the roof up as it was dark. On the way home, he drove down some lane off the main road and pulled over onto the grass verge overlooking a field. She said he started kissing her, which was okay, but then he turned aggressive. He pulled her sweater up and began groping her breasts. Then he went to put his hand up her skirt; all the while, she said she was trying to push him away. Luckily, a car pulled up behind them, with its lights flashing. She said she had never been so pleased to see a police car in her life. The police officers walked to their car and shone their torches inside. They told Sarah and Paul to step out of the car. From the look on Sarah's face and the state of her clothes, they could see all was not as it should be. They asked if she was alright, and although she nodded, they told her to fetch her bag; they would take her home. They took down Paul's details and told him to be on his way and that he was lucky not to be arrested. Then the police took Sarah home and told her parents what had happened.

"Sarah said that after the police left, her father told her to go to her room. He looked furious. She said she was about to complain, but from the look on his face, realized he was not to be argued with, so she went upstairs. As she walked into her room, she heard her father shouting at her mother. He was blaming her for what had happened. He yelled at her about the embarrassment of having the police involved

164

and how it would look if the newspapers found out that his daughter was caught with some thug from the East End having sex in a car in a field. He said Sarah was just like her mother, that she had no morals and was a slut just like her. He said something about marrying her mother was the biggest mistake of his life, and if she hadn't been pregnant, he wouldn't have.

"Her mother, who was crying by now, apologized for letting this Paul take Sarah out, but her father roared back that all her friends were criminals and lowlifes, and she should have known better. He said thank goodness the police arrived when they did, as God knows what this thug would have done to her. He forbade Sarah's mother from seeing Barbara Russo ever again. Sarah said that when she was growing up, her father constantly reminded her mother that she would still be in the gutter if it hadn't been for him taking pity on her when she was pregnant.

"Sarah never heard from Paul again, and as far as she knew, her mother never said anything about it to her friend Barbara. But she continued to go to London and meet her for lunch, though Sarah was never invited again. I only brought up this particular story because I found it interesting that the uptight Mrs. Weston could have been associated with the criminal class."

Camille, who had been furiously scribbling, asked, "Do you know anything about these people from the East End? How would Sarah's mother know a bunch of what sounds like unsavory characters from there? I think this warrants a bit of investigation, don't you?"

165

"Absolutely, I would love to learn more about that family. In the meantime, I have another story to tell you about that same visit with Sarah. The following evening, I had dinner at my Aunty Bridget's house. She was the village hairdresser back then, and she and I were very close. We spent the evening catching up on all the latest news, although I think I monopolized the conversation with my stories about uni. My parents were never that interested, but Aunty Bridget wanted to know every detail, and it was so much fun relaxing in her living room over a couple of glasses of wine.

"Later that evening, I walked back to Sarah's house and was surprised to find Mr. Weston there alone. Sarah and her mother had taken advantage of my plans to spend the evening with Aunty Bridget and gone out. In the past, Sarah's father had always ignored me, but that evening, he was uncharacteristically chatty. I'd always thought he was a good-looking man, quite tall, about six feet, his black hair starting to go grey over the temples, making him look even more distinguished. I could imagine him making impressive speeches in Parliament. Sarah had told me he went to the gym whenever he could, and he certainly looked pretty fit. Looking back, I realize it was a huge mistake, but when he offered me a drink, I accepted, even though I was already a little tipsy from the wine at Aunty Bridget's. He gave me a gin and orange juice that was extremely light on the orange juice, making me shudder at my first sip.

"We sat outside in the garden as it was a lovely, warm evening, and he was very friendly. He appeared genuinely interested as he asked me about university. Foolishly, I was flattered that he wanted to spend time with me. I was on my second drink when I recall feeling a bit woozy, and I excused myself and went upstairs to bed. I was almost asleep when the door creaked open, and Sarah's dad was silhouetted against the landing lights. Not saying a word, he walked in and sat on the side of the bed.

"I felt the hairs on my arms stand on end. Why was he in my room? What did he want? He leaned over me, and I could feel his breath on my forehead as he brushed some hair off my face. He continued to run his fingers gently through my hair as he spoke, almost whispering, 'I always thought you were a very pretty little girl, Margaret, but you have turned into a beautiful young woman. In fact, you are a very *desirable* young woman,' he added creepily. His right hand was now massaging my neck. I held my breath, my heart pounding in my chest. 'Do you have a boyfriend? I'll bet you are very popular with the boys,' he chuckled suggestively. 'I'm sure a body like yours could make a man very happy.'

"I lay there, not knowing what to do, as he picked up my hand, which had been outside the covers, and started to tickle it, drawing circles slowly around the edge of the palm. Leaning forward, he tried to kiss me. I turned away, but he wasn't having any of it. 'Come on, my little darling; I know you want me. You know those boys you have sex with have no idea how to please a woman. I know just what you would like. I can make you so happy, so fulfilled.'

"Foolishly, I'd told him earlier that I'd had a couple of boyfriends, so he probably assumed I wasn't a virgin, and I was easy. Anyway, he then pulled the bedclothes back a little way and started to massage my breast, squeezing my nipple so hard. I began to cry as I wriggled and tried to shrug

167

him off. I told him to leave me alone and started to scream, but he put his other hand over my mouth and shook his head. Then he pulled the bedclothes back and put his hand on my leg. Why hadn't I worn pajamas instead of that stupid night dress? Moving his hand purposefully up my inner thigh, he found what he was seeking and painfully stuck his finger inside me. I started screaming louder, and he slapped me hard across my face, then, laughing, told me there was no point screaming — Sarah and her mum wouldn't be back for ages.

"Standing up, he unzipped his trousers while I made another attempt to move off the bed, but he put his hand around my neck while he took out his penis, which by now was erect and red. He took my hand and tried to make me touch it as I tried desperately to pull my hand away. Then he got on the bed and straddled me, pinning me down as I kept struggling. 'It's going to be fine, my dear. I won't hurt you. I want you to enjoy it, now relax. I know what I'm doing.'

"He forced himself into me as I squealed in pain. I'd had sex before, but not like that. It was incredibly painful. He was so rough as he thrust himself back and forth, the drops of sweat dripping from his contorted face directly down onto mine, until, with a grimace on his face and a loud groan, he came.

"I had never felt as dirty as when he clambered off that bed. But finally, he stood up and zipped up his trousers. I was sobbing uncontrollably — unable for the first time to control my tears at will. Callously ignoring my distress, he bent over me and, in the most menacing tone, threatened that if I ever told anyone what had happened, he had the power to

168

have me thrown out of college. With that final attempt to intimidate me, my rapist left the room. I immediately stood up, went into the bathroom, and threw up. I jumped in the shower and let the scalding hot water wash over me as I scrubbed my body, trying to remove every trace of that evil man. I couldn't face sleeping in that bed and instead curled up in the armchair in the corner of the room, pulling my coat over me.

"I hardly slept and eventually gave up at five o'clock, threw my things into my bag, and wrote a note for Sarah and her mother telling them that I'd had an urgent summons from my mum while I was at Aunty Bridget's. I thanked them for having me, left the note on the hall table, and then, as quietly as possible, opened the front door and left. I walked to Aunty Bridget and made some excuse about having a fight with Sarah, and talked her into taking me to the railway station. I wanted to go home. I would normally have confided in Aunty Bridget, but after his threat of how he could ruin my life, I didn't want her to be suspicious and guess it was him."

Up until that point, I hadn't looked at Camille as I told her what had happened that night. That was the first time I'd ever told anyone about it. I was so embarrassed, but I needed Camille to know about Sarah's father, as I felt it was necessary for the investigation.

"Oh my gosh, Margaret, that's horrible. Did you ever report it? Was he arrested? He would surely have lost his seat in Parliament over that." Camille had become quite distressed and leaned across the table and took my hand.

"You are the only person who knows his identity, and I'm only telling you now because he's dead," I admitted.

I sat up straight, letting go of Camille's hand and brushing off what I felt was her pity, which I loathed. I took a sip of water and continued.

"Unfortunately, it wasn't the end of my ordeal. Three weeks later, I missed my period and realized I was pregnant by that vile creep. I had no idea what to do. I wasn't about to tell anyone at university, and I obviously couldn't tell Sarah, 'Oh, by the way, I'm pregnant because your dear old Dad raped me.' I had no intention of telling my unsympathetic mother and having her say it was my own fault — that I had probably led some nice young man on. So, the only person I could think of to confide in was Colleen Ryan. She and I were still close friends, and I felt she would understand my predicament. Not that she would know what to do, but I thought she'd be there for me. I rang her and asked if we could meet somewhere other than Lower Naughton. When she asked why, I told her I couldn't talk about it on the phone, but I emphasized how desperate I was.

"Colleen agreed without hesitation, as I knew she would, and she kindly said she would come down to Oxford to my flat. Unable to drive, she asked if I would mind if Harry, her brother, brought her down. I was a bit unsure if I wanted to unburden myself in front of him as I hardly knew him, but I didn't have an option. I don't think I'd realized at the time that he was gay. I was so naïve I probably didn't even know what that meant. He'd left school at fifteen and had begun his working life, helping his dad with his bakery delivery job. He used to take painting and drawing classes at the local

170

technical college in the evenings. Colleen used to boast about what a great artist Harry was, and she was right; he had a lot of talent. I just hoped he'd be supportive, and god was he!

"Harry asked who the bastard was, but after Mr. Weston's explicit threats, I was too afraid to admit who it was. I was concerned that, with his position as an MP, he really did have the power to have me thrown out of uni. I didn't even admit it had happened in Lower Naughton in case they put two and two together and guessed who it was — after all, they knew I'd stayed with Sarah. I told them my rapist was one of the professors at uni and that he'd threatened to have me thrown out of uni if I told anyone. Harry asked what I wanted to do about the pregnancy, and I told him I wanted an abortion — I wanted nothing to do with it. The last thing I wanted was his or anyone else's baby.

"He immediately went into action and grabbed the phone book to look for clinics in the area that would take care of it. Panicking, I stopped him, explaining that I didn't want to go anywhere near Oxford — I was worried someone would see me going into a clinic and guess why. Colleen cleverly suggested we look for clinics in London, and we trekked off to the library to find a London phone book. After a bit of research, we found somewhere. When I rang, a pleasant-sounding receptionist told me they could take me in two days. She kindly warned me about the cost, but I assured her it would not be a problem. She also told me that I would need to talk to a counselor so they could be sure I wanted to go through with it and it wasn't just on a whim. The cost took all my savings, but I had no choice. Harry said I should send the bill to the arsehole who did this to me, although he knew I couldn't do that. Realistically, we both knew my rapist would deny all knowledge of the event.

"Colleen, by that time, had a young baby, which meant she needed to return to Lower Naughton as soon as possible, so Harry, bless his heart, drove her home, then turned around and came back to stay with me through the rest of the ordeal. I'd barely known him before this, but throughout it all, he became my hero. He drove me to the clinic, even coming into the room with the counselor as she asked me why I needed to have the procedure — holding my hand as I told her about the rape. The counselor asked me why I didn't go to the police and press charges, but I told her it wasn't possible, that the arsehole, yes, I even called him that, was in a position of trust and that he would deny it and I would be in a heap of trouble. All I wanted was to make it disappear and forget it had ever happened."

I was by now quite upset as I recounted the details of that experience. Poor Camille, this was more than she'd bargained for when she signed up for this detecting thing. I stopped talking, blew my nose, and sipped my water.

"I won't go into the details of the actual procedure except to say it wasn't the best day of my life. Harry took care of me for two more days, then drove back to Lower Naughton while I tried to return to as normal a life as possible. In some ways, the episode was one of the worst times in my life, but having Harry there with me through it all made me realize there are good people in this world, and he was up there as one of the best. That was the last time I saw Sarah or went to Lower Naughton until I returned for Aunty Bridget's

172

funeral just after Sarah's mother was murdered all those years later."

Camille looked up from her writing pad and asked:

"Could Mrs. Weston have found out about the rape? Could she have threatened her husband? You said earlier that he was dead; when did he die, and how did he die? Was it before or after his wife? He obviously had no affection for her. Should we add him to the list?"

"Unfortunately, he died a few years before Mrs. Weston was murdered. He was in a car accident. There was a young girl in the car with him who also died. Rumours were flying around that he liked young girls, and he was about to lose his seat at the next election. Unfortunately, that doesn't help us, but regardless, I do think we're onto something important about the Weston family, don't you?"

Camille nodded and made a move to clear away the lunch items. We both felt we'd had enough serious talk for the day. I stood up to help, but Camille told me not to worry. Over coffee, we chatted for a while about Camille's lovely garden, and we arranged for the next meeting to be in two weeks at my house before I headed home.

Chapter 8

Two weeks later, and the weather forecast was bang on for once. It was a beautiful, warm day, and as we'd be eating outside, I'd prepared a cold meal of poached salmon and a salad. I had also made a jug of peach-flavoured iced tea.

I was quite eager for this next session. There wouldn't be any more personal admissions and embarrassments this time, as I had decided what I wanted to talk about. When Camille arrived, she was dressed in a flouncy, heavily patterned silk skirt with a long shawl draped over her shoulders, looking fabulous as usual. I suggested we eat in the garden, which Camille readily agreed to. We quickly set up lunch on the table on the patio, keen to get to work. Rocco, my cat, was already ensconced in his usual spot on the wall in the sun. After helping ourselves to the food and iced tea, I began the next chapter of my life and my memories of the cast of characters involved in the case, hopeful that it would produce another suspect or perhaps confirm one of the suspicions we already had. It was good to have a second pair of eyes and ears on the case.

"You may remember I briefly mentioned that I was married. It was a long time ago, but if you don't mind, I would like to tell you about it. My husband's name was Chris."

"Oh yes, I'd love to hear about it if it wouldn't be too painful," Camille added. I could tell she was hoping not to offend me with the eagerness of her curiosity.

"So, apart from my degree, I also found a husband at uni and a very rich one. That meant I could give up my tiny, drafty bedsit and move into his much larger and much nicer flat. I think I've already told you that Chris went to the same primary school as me in Lower Naughton, but he was a couple of years ahead of me. He knew Harry and the blacksmith's bullying son, Alan, as they were in the same year. As I mentioned, Chris' family, the German-Browns, were minor members of the aristocracy and owned Nawerton Manor in the village. Chris was up at Oxford reading microbiology, taking all manner of classes that were way beyond my grasp. He was fixated on bacteria, parasites, and other unpleasant stuff. We started going out in my second year after meeting by chance, and we moved in together in my third year.

"When we lived together at uni, I'd find him dissecting frogs and other poor, defenseless creatures on the kitchen table — making him not the easiest of boyfriends. There were times when I would be looking for the le Creuset pot to make a casserole for dinner, only to find it already on the stove. Chris was using it to boil up a rat or some other equally disgusting animal as he needed to remove the skin and flesh so he could examine the skeleton — quite revolting. Maybe I should have gone for a stockbroker or banking type, so much less disgusting, don't you think?"

Camille made a gagging gesture and nodded in agreement. "I had a boyfriend at uni who was studying medicine. He'd go to the butcher and return to my flat with all manner of discarded cow's parts: eyes, hearts, intestines, tongues; I can't believe anyone eats tongue and all that gross stuff.

175

He'd lay them out on the kitchen table before dissecting them. I gave him up pretty quickly and, as you know, went for the lawyerly type."

I burst out laughing.

"Considering the dramatic difference in our backgrounds, Chris and I had much in common. We both loved the theatre. Although the only theatre I'd ever known growing up was going to Derby to see the annual Christmas pantomime, even so, I could still appreciate and enjoy watching actors on stage. I mean, some of the best acting in the world is Widow Twanky in Aladdin, don't you think?"

There was more laughter and nods in agreement from Camille.

"I have to admit there were a few advantages to dating Chris. Apart from being quite good-looking and having a brain in his head, unlike the other boys from Lower Naughton, he had a substantial income from a trust fund set up by his grandparents." I stopped and took a sip of iced tea.

"We used to love taking walks in the countryside. Admittedly, Chris would be looking for some new species of something or other, and he'd end up with a backpack full of all sorts of flora and fauna. I think he may have had a witch or two in the family back in the day, as he certainly knew a lot about how plants were used medicinally to make various potions, when to add 'eye of newt' or 'tail of rat' to cast a spell — it certainly seemed that way. Unfortunately, his habit of acquiring dubious specimens could make our lunch at a pub somewhat awkward, as his collections could give off quite an unpleasant stink.

"Although I had seen Chris' parents around the village, I had never been formally introduced, and it was quite intimidating when I eventually met them at the 'Big House.' I also met his brother Patrick and his two sisters, the twins Fiona and Felicity. They were nice, but his parents barely spoke to me. My mother loved Chris, of course, and he was friendly and respectful to her, but he and my dad didn't have much to do with each other. Dad was a Labour supporter, a union man all his life, and he had an inherent distrust of anyone from Chris's social class; sorry, Camille, that would also be your social class."

Camille shrugged her shoulders, accepting the criticism.

"Dad begrudged them their titles and large houses and fancy cars and hated their sense of entitlement, but he was polite and would manage to grunt out a 'hello' when Chris and I dropped by. It's ironic when you think about it, me ending up with precisely the life he abhorred.

"Anyway, after uni, Chris and I moved to London, where we found a flat in Marylebone. We hadn't been there long before Aunty Bridget sent me a letter to tell me that Harry had also moved to London and was working at a florist on Marylebone High Street. I told Chris, and knowing how important Harry was to me, he suggested we wander down there one Saturday on the pretense of buying flowers to see if we could find him. Despite being in the same class at primary school, they didn't know each other that well. The following Saturday, we set off, and after passing a couple of florists and not seeing Harry, I spotted him coming out of a newsagents. We hollered and waved like lunatics as we sprinted up the road. When he turned and looked in our direction, I could tell he didn't recognize us. Then suddenly, he beamed his beautiful smile and came running towards us, shopping bags swinging dangerously back and forth, hitting a couple of people as he passed them. I flung my arms around his neck as Chris grabbed his bags before he injured someone.

"He was so pleased to see us. I remember him saying something like, 'Oh my God, what on earth are you doing here? How did you know I was here?' I asked him if he had a few minutes to grab a coffee, and he told us there was a greasy spoon just by his florist shop.

"His shop was only a few steps further, and he nipped in, left his bags behind the counter, and asked the salesgirl to hold the fort while he came with us. The cafe was literally next door. Chris took our orders for coffee and tea, which he brought back to our table along with a couple of slices of lemon drizzle cake. Isn't it weird what you remember?

"Harry asked how we'd found him, and I explained that his mother had told my Aunty Bridget that he'd moved to London and was working at a florist on Marylebone High Street but didn't have an actual address. Aunty Bridget, being the source of all village gossip, had immediately written to tell me. Harry said he was so pleased to see us as he'd only been in London a few months and didn't know many people and was feeling a bit homesick and wondering if he'd made the right decision moving there.

"We'd just finished our drinks when Harry apologized and said he needed to return to the shop. We exchanged phone numbers, and he left with a promise that we would have dinner together really soon and have a proper catch-up.

"A couple of days later, I rang Harry to see if he would like to meet us for a drink and a bite to eat one evening. He was so eager, and we arranged to meet the following Saturday evening at a Greek restaurant in Soho.

"We had a lovely time discussing what we'd all been doing for the last few years. I must admit, Camille, that back then was the happiest I've ever been before or since. It's sad when you think about it, but you'll come to understand why. Harry wanted to know how Chris and I had met. I remember him teasing me that I'd done alright for myself, snagging the only bachelor in the village worth having. He said he bet my mum was over the moon. 'Scored one for the council houses,' he laughed.

"I told Harry we'd started dating at uni. I was sitting in a coffee shop on the High Street, drinking a gallon of black coffee while cramming for an exam, and Chris walked in. He ordered his tea, looked around for somewhere to sit, spotted me, walked over, and asked if he could sit at my table. At that point, neither of us recognized each other. After a couple of minutes, he asked if he could interrupt my reading and if we knew each other since I looked vaguely familiar. I told him my name and that I lived in Luton, and he said his name was Chris German-Brown from Lower Naughton. Who would have thought? Anyway, we chatted about our recollections of the village, and he asked if he could take me out to dinner, and that was it.

"I asked Harry if he and Chris were in the same class at primary school, and Harry chuckled and said yes, though they didn't have much to do with each other as Chris was the sporty type, and he was definitely not. Chris, not very tactfully, said he remembered Harry mainly because he had a sister. He didn't remember her name, just that she was pretty. Typical man! Harry said he thought most of the boys remembered Colleen, unfortunately not for the best reasons. He said she was fine and had married Kevin Ryan and started a family."

Camille was writing again, pleased, I think, to recognize some names from the trial and to be able to pick up on how Colleen was regarded in the village.

"I asked Harry what had happened to him and why he'd left the village. His reply was a bit of a shock. It wasn't too bad to start with when he was younger, he said. Nobody paid much attention to him growing up. But then he told us, 'After I left school, I worked with me dad on the baker's delivery round and went to art school in the evenings. You do know I'm gay, right? Well, as I got older, the local lads twigged it, and it started getting unpleasant. There weren't many gays in the village, and there was even less tolerance. In fact, I only knew of one gay couple; they lived up the road from your grandad, Peggy.'"

Camille choked on her glass of iced tea, "I'm sorry to interrupt your flow, but who is Peggy?"

I went bright red with embarrassment, "I'm Peggy. My given name was Margaret Holmes, but as a child in the village, I was known as Peggy. Growing up, I hated that name and

180

insisted that anyone I met call me Margaret, but everyone in the village still calls me Peggy."

"I really can't picture you as a 'Peggy,' so I shall continue to call you Margaret. Sorry for my rude interruption. Please go on."

"Thank you. I appreciate that. Anyway, Harry went on to describe these elderly gay gentlemen. They were quite old, maybe in their fifties, and he assumed everyone thought they were brothers. He used to see them in Burton at one of the few gay bars. He said you had to be so careful back then as you could find yourself having the living daylights punched out of you by a bunch of thugs if they thought you were gay, so the two old men were very careful about making sure no one in the village found out. It must have been awful to have been gay back then. I can't believe that homosexuality wasn't legalized until 1967, and then only if you were over 21, which Harry wasn't."

"Yes, I know." Camille interrupted. "My brother's gay, and fortunately, my family doesn't have a problem with it. I'm so glad it's not such a big deal these days, thank goodness. Back then, it must have been dreadful. Trying to hide who you were from everyone."

"Harry told me that about a year before he moved to London, he was in the Post Office in the village, and a couple of men came in. He didn't recognize them, but they took one look at him and nodded to each other. When he went outside, they started calling him names, you know, things like fag and pervert, but the thing that really upset him was when they accused him of molesting little boys. He

181

said he tried to ignore them and started to walk away, but one of them came up behind him, grabbed his arm, swung him around, and the other one punched him in the stomach. They pushed him to the ground, and one of them started stamping on him and kicking him. The strange thing was they knew who he was; they called him by his name. They blamed him for the murder of a little boy who'd been molested. He was stunned. He said he wouldn't molest a child. He wasn't like that. Yes, he liked men, but men his age, not children. At some point, he heard somebody shouting at them, and they ran off. The next thing he knew, he was in hospital. They'd broken a couple of ribs, and he had a concussion where they'd slammed his head on the ground. After leaving the hospital, he decided to leave the village and move to London, where nobody knew him."

Camille looked intrigued. "Two questions: One, should we add this new little boy to our list of victims, and two, were these two men charged with the attack on Harry?"

"The little boy's murder was solved, but yes, let's add it to the list as it constitutes another dramatic murder in the village. And no, nobody was charged for the attack on Harry. Mrs. Layton at the post office told the police that she had never seen the men before. The police asked Harry if he could describe them, but all Harry could remember was that they were dressed in black, and they had distinct cockney accents that he recognized from watching television. He did hear one of them shout, 'Paul, let's go' to the other one. Harry said that beating was the last straw. It made him realize that life in Lower Naughton was not for him anymore. He said he was much happier in London. He'd found a small flat and made a few friends. It was very different in London; nobody seemed to care what or who you were. It felt safer."

"Sorry to interrupt again, but although Harry wasn't murdered, I wonder whether to add him to our list of victims. It was an unsolved crime, and the name 'Paul' rings a bell. Haven't we had a 'Paul' from the East End of London mentioned before? It's fascinating how the Cockney bits of the puzzle seem to keep intersecting."

"Yes, you're right, now I think of it. Paul was the man Sarah had the unfortunate date with. Good memory! And I think that's a good idea to add Harry's attack to the list. I had only thought of victims who were murdered being on the list. But anything that could be a clue to one of the actual murders would help us. And certainly, anyone from the East End may help with Mrs. Weston's murder, as we know she had connections there.

"Going back to Harry, we saw him about once a fortnight. Sometimes, he'd come over to our flat, and I'd cook Sunday lunch. Other times, we'd meet up after work for a drink. Harry, like us, loved the theatre, especially the opera, and he'd often come with us.

"Since living in London, He'd really blossomed and was finally able to be his authentic self. He became this wonderfully flamboyant character and was so much fun to be around. He had such an eclectic design aesthetic. He'd spend hours poking around local antique markets in search of unusual accessories for his flat, which was in an old Victorian terraced house. And what a deal-maker he was.

Many of his gorgeous Persian rugs were acquired with some strategic paddle waving at the auction houses where he'd spend his Saturday afternoons.

"His flat was uniquely exquisite, and the man himself was a sight to behold. He certainly knew what to wear to make an impression. Whether he was strutting his stuff in the Soho clubs in drainpipe jeans, V-neck T-shirts, and sharp sharkskin fitted jackets or hippie flared trousers, blousy shirts, and old-man woolen waistcoats chatting up the Mothers of the Bride who were organizing their daughter's society weddings, he had the originality and confidence to pull it off.

"And his business really took off, too. Harry established himself as the go-to florist for high-society weddings, which, in turn, had generated some great publicity, and from that came name recognition. He bought a shop on Marylebone High Street, then opened a second shop on Kensington High Street and was very much in demand for a wide array of social events — such was his skill and creativity."

"Gosh, I wish I'd had the opportunity to meet Harry; he sounds like such a wonderful man. I'm quite jealous of you. I wish you had shared him with me," laughed Camille. I smiled wistfully; I wish I'd been able to introduce her to him, too.

"Chris and I had been together for over six years when he took me away for a weekend to a lovely old hotel in the Cotswolds. After breakfast, we were walking in the grounds when he suddenly dropped to one knee, produced a little blue Tiffany box, and asked me to marry him. Of course, I said yes; I knew he was the only person I wanted to be with. The ring was stunning, a solitaire diamond in a white gold setting. I immediately called my mother to tell her, and her response was less than warm, as usual: 'Took him long enough. And you needn't think we're paying for the wedding; his family has enough money; they can pay.'"

"Seriously, she said that. No congratulations or anything?" asked Camille, looking both horrified and full of sympathy.

"Nope, no, 'we are so happy for you,' nothing. Oh well, I shouldn't have expected anything else. However, you can bet your money that as soon as I hung up the phone, Mum rang everyone she knew to tell them that her daughter was marrying Lord German-Brown's son.

"Ever since I was a child, I'd been determined to make something of myself, to be someone. And from then on, I'd be part of the family in the 'Big House.' Not, I hasten to add, that I was marrying Chris just to escape my old life; I genuinely cared very deeply for him. But I intended to build a reputation in my own right; I didn't need a husband for that. However, there is a certain prestige in some circles that comes with being married into the 'right' family, as I'm sure you know.

"The wedding was planned for the sixteenth of June, which gave me just three months to arrange everything. We picked the Marylebone Registry Office for the ceremony. As neither of us was particularly religious, we felt that a church wedding would be unnecessary. It was a small affair with Patrick, Chris' brother, as best man, and instead of a maid-of-honour, Harry would be my man-of-honour. My parents and sister were invited, and so were Chris' sisters, who we asked to be witnesses. We asked Chris's parents, but they declined as they apparently had a 'prior engagement.' I was upset for Chris, but he said he didn't care one way or the other; at least his brother and sisters would be there. We chose Durrants for the wedding breakfast and ordered a cake from Harrods.

"The only thing left was my dress. Harry, with his impeccable sense of style, helped me figure out what I should wear. And what fun we had. I tried on traditional full-length meringue dresses, sophisticated ankle-length satin slip dresses, and flouncy, broderie anglaise numbers, very hippie. Eventually, we decided that, as I was to be married at a registry office, something short would be more appropriate. And finally, at a small shop just off Bond Street, Harry and I found the perfect frock: an ivory-coloured satin shift with a lace coat. I chose a fashionable pillbox hat with a veil to demurely, I thought, cover my face and the most gorgeous high-heel pumps with a diamante flower-shaped attachment on the front. I have a photograph from the wedding in my bedroom; I'll show it to you, and then you can see Chris and Harry and, of course, my dress."

"Oh yes, I'd love to see your dress and put a face to Harry and Chris," Camille said enthusiastically.

I realized this meeting was in danger of devolving away from anything related to the investigations and into my personal reminiscences. Still, as I had an audience who seemed interested, I continued.

"The wedding day was perfect, warm and sunny, and as I was putting on my dress in my room at the hotel, Harry arrived. The ceremony was to be relatively informal, and I hadn't planned on carrying a bouquet — I'm not the sort to make a showy statement by marching down the aisle with a huge bunch of flowers. Darling Harry, however, was having none of it. He brought me the most fabulous posy of wildflowers: forget-me-knots, purple scabious, sprays of rose hips, and honeysuckle; he had even included a sprig of heather for good luck — it was just stunning.

"Everyone dressed up for our big day; even my family had outdone themselves. Mum, for once, was in a good mood and looked lovely in her coffee and cream-coloured silk dress and beige sandals, her hair in an updo. Dad was in his best dark brown pin-striped suit, his shoes so highly polished you could see your reflection in them. My sister looked very pretty in a cute navy blue and white mini dress, and Felicity and Fiona looked stunning in what I'm sure were haute couture dresses.

"Chris, so handsome in his dark grey three-piece suit, white shirt, and kumquat orange and white striped tie, was grinning from ear to ear. Harry had taken charge of the men's flowers and had made sprays of blue bachelor buttons and asparagus ferns for Chris and his brother to wear in their lapels. And as for Harry, true to form, he looked fabulous in his scarlet hunt coat with the blue velvet collar. He had found it at the Portobello Road market along with three gold blazer buttons that he had exchanged for the ones that were originally on the jacket. The new buttons glistened in the sun, giving the coat a dash of glamour and style. He'd even managed to find blue trousers that matched the collar perfectly. I could not have asked for a more marvelous attendant.

"The ceremony was short but sweet. We said our vows, which we had written ourselves, just a few sentences promising to be there for each other and always love each other. I promised I would not be upset if Chris used our best dishes to disembowel some poor creature for one of his experiments, and he promised he would not be upset if I threw said dissected animal in the dustbin. When we arrived at Durrants for the wedding breakfast, I found that Harry had popped in earlier that morning and placed Kilner jars filled with white roses and more wildflowers, purple scabious, and wild orchids down the centre of the table.

"Much as Dad hated speaking in public, he gave a heartfelt and, to me, emotional father-of-the-bride speech. Setting aside his biased views against anyone from Chris' social class, he welcomed Chris into our family. He asked the guests to raise their glasses as he gave his blessing to our union. I was in tears by the time he'd finished his speech."

"Oh, Margaret, it sounds like the perfect wedding. And you two were obviously the perfect pair. I do so wish I could have met Chris."

"Yes, I think you would have liked him. We lived together for some years before we were married. We enjoyed each other's company, liked similar things, shared a sense of humour, and I couldn't complain about the sex, either! So it was sad and remarkable how quickly Chris and my relationship began to unravel once we were married, all over a topic we should have discussed but completely overlooked — children. Unfortunately, I hadn't even considered this one big hurdle to my career strategy! Having been fortunate to be hired as a junior barrister straight out of university, I knew I wouldn't be working nine to five. I had thrown myself into my work, putting in some long hours. Chris, however, expected once we were married, life would be very different. His mother had never worked, and he expected me to give up work, too, once we had children. He wanted children, and he expected it to happen immediately.

"In my mind, it was never going to happen. I had worked too hard, and I was not about to give it all up to stay home with a baby. I don't know what Chris' definition of a good wife would have been, but I'm sure I fell short — domesticity was not in my DNA. My lack of desire to have children certainly did not meet Chris's expectations of what a marriage was supposed to be. But I'm not taking all the blame; we undoubtedly should have discussed the topic before we were married. It's extraordinary thinking about it now that such an important conversation had never arisen before. I suppose we each had our fixed assumptions and never thought to raise the issue. I stupidly had not understood how important having a child was to his family. On his father's death, Chris would inherit a title and a small fortune, so he was expected to produce an heir, preferably a son, to whom he could pass everything on, thereby perpetuating the family name. He should have warned me!"

"I understand how you felt, Margaret. The same thing happened to me. I was a professor of criminal psychology at Cambridge when I married Hywell, and he too, wanted

189

children. It was expected that, as fine, upstanding members of the community, we would start a family as soon as the vows were made. The problem was I was hesitant to give up my position. In the end, we made a compromise. I would be willing to have a child as long as I could continue working, and a nanny could be employed to help out. Obviously, as I was teaching at a university, I would have long vacations and be there some of the time, and so we had Finley followed by Agatha, and it all worked out. I'm just sorry you weren't as lucky." Camille said.

"Unfortunately, there was another reason it didn't work out. Two years after the wedding, I reluctantly agreed to accompany Chris on a trek in South America. The arguments over children, or lack thereof, were worse than ever. The hours I was putting in meant we barely saw each other. The requirements of my junior position necessitated me being at the beck and call of the more senior barristers, drafting pleadings and other documents.

"However, Chris thought a break away from life in London and the stresses that go with it might help us rekindle the relationship we'd had before we were married. I think he also hoped I would change my mind when I was away from my job, and the baby thing might happen. And I was hoping he wasn't holding his breath. Anyway, we picked a date when I was between court cases, booked tickets, hotels, and tours, or I should say treks, through the jungle — joy of joys. But I had no choice; I sensed that the alternative, divorce, was floating ominously in the back of his mind.

"As I expect you can appreciate, on the odd times Chris and I had gone away together, I'd become used to the pleasures

190

of packing Louis Vuitton suitcases full of pretty dresses and beautiful shoes and flying to fun, exotic locations. But this time, I found myself packing a large backpack, almost as big as me. In went hiking boots, those awful trousers with the zip-off bottoms and enough pockets to hide an entire family of refugees, plus long-sleeved shirts, gallons of bug repellent, and suntan lotion, that unfortunately was not going to be used for lying by the ocean — ugh! We flew from Heathrow to Bogota. At least that part was First Class; there was no way I was flying that distance in Economy. The hotel was surprisingly quite comfortable, and we enjoyed the first couple of days exploring our surroundings — so far, so good. I did a little shopping and attempted to show some interest in why we were there. We were only allowed a few items for the actual trek: one change of clothes, essential toiletries, headlamp, water, rain jacket, that sort of thing, which we put into smaller backpacks. I remember thinking that if Chris harbored devious plans about using this opportunity to impregnate me, then trekking was certainly not conducive to romantic nights of uninhibited sex."

Camille was now laughing so hard, "Oh Margaret, you do tell a good story. I haven't laughed so hard for ages."

She was kind not to point out that the stories weren't advancing the detective work, but it was the first time I'd been able to talk to anyone about that trip in years.

"The day of the trek, we met the other 'adventurers' and our guides, then piled into rickety old jeeps and were driven to the town of Leticia, on the edge of the Amazon. Burdened by the weight of our backpacks, we started to trek through the jungle. It was so dark once you were in among the trees and vines, which were so dense you couldn't see the sky, so we finally understood the reason for the headlamps. More importantly, we found out why we were issued Wellington boots. If we didn't look where we were going, we could sink into the boggy, leech-infested waters. And Chris expected me to be eager for rampant sex after that — pigs might fly! Anyway, eventually, after what felt like hours of walking, we found somewhere to make camp. Setting up camp meant hanging hammocks between trees and, once in the hammock, pulling a tarpaulin and mosquito net over ourselves as protection from any sudden downpours and the vast array of flying insects, particularly mosquitos — hence the gallon of bug spray we'd hauled around in our backpack.

"The following day, we went on a boat trip down the Amazon, something even I, ever the cynic, loved. The boat slowly meandered down the vast expanse of the muddy, brown river as the guide pointed out spider monkeys jumping from tree to tree and three-toed sloths reclining along the branches. There were river dolphins and giant otters on the edge of the water. I remember feeling quite moved by the whole experience and actually grateful to Chris for bringing me on his adventure. There was hope for us yet.

"When we reached our destination, we had a short walk from the boat ramp to a more permanent campsite, where we were to spend the rest of the day and the night. The good news was we were staying in little huts, slightly more comfortable than a hammock and a tarp. There were even showers with warmish water — quite a luxury. What a feeling of relief, knowing I would be sleeping in a bed, albeit on a wafer-thin straw mattress. I unpacked our bits and pieces, hung up our wet garments in the hopes they would be dry for the next day and then relaxed. Chris, on the other hand, decided to go off by himself back down to the Amazon with his plastic bags to collect some specimens. He gave me a quick kiss and headed out. Alone, at last, I delved into my backpack, found my book, and curled up on the inch-thick mattress to lose myself for an hour.

"I remember looking at my watch and realizing a couple of hours had passed, and I began to worry. Even though Chris had a habit of losing track of time when he was doing fieldwork, I thought he should be back by then. I went outside and told one of the guides that Chris had gone for a walk alone, but surely, he should be back by that time. They reassuringly told me not to worry, that they would find him. About half an hour later, I heard a lot of whistling, and somebody came running. To my horror, they had found Chris collapsed on the side of the river. The whistling guide had been sent back to camp to fetch a stretcher. I tried to go back with him, but they wouldn't let me — I began to panic.

"Eventually, the guides arrived back, carrying him on the pallet. I rushed over, and my fear increased tenfold — Chris looked dreadful. They lay him on a bed in a hut reserved for medical emergencies, where the camp doctor examined him. Finally, when I was allowed to be with him, I asked Chris what had happened, and he told me he'd felt weak and nauseous. I had always made sure he had some chocolate or a granola bar in his pocket in case he got

193

peckish when he wandered off on one of his little expeditions. He'd eaten it and started to feel a bit better but then was violently ill and had collapsed. I found a glass and poured him some water, suggesting he drink some to avoid dehydration. The poor man had a few sips and then fell into a deep sleep. I insisted on staying with him, telling the guides they could go as I wouldn't leave him. Unfortunately, I was so exhausted from the lack of sleep the night before, and from all the walking, I also fell asleep.

"I was woken by someone coming into the hut and heard them go over to Chris. I sat up and asked if something was wrong; the distraught man looked up at me and said he was very concerned because he didn't seem to be breathing. I rushed over to check for myself. Oh God, had he died while I was napping? The doctor who examined him could only surmise that he had eaten or touched something poisonous while he was wandering about by himself. There are so many toxic plants in that area. The guides refused to accept any liability for Chris's death and to be honest, I agreed with them. It was Chris's fault for leaving the campsite without a guide. They could not be blamed for his rash behaviour when it was actively discouraged for anyone to leave the camp alone."

"Oh no. Oh, Margaret, I am so sorry. I knew you were called 'Mrs.' and assumed you had been married, but I wrongly thought you and your husband had split up. I had no idea he had died. What on earth did you do?"

"Thank you, but it was a long time ago, and I have put it behind me; though, having said that I wonder what would have become of us if we'd had that child? Anyway, back to

194

the story: there was no postmortem, so I could never be sure what exactly had caused Chris's death. He was young and healthy, in the prime of his life, and, just like that, he was dead. There I was in the middle of nowhere. What the hell was I to do? Thank goodness for the tour company, who were terrific once they understood they wouldn't be blamed. They arranged to have Chris' body transported back to Bogota, where I had him cremated. I regrettably made a snap, albeit emotional, decision that, rather than bring him back to England, I would leave him there in a place he had always wanted to visit. The top of his bucket list, I suppose you could say. I found a guide to go with me, and I sprinkled his ashes into the Amazon for what would be his final adventure.

"When I returned home from the Amazon trip, I received a scathing letter from his father demanding to know why I hadn't brought him back to be interred in the family mausoleum on their estate. Just who the hell did I think I was, he demanded to know, deciding to leave him there without consulting them. It should have been a family decision; he was, after all, the son and heir to a titled family. Besides which, how could I have done that to his poor mother? She didn't even have the opportunity to say goodbye to her son. And then came the final paragraph, the piece de resistance; Lord German-Brown thanked the Lord that Chris had the good sense to insist on a pre-nuptial agreement. Chris and I had discussed the pre-nup, and I had willingly signed it. If Lord Cecil had asked me, I would have told him I didn't want or need their money. But still, his attitude infuriated me. How could they profess to love Chris when they'd had virtually nothing to do with him for the past five years?

"Harry, who had been a tremendous support after Chris died, was beside himself when he read the letter. Who did *they* think *they* were? Harry reassured me that Chris had loved me; he had wanted to spend the rest of his life with me. His parents had never respected his choice of bride and hadn't even been gracious enough to attend our wedding. Good riddance to them was his attitude, and so it became mine, too.

"Back home in London, I threw myself into my career. Step one of my plan, which was to marry well, had not turned out as I had hoped, so now it was all up to me. I was so determined to take Silk, to be appointed Queen's Counsel, that I ignored any other romantic overtures that came my way and remained single. I wanted so badly to be admired and respected as a lawyer so, whatever it took, I would not be distracted from my goal. From then on, it would be all about me and my career. I suppose it makes me sound bitter, but, at the time, the only way I could cope with losing Chris was to tell myself that a husband would be superfluous to my needs."

"Goodness," Camille said, looking a little shocked, "But, on the other hand, I can understand you feeling that way."

"I stayed away from Lower Naughton after that. The last thing I wanted was to bump into any of the German-Browns. I doubted that Chris's brother and sisters felt the same about me as their mother and father, but I couldn't be sure that his mean-spirited parents hadn't tainted their viewpoint.

"As time passed, Harry and I became closer than ever. Yes, he had boyfriends, and there was one chap, Michael, who I really liked and who worshipped Harry. They were a perfect match, and over time, they developed a deep and passionate relationship, which lasted until that fateful night on 30th April 1999. The three of us had gone out for dinner in Soho. After a lovely meal, I left them at the restaurant to finish their bottle of wine and went outside to find a taxi to take me to Victoria Station for my train back home. After Chris died, I sold our flat and bought this house. Harry and Michael were going bar-hopping, and much as I loved spending time with them, bar-hopping was never my cup of tea.

"I had no idea they'd gone to The Admiral Duncan until the following day when I received a phone call from Harry's sister, Colleen, who wanted to know where Harry was. I had no idea what she was talking about, and she told me to turn on the television and watch the news. I told her not to worry; they were probably still in bed as they'd been on a bit of a bender the night before. Meanwhile, I turned on the television; a bomb had exploded in the pub, targeted for being a noted hangout for the gay community. I was in a complete panic, praying that Harry and Michael hadn't gone there. I tried ringing Harry, but nobody picked up the phone. I tried Michael, and nobody picked up there either. I rang a policeman I knew from one of my cases, who worked the Soho area, and I asked if he knew what had happened to the victims. He told me they had been taken to various hospitals

197

across the city, and there was a phone number to ring to hear the names of the dead and injured and which hospital they were taken to. I tried ringing, but, infuriatingly, I was told I needed to be a close relative. So I rang Colleen and gave her the details so she could check. After the longest ten minutes of my life, she rang me back to tell me they were both in St. Thomas' hospital — thank God they were still alive."

"Oh yes, I remember the bombing. It was dreadful. I can't believe people can be so cruel."

"Colleen caught a train down to London, and I met her at St. Pancras. I spotted her as soon as she pushed through the barrier; she looked so pale and scared. I took her bag, and she held onto my arm as we walked across the concourse to find a taxi. Once we arrived at St. Thomas', we were surrounded by crowds of people, all looking nervous and frightened. Like us, they were trying to find their loved ones. I suppose I should have expected it, but it was still a shock to see the press and television cameras hovering about trying to interview members of the families of the injured. Asking the usual ridiculous and insensitive question, 'So how does it feel to know your relative was blown up last night?' Bloody parasites.

"We managed to make our way through the crowd and went up to the front desk, where we explained who we were. In a side room, a social worker sat us down and very gently warned us what to expect. Harry was very seriously injured, having lost his left leg and left hand — my stomach turned over. I could not even imagine how Colleen was feeling. I took a deep breath and asked if we could see him, and the social worker told us which ward he was on. Holding on to each other for support, we walked through the hospital and found a bank of lifts that took us to the fourth floor. The ward was straight ahead of us as the lift doors opened. Apprehensively pushing open the swing doors, we approached the nurses' station, and Colleen asked where Harry, her brother, was. The nurse told us he was only allowed one visitor at a time, and they must be a close relative. I indicated to Colleen that she must go and I would wait in the corridor. After what seemed like an eternity, she came out of the ward, sat down beside me, and burst into tears. She described how dreadful he looked; his handsome face was covered in cuts, some severe enough to warrant stitches. Apparently, Harry didn't say a word, but he let her hold his hand, and she felt him squeeze it. She told him that she was staying with me and would be back to see him the following day.

"Colleen stayed with me for a week, but she needed to return to Lower Naughton for the children. Kevin had managed with help from his mum, but understandably, they wanted her home. By that point, I was allowed to visit Harry, but it was so sad and so distressing to see him like that — such a vibrant, gorgeous man who one minute was so full of life, so successful and so happy, reduced to a shadow of his former self.

"A couple of months later, after his wounds were healed, he was moved to a rehabilitation facility. Michael, who was luckier than Harry and had not lost any limbs, was back home. He visited Harry for a while, but his lover had become withdrawn. He didn't want to see anyone and was going through the most dreadful depression, which, of course, was absolutely understandable. He took his anger and frustrations out on Michael, telling him repeatedly how lucky he was to be in one piece, and in the end, the tension between the two of them became too much to bear, and they decided to end their relationship. Harry, struggling with therapy and refusing to wear either the prosthetic leg or hand, closed his flower shop, shut down his business, and decided to move back to his parent's home in Lower Naughton.

"Selfishly, I took it personally. I thought that as we'd been so close for so long, Harry should move in with me. We had both suffered losses, and I truly believed we could love and support each other. Logistically, there was plenty of room downstairs. I could turn my drawing room, which I hardly ever used, into a bedroom for him and adapt the downstairs toilet to add a shower. I could hire all the help he would need, and we could still go out to restaurants and the theatre as I would be quite capable of pushing a wheelchair — but he would have none of it. Eventually, his father drove down to the skilled nursing facility, picked him up, and drove him back to Lower Naughton. Whenever I tried ringing him and writing him letters, he ignored me. I never saw him again.

"I heard from my Aunty Bridget that he went downhill rapidly once he was home. He wouldn't eat, he wouldn't go to rehab, and he still would have nothing to do with wearing his prosthetics. The doctor put him on anti-depressant medication, but it didn't help — it could be he never even took them. One terrible morning, his mother went into his room with a cup of tea to wake him and found that my wonderful Harry had died during the night. When the coroner did the postmortem, she found large amounts of the anti-depressants in his system. He must have been storing them up for just such a moment."

Camille, who had been silent until now, shook her head, "Oh, Margaret, I am most dreadfully sorry. First, to lose Chris, but then to lose Harry in such a way must have been devastating. How could you bear it?"

"I couldn't. For a long time, I found it difficult to accept that Harry was gone. He was too young, too talented, and too amazingly wonderful to die. It wasn't fair. The two most important people in my life were gone, and with them, any feelings I may have had for anything or anyone. I wanted nothing more than to become an emotionally-stunted eunuch. Of course, that was many years ago. I'm fine now, obviously, but at that point, I hated everything and everyone.

"And then, the icing on the cake — Sarah's mother. My Aunty Bridget called to tell me that when she told Mrs. Weston of Harry's death, her response was, 'Good riddance, one less pedophile, one less perverted homosexual on the planet.' What a bitch."

Camille looked at me with a concerned frown, "No wonder someone wanted to kill her. I know they say time does heal most things, but that must have taken a lot to come to terms with. You are such a sweet and kind person; you did not deserve anything like that to happen to you."

Sweet and kind! I certainly hadn't felt sweet or kind after that.

Camille started writing in her notebook, and I asked her what she'd written. "Oh, I was making a note about Sarah's mother and the awful things she had said about Harry. Just a thought: could that be connected with the two men who had attacked him for being gay? We'll give it some thought. Anyway, I should love you and leave you — but another fascinating lunch meeting. The food was delicious, and thank you for sharing your story. It means a lot to me that you were able to confide in me."

I smiled, grateful to have someone to tell my story to. These so-called detecting sessions were turning into therapy sessions for me.

"Thinking about our victim's list, do you think we should do some research into Mrs. Weston? She seemed to have problems with gay men, and in particular, Harry. I just feel there must be a reason. Why don't we both do some research into her background and hopefully, we can come up with something for our next get-together." Camille said earnestly.

We decided our next lunch meeting would be in Kingston-upon-Thames. Camille offered to find a restaurant and said she would ring me closer to the date to let me know the venue and the time. I think she must have been thinking that I needed some downtime and that she should take hold of the reigns of this project and organize our research, as I seemed to be off with the fairies at the moment. I needed to pull myself together.

Chapter 9

It was an easy drive into Kingston, with not too much traffic, and after parking my car in a nearby carpark, I walked to the restaurant, arriving at the same time as Camille. After the usual hugs and salutations in front of the restaurant, we went in together. A young girl seated us at a table by a window overlooking the Thames. It was a chilly day, so we ordered coffees, hugging the mugs to warm up our hands. As soon as the waiter had taken our orders, I put a folder on the table and opened it.

Camille looked at the stack of papers and then at me, "Good heavens, you have been busy. I've done a little research myself, so it will be interesting to see if we've come up with the same information. Why don't you begin."

"Do you remember I told you about the first time Chris and I saw Harry in London? He told us the reason he had moved there was because of an incident that happened back in Lower Naughton when a couple of thugs had set on him and beaten him badly. Chris, at the time, tried to do some digging and had even spoken to the Chief Constable of Staffordshire, a friend of his father, and asked him whether he could have an unofficial look at the case notes filed in Burton. There was not a lot of information, just the description of a car, dark blue, parked down by the brook, possibly a Ford Cortina. A passer-by said they had seen the car and two young men climbing into it and roaring off at breakneck speed. The witness said both men were dressed in black suits, white shirts, and skinny black ties — strangely formal attire for rural Staffordshire. This description matched the two thugs who had attacked Harry. He also told the police they didn't sound like they came from around Burton, and he was reasonably sure they had cockney accents. He remembered one of them calling the other 'Paul.'"

Camille flicked back to a page in her notebook where she'd written all her notes from that day and nodded in agreement. "Yes, here it is."

I looked at Camille, "It would be a heck of a coincidence, but could he be the same Paul who had taken Sarah out and whose mother, Barbara Russo, was a friend of her mother? Unfortunately, the police, having assumed the two men were out-of-towners, possibly from London, had closed the case. I thought that very strange until I realized the police wouldn't make much of an effort to find someone who'd beaten up a gay man. Back then, being gay was not exactly going to evoke much sympathy."

"Where did you find this out?" Camille asked.

"Well, believe it or not, after Chris found this out, I'd kept all this information in a file in my office at home just in case I might need it in the future. Who knew? I'm probably grasping at straws, trying to connect Harry's incident with the murder of Elizabeth Weston, but there are so many unexplained elements to the Weston family. We know that Sarah's dad was furious about Sarah going out with that Paul fellow just because he came from the East End of London, and he accused his wife of hanging around with lowlifes. I admit I'm becoming a bit obsessed with Elizabeth Weston's background.

"Sarah knew her mother grew up in the East End, and her grandparents had died when Elizabeth, her mother, was a baby. She said an aunt had brought her up but that the aunt died when Elizabeth was a teenager. I'm not sure if that's true. I have a feeling Elizabeth Weston kept her past to herself. The only other person from her past that Sarah knew of was Barbara Russo, Paul's mother. I decided to see if I could obtain a copy of the Weston's marriage certificate as there must have been witnesses to the wedding, and it should give me Elizabeth's maiden name. I asked Amanda, my PA in chambers, if she would mind doing some work for me and if she could track down a copy of the document. I don't know about you, but I have a gut feeling about Elizabeth Weston and her past. What did she know about the notoriously crime-ridden East End?"

Camille leaped in, "And what about the dreadful car accident that killed Colleen and Kevin's little daughter, Tiffany? Could that be a part of all this? The police never did find out what happened."

"I don't know, Camille. It's a bit of a stretch that an accident that happened around ten years ago could possibly be related to Harry, who was attacked, what, thirty years previously. Or, come to think of it, the murders of Elizabeth Weston and Richard Slater."

"I agree it's a bizarre hunch, but I have a feeling they tie together somehow. And I'm sure Elizabeth Weston is in the midst of it all. Why would two cockney thugs visit a small village to brutalize a local gay man, and why would two more unpleasant characters run over a little girl? It all seems like too much of a coincidence," she said quizzically.

I nodded, and Camille continued, "I've done some research myself. I rang Burton police station and asked if they could track down the notes from the hit-and-run accident that killed little Tiffany. I could hardly believe it when, an hour later, I received an email with a scanned copy of all the documents and photographs. It's amazing the strings I can pull using Hywell's name. Nobody had actually seen the accident, but a woman coming out of the Post Office heard a bang and a scream and saw a car with two men careening down the road beside the brook. She described the car as a large black SUV, possibly a BMW. She couldn't be sure. The police interviewed the staff at the Falconer's Arms in case the driver had stopped in there for lunch or drinks, but they said that only locals had been in there that day. They tried to find the car, assuming there must have been some damage to the front, but after checking with all the local garages, they gave up as none of them had been asked to mend the front of any cars fitting that description. Again, an out-of-towner? Until then, I'd never been a great believer in coincidence — but now?"

"That description of the car, a black BMW SUV, is how Colleen described it to me when she and I had a cigarette at the trial."

The waiter came over to see if we were ready to order lunch. I was starving and ordered steak frites, and Camille asked for a tuna niçoise salad.

I then handed over a copy of the Weston's marriage certificate that Amanda had sent me. Camille looked it over, then looked at me.

"I admit I felt a mixture of apprehension and a degree of excitement when I tore open the envelope and pulled out the certificate. I hoped it would give us some insight into the enigmatic Elizabeth Weston. What do you think? At first glance, much of the information seems unremarkable. The wedding took place at the Richmond registry office. The bride, Elizabeth Sarah Johnson, was just eighteen. Her profession was listed as typist, and her residence was Whitechapel, smack bang in the East End of London and a hive of activity for London's criminal gangs. Did you notice that rather strangely, in the Father's Name column, there's just a dash? Even if Mr. Johnson had died as Sarah had been told, there should have been a name. So, was it a simple clerical error or a sign of something fishy?

"The certificate shows the groom, Charles Michael Weston, was a thirty-year-old accountant from Kingston. In the Father's Name column, it says Charles, so father and son have the same name. And he's listed as a Publisher. Finally, at the bottom of the certificate are the signatures of the two witnesses, Fanny Purcell and David Weston. I have no idea who Fanny was, but I assume David was Charles' brother. One interesting point: knowing Sarah's birthday, the date on the marriage certificate confirms that Elizabeth must have been pregnant at the time of the wedding. And another point: I hadn't realized there was such a significant gap in her parent's ages."

Camille, smiling, looked at me, "Can you imagine how thrilled Charles Weston senior must have been when his son, thirty-year-old Charlie, told him he was about to be married — oh, and by the way, Dad, she's pregnant. Oh, and she's from the East End of London. Oh, I almost forgot, Dad, she's only eighteen!"

"Absolutely. I would have loved to have been a fly on the wall when that conversation occurred. I knew from what Sarah had told me that her mother and father met at a publishing company, and after spending some time Googling, I discovered that her grandfather, Charles Sr., had owned the company."

"Well, well," said Camille, "So it looks like our Charlie was messing about with the girls in the typing pool, and Elizabeth was the lucky one who snagged him. This begs the question: was the pregnancy by accident or design?"

"That's a good point. From what I've learned about Sarah's mother, I'd lay money on the pregnancy being planned. It was her way out of poverty and the East End and into a good family. Not unlike me, I suppose. I, too, found a good family to marry into if only I hadn't been careless and lost the husband."

Camille smiled awkwardly and took a sip of her coffee as she looked out of the window. Luckily, at that point, the food arrived, and after having a few bites, I continued.

"From Elizabeth's snobbish attitude in her later years, you would never have known that she was not quite what she made herself out to be. If I had a chip on my shoulder about where I came from, Sarah's mother must have had a chip the size of the New Forest. Talk about no better than she ought to be. Elizabeth acted the proper lady with all her airs and graces — it was as if she was born to it. She'd have been mortified if anyone had ever found out where she actually came from and the reality of her background. It also explains why Sarah's dad shouted at her mum when the police brought Sarah home after her date with Paul Russo. If you remember, Sarah said he'd told her mum that she was lucky to have him, that she was common as muck, that he'd dragged her out of the slums in the East End, and she needed to act as if she were more grateful."

I stopped to have a couple more bites of my steak, then said,

"After the revelations of the marriage certificate, I asked Amanda if she could find a copy of Elizabeth's birth certificate. It would give us her parents' names, and she came up trumps once again. It turns out Elizabeth was born in Whitechapel, and her father was a George William Johnson. The certificate listed him as a labourer. I had my doubts about that, knowing he came from a gang-riddled section of the East End. It seemed far more likely he was a petty criminal. Elizabeth's mother was Alice Johnson, formerly Purcell, a maid."

Camille leaped in, "Ah, so Fanny Purcell, who was listed as a witness at Elizabeth's wedding, was a relative. Could she have been the mysterious aunt Elizabeth lived with as a teenager or was that all made up by Sarah's mother to put Sarah off the scent and cover up a more bleak reality?"

"That's a good point. Anyway, next, I set about researching Elizabeth's father, George, and, after a few Google attempts, found a newspaper article that described a burglary that had taken place at a house in Blackheath. George, who had previously been in prison for several burglaries, including one for grievous bodily harm, was charged along with a couple of other unpleasant characters. Looking them up, I found that one of them, years later, was acquainted with the infamous Kray twins, having been a driver for a couple of their heists."

"Good heavens." Camille nearly choked on her tuna. "I bet Sarah knew none of this if she'd been told her grandparents died when she was a baby. It was an excellent subterfuge if Grandad was actually serving time at *His Majesty's Pleasure* in Wormwood Scrubs Prison. Could that explain why he was not on Elizabeth's marriage certificate? It seems as if every piece of information you found leads us to more questions. And what about Elizabeth's mother? Why did Sarah never meet her grandmother, or did she? And did Elizabeth have any brothers or sisters?"

We stopped talking for a while and tucked into our lunch, trying to process all this information and make sense of it.

"You know, Camille, it's possible Elizabeth's parents really were dead when Sarah was born, but somehow I doubt it. We need to find out when they actually died."

Camille lifted her bag onto her lap, "Let me boot up my laptop and do a quick search."

After a few minutes and a few dead ends, she found the General Register Office and searched for death certificates for George and Alice Johnson. After hunting and pecking around, she found them and immediately requested copies to be sent to her home address. She swung the laptop around on the table so we could both read the certificates, and I was not at all surprised to find that George had died in prison at the ripe old age of 51. As for Alice, she died in Brighton aged 54.

"So the story about Elizabeth's parents dying when she was a little girl and her being brought up by an aunt was a complete fabrication," I said, feverishly scanning the page.

Camille turned to me. "It's become apparent why Elizabeth didn't want Sarah to know the truth about her grandparents, especially with her father's questionable history. She had effectively disowned her parents."

Still curious to see if Elizabeth had any brothers and sisters, I asked Camille if I could borrow her laptop. She passed it across, and I tried searching for George Johnson. Eventually, I found what I was looking for — a Daily Mirror newspaper article.

"Camille, look at this." I pointed to the screen and turned the laptop back toward Camille.

The article described how a young boy, Wilfred Johnson of Whitechapel, was found sexually assaulted and strangled under Tower Bridge beside the Thames. He had been in the water for a few days, judging by the state of his body. The little lad was only five years old. His parents, George and

Alice Johnson, had reported him missing to the police three days before. A man out walking his dog had seen something that looked like a pile of old rags on the edge of the water. His dog had gone over to it and was sniffing about, so he decided to see what the dog was looking at and realized it was a boy's body. Initially, the police thought the boy had fallen into the Thames and drowned. However, when his body was examined at the morgue, the coroner determined the lad had been strangled and, on further inspection, discovered he'd been physically and sexually assaulted. A description of the clothes the little boy was wearing when he was found was circulated to the local police stations. The station where George had reported Wilfred missing realized they matched the clothing little Wilfred wore at the time of his disappearance. George, who identified the body, was interviewed afterward by a journalist working for the newspaper. He told him that Wilfred's killer should be very afraid because if he ever found him, there wouldn't be much left of him.

Then, I did another search to find out more about the murder and whether the murderer had been caught. After more hunting and pecking, I found a couple more newspaper articles. I clicked on the first one and started reading it out loud to Camille.

"The first person interviewed was Wilfred's older sister Elizabeth, our Elizabeth, who was six at the time. She had been babysitting her little brother while her mother was at work. The two children had been playing in the street with some other kids from the neighbourhood. Elizabeth said she left Wilfred for a few minutes while she went to the lavatory. When she came back, her brother was gone. She asked the other kids where he was, and they said a man had dragged him off down the street. She ran to the corner to see if she could see them, but there was no sign of them. The police asked for the names of the other children they had been playing with, and she gave them names and, as best she could, where they lived. When a detective interviewed the children, they managed between them to come up with a vague description of a youngish man with orange hair, wearing overalls covered in black stuff (oil, the notes said, possibly worked in the docks?) One of the children said the man had a strange accent; he sounded like the priest at the local Catholic church. When the detective met with the priest, he found a middle-aged man with a strong Irish accent.

"The police looked at all the known paedophiles in Whitechapel and the surrounding area. A couple of men were brought in and interviewed, but they had alibis for when Wilfred went missing. However, one suspect in the police files was a known paedophile named Harry O'Mara. He worked in the docks and had been accused of molesting a young boy several months before, but it was never proven, and he was subsequently released.

"About a month after Wilfred was murdered, a man down by the docks was seen holding the arm of another little boy and dragging him along. An off-duty policeman who was headed to his local pub saw him and, remembering the description of Wilfred's suspected killer, ran after him. The man, realizing he was being chased, let go of the child and ran in the opposite direction. That was the last time he was spotted. It was assumed that Harry O'Mara had boarded a boat to Ireland."

I looked up from the laptop at Camille, "The more I read about what happened, the more I'm convinced Elizabeth Weston's attitude toward my dear Harry could be explained by the murder of her little brother. I'm guessing she remembered Harry O'Mara; how could she forget him after what he'd done to Wilfred? From what it says, this Harry had been just twenty-five years old when he was first picked up, and he was an Irish man with red hair, just like my friend. So, was that the key to her irrational hatred of Harry? I could imagine she would have been incensed at the sight of a young red-haired man of Irish heritage in the village, matching the description of the man who had raped and brutally killed her brother."

"Oh, absolutely. I imagine Elizabeth had been wracked with guilt all her life for leaving her little brother alone in the street that day. She was probably so traumatized by his death that I wouldn't be surprised if her deranged mind subsumed the two Harrys into one incarnation of evil. She also knew Harry was gay and, in her crazy, warped mind, erroneously connected homosexuality with pedophilia and decided the two Harrys were one and the same. Making up her mind to exact her revenge, could Elizabeth have had a couple of thugs she knew from the East End come up to Lower Naughton and attack your Harry in the hope she could drive him away? I think we've worked it out, Margaret, don't you? Obviously, Sarah's mother was a psychopath. All her adult life, she'd been a schemer. She had it in her mind to find a rich man, and I bet Charles

215

Weston didn't know what hit him when she got her claws into him. She knew that if she were pregnant, he would marry her. I was going to say poor, innocent Charles, but after what he did to you, I think not. Maybe they deserved each other. The only problem is, we have worked out how her mind worked and why someone might want to kill her, but we don't have any more suspects — or do we?"

"Anyway, look at the time, Camille. We should probably call it a day — plenty to think about. We have so much new information. Just a thought: do you fancy the idea of a field trip? We could drive up to Lower Naughton just for the day. It's doable, I've done it a couple of times. I can book a table for lunch at the Falconer's Arms, and I can drive you around the village so you can have a feel for the place. Shall we say a week from today?"

"What a splendid idea. I would love to see Lower Naughton. Perfect. I can't wait. A field trip, how exciting." And on that note, we exchanged goodbyes and parted ways.

After arriving home, I rang the Falconer's Arms and booked a table, then emailed Camille with the details. I arranged to pick her up at eight, giving us plenty of time to drive up to my childhood home, the site of all the intrigue!

Chapter 10

The following week, after picking up Camille, we set off on our little adventure. Being very organized, Camille had packed a few essentials for the drive: a flask of coffee and a pastry to keep us going until lunchtime. The drive up was uneventful. The traffic wasn't too awful once we'd passed through London, and even that hadn't been too horrendous, thanks to the satnav. Once we were on the M1, I felt more comfortable chatting. Camille, who had been quiet until then to let me concentrate on the London traffic, asked me about the last time I'd seen my Aunty Bridget, as she'd been the source of so much information, or I should say *gossip* about the village.

"Unfortunately, I hadn't seen her for several years. We kept in touch via Skype and texts, and then I heard from my cousin that she'd died. It was sudden, a heart attack, so the last time I came up here was for her funeral."

"Oh no, I am sorry."

"Thank you. I was annoyed at myself for not taking the time to drive up and see her before, but you know how it is; the time just gets away from you. Anyway, I was determined to go to her funeral to pay my respects. She was, after all, one of the most important people in my life — I certainly preferred her to my mother. I stayed at the Falconer's Arms in the village. I think you'll like the hotel. I remember being pleasantly surprised and relieved that the hotel had not been 'modernized.' You almost feel like you've gone back in time when you walk in. The low ceilings and the walls are an antique off-white colour. The supporting oak beams are painted a glossy black. Horseshoes climb up either side of the mirror behind the bar, and pewter tankards hang across the beams above the mirror. The tables and chairs in the bar look like they've been there a good number of years. Quite a few bums have sat there before us, and there aren't any red plastic banquettes, thank goodness. The ceiling in the snug bar is still slightly yellowed from the years before smoking was banned. In fact, there is only one thing missing — the smell of stale beer and cigarettes. Don't you hate it when you walk into an old pub these days, and a tantalizing aroma of disinfectant greets you."

Camille, who had been looking out of the window at the passing scenery, agreed, "Absolutely. I've never been a smoker, but there was something about that smell that seemed fitting in a pub."

"Right, we have reached our destination, as the satnav would say. Before we have lunch, I thought I'd drive around the village to give you an idea of where all the places we've talked about and were mentioned in the trial exist in relation to each other. Then, after lunch, we can have a bit of an amble."

"Wonderful," Camille exclaimed with the excitement of a schoolgirl.

"So this is the north end of the village, and the first place I'm going to take you to is Elizabeth Weston's house; this is where the first murder occurred. Next, we'll drive to the school and then head back up the road to the village shop. My Aunty Bridget's hair salon is next door to the shop.

Lastly, we'll head over to the brook so you can see where Sarah lives. If you remember, Sarah supposedly went from the school to the shop to buy milk and biscuits for her mum. Hywell reasoned she had the time to pop into her mother's house, kill her, and then go on to school. It's certainly possible, as you'll see."

Camille took her notebook and a pen from her bag and wrote this all down as I drove through the village. Camille looked at her watch as we passed each location and wrote down the times. She was clearly a prolific note-taker. I turned left off the main street and drove up the road until we reached a large red-brick detached house set back a bit from the road. I pointed to the house. "That was the Weston's house."

"It's a nice house." Camille said, "Does Sarah still own it?"

"As far as I know, she does. It must be worth quite a lot. I wonder, if now the trial is over, she'll move into it and sell hers and Richard's house."

"Ugh, Margaret, I think not. Surely, she wouldn't want to live in the house where her mother was murdered so brutally. Especially if she was the murderer."

I smiled, "Sorry, that was a rather gruesome thought. Imagine sleeping in the same bedroom where it happened. It gives you the shudders just thinking about it."

Camille made a note as I did a three-point turn and drove back to the main road. About a mile further on, I stopped outside the school. "This is the village school where Sarah is the principal."

Camille checked her watch, "You know it only took a minute and a half to drive here from the Weston's house. Let's time the drive from here to the shop."

I set off again, and within a couple of minutes, we arrived at the shop.

"Goodness, that was quick. This is a small village. Sarah certainly had plenty of time to drive from the school to the shop and back to her mother's house. Now we need to add in how long it would take to drive from the school to Sarah's house. Do you mind driving back to the school and then to her home?"

"Of course not." I managed a U-turn and headed back to the school as Camille timed the journey from the school through the estate to Sarah's house.

Looking at my watch, I realized we were due to be at the Falconer's Arms for lunch in ten minutes.

"We'd better start moving to get to lunch, but we just have time to drive past my old house."

I turned right and drove down the hill, stopping directly across the road from the house.

"You see those houses over there; that's where I lived as a child. Next door on the left is Richard's old house, and next door to him is Kevin's house. He still lives there with Colleen. Hopefully, they removed the chicken coop from the bottom of their garden."

"Yes, hopefully so!" Camille agreed, looking horrified.

Not being one for sentimentality, I started the car up again and drove alongside the brook.

"Now you can see the brook where I would fish for tiddlers. The estate where Sarah and Richard lived is built on what used to be the woods where we used to play when I was a child. Oh, and on your right is where the blacksmith used to be. That's where Alan, the little boy who died, lived with his mum and dad. And just over that bridge is the pub. We should be just in time for our reservation."

Once I'd parked the car, we walked to the pub entrance and went inside. "Oh good, it hasn't changed since I was last here. Maybe a coat of paint, but all is how I remember it."

The hostess sat us at a table beside the window and left us with menus.

"This is just as I'd imagined," Camille said, looking around and spotting a couple of workmen in overalls seated at the bar with their pints. "The pub's quite old, isn't it? It has so much character. You can feel it's the heart of village life. Thank you for bringing me on this trip, Margaret. It is so interesting putting the faces and names to the buildings."

"You're welcome. It's a trip down memory lane for me too. Now, I'm starving, and I noticed shepherd's pie was on the board of today's specials. It seems to fit this place, so that's what I'm going to have, and I'm in desperate need of another cup of coffee."

"That sounds perfect. I think I'll join you. Does this mean I've seen everything?"

"Not quite. I thought after lunch we'd have a walk to the church which is next door and, if you don't mind, I'd like to walk over to Chris' old house, or the 'Big House' as all the villagers called it. I don't know if you remember, but Chris, my late husband, also came from Lower Naughton?"

"Of course. I'd like to see where your husband was brought up. I'd also like to see the church."

We had a few bites of our lunch when Camille said, "You know, Margaret, having seen where Sarah lived and the distance to her mother's house and the school, I can understand why the police thought she'd done it. Time-wise, it's certainly possible, although it would have been quite a challenge to clean up all that blood from her clothes and car in such a short time frame. And there's something else I'm curious about. During the trial, you asked a couple of witnesses about a car that was seen outside Mrs. Weston's house around the time she was murdered. This had a significant impact on the course of the trial as the car fitted the description of the one Sarah owned. And yet, neither of the witnesses could categorically state it was actually her car. I find that odd. It was the same make, the same colour, and someone fitting her description was seen driving it. Has anyone investigated further into who the car belonged to? Did someone borrow Sarah's car while she was at work? Who else has a car like that? Oh no, don't tell me, it was out-of-townies again? Could Mrs. Weston have upset one of her East End cronies, and they had put out a hit on her?"

Laughing, I replied, "You're right; it is a popular make and colour. But somehow, I don't see professional hitmen driving a Prius. And the answer to your question is 'No.' I didn't bother checking on the car any further once I had the postman and Mrs. Woods give their evidence. It was up to the police to investigate further. Though I'm beginning to see where you're coming from. Was it Sarah, after all? You always had a feeling she was guilty, didn't you?"

After lunch, we left the pub and walked down the road past the church. I spotted the turnoff to Nawerton Manor, and as we strolled up the lane toward it, I thought I should give Camille some context about the home and the family.

"Patrick, Chris' brother, inherited the estate after their parents died. I didn't marry Chris for his money, or I would have made more of an issue of the pre-nup, but I certainly hadn't expected him to die so young. After he was gone, I never saw the family again. I think, in the back of their minds, they thought I'd had him killed so that I could inherit everything. But that was deluded — there was no way that could happen as I'd signed the pre-nup, which they knew all about anyway."

I stopped at the bottom of the driveway to look at the estate.

"Funny to think that if I hadn't been so eager to sign that piece of paper, I could have been living here, but truthfully, would I have wanted to? It would have meant giving up my career in London, and I would never have done that."

Camille nodded, "Of course, but I can see how you can still appreciate the place. The grounds are beautiful, and that white house is gorgeous. The formal gardens set out in front are stunning. Knowing what a keen gardener you are, this must be the one aspect of country life you would have enjoyed. There must be acres of land. Are there horses over there in the paddock?"

"Yes, it's a vast estate. Every year, Chris' parents used to host the village flower show on the lawn in front of the house. The villagers loved it; they'd compete against each other for the most enormous onions, the most beautiful roses, and, of course, the tastiest Victoria sandwich and apple pie. It was quite a show.

"Lady Celia, Chris' mother, was a serious equestrian. She won quite a few competitions in eventing. Seeing the horses wandering around the paddock, I assume Patrick's children are riders. Oh well, I shall console myself with the knowledge that I really wasn't cut out to live such a rural life, and I certainly can't see myself as the Lady of the Manor."

Camille put her arm through mine, I assume, in an effort to console me, but it just made me feel more uncomfortable. "I tell you what, if that place ever comes on the market, I'd love to make an offer. You can come and stay here with me and enjoy the gardens."

I laughed, "You have a deal."

On that note, we set off for the walk back toward the Falconer's Arms to pick up the car. I would have liked to have had a stroll around the churchyard, but we were short on time and had to set off for the drive home. On the way, I told Camille about the night before Aunty Bridget's funeral:

224

"That evening, I had dinner downstairs in the hotel's dining room, opting for a table in the corner by a window that allowed me to watch the other patrons coming and going to see if I recognized anyone. I remember having a glass of red wine and French onion soup, which was delicious.

"I was about to head upstairs when I noticed a man sitting alone at the bar. I was reasonably sure it was Richard Slater, Sarah's dead husband. If you remember, he was my old neighbour. I hadn't seen him for years, well, apart from the family photo Sarah always included in her Christmas cards, but I was convinced it was him. He had a bit of a paunchy belly, but it was the full head of jet-black hair, albeit streaked with grey, that convinced me. There was an empty stool beside him, so I walked over, tapped him on the arm, and asked if I could join him. He looked a bit surprised, having not recognized me. I introduced myself, explaining we used to live next door to each other. He apologized and said that Sarah had told him I would be in the village for my aunt's funeral. He was a bit flirty, saying my offer to join him was the best offer he'd had all day. It was a bit pathetic, but anyway, he bought me a drink, which was nice of him. Jake, the bartender who had a nasty case of acne, if I remember correctly, brought the drinks over, and Richard and I had a nice chat about the old days.

"I teased him about marrying Sarah and told him he'd done well for himself. I asked him how he'd persuaded Sarah's parents to agree to it, and I was surprised when he said Sarah's father was fine about it, but her mother had a fit; some layabout marrying their dear daughter is how she phrased it. Fortunately, Sarah's father stuck up for her and

225

said it was fine, that he was sure Richard would keep their Sarah in the manner to which she was accustomed, and told his wife to leave him alone. He told me how he and Sarah's father were quite friendly initially. They sometimes watched football matches together, which, Sarah said, drove Mrs. Weston crazy. She didn't want him in the house, but Mr. Weston used to tell her to back off. Richard reckoned there wasn't much love lost between Sarah's parents. He told me he'd heard Mr. Weston shouting at Mrs. Weston, telling her how lucky she was to have him.

"Anyway, once Richard and Sarah were married, Mrs. Weston was even worse to Sarah. Richard said she was a real battle-ax. She had Sarah constantly at her beck and call. He said it was a relief when she died. 'Good riddance' was how he described it. He couldn't stand her. He even said there were times when she'd been particularly unpleasant to Sarah, that he'd been tempted to put a pillow over her face. She was so possessive of Sarah, and he had a couple of run-ins with her over it. I asked him how she treated his mother, as I'd heard she was quite nice to her, and he said not to believe everything I heard. She was horrible. His mum was never invited to any family functions. In fact, Mrs. Weston wouldn't even let her in the house. Apparently, one time, when Richard's mother invited Mrs. Weston for tea, she was given short shrift and told to leave her family alone. She told Sarah she wouldn't be caught dead in that hovel and that Richard's mum was the last person she'd want to spend time with."

Camille was busy writing again. Shaking her head, she looked up, "Now there's a thought: could Richard have become so enraged about his mother-in-law that he'd taken matters into his own hands? Suppose he'd taken Sarah's car from the school car park and driven over to Mrs. Weston's house, and he'd killed her. What do you think? I'm putting him on the list of suspects. Just because there were two murders in the same family, the police simply assumed there was only one perpetrator. But what if the two killings were entirely separate?"

"You know, Camille, I'd wondered the same thing. It would certainly explain why a car that looked like Sarah's was outside Mrs. Weston's house around the time of the murder. But that means he was setting Sarah up as the murderer, right? I wonder if he and Colleen were still having an affair. Maybe they were planning on running away together. It's possible, I suppose. In the trial, the postman said it was difficult to tell who was driving the car as it was going so fast. But I do wonder if the police ever suspected Richard."

Camille shook her head and looked at me. "No, I don't really think it was Richard. I still think Sarah did it. She had the means, the reasons, and the opportunities to murder both of them. The Weston house would fetch quite a large amount of money if Sarah sold it. Suppose her mother *had* told her about Richard and Colleen and the baby. I can imagine Elizabeth Weston, in her passive-aggressive way, telling Sarah how she was right all along. Richard was a good-for-nothing drunk who took advantage of poor Sarah. So, in that scenario, the red car was indeed her Prius. She was hoping not to be seen, but Mrs. Woods and the postman did see her, and so in a panic, she slammed her foot on the accelerator to move away from there as fast as possible in the hopes they hadn't recognized her."

I nodded in agreement, "You're right. In Sarah's mind, Richard deserved to die for having an affair with Colleen that produced poor little Tiffany. Do you think Sarah might have had the little girl killed out of anger and jealousy?"

"Good Heavens, Margaret, that would be unthinkable," Camille said, shocked at the idea.

"There was a bit more Richard said that night, but I'll tell you next time. But I think that's enough to think about for now."

We were close to London, and I needed to concentrate, so we drove the rest of the way in silence. I dropped Camille off at her house, refusing her offer of a cup of tea as I was exhausted from the drive and just wanted to go home.

#####

Later that evening, a glass of wine in hand and nibbling on some cheese and crackers, I thought about what Camille had said; she still believed Sarah had killed both Richard and her mother. What I hadn't had the chance to tell Camille was what happened later that evening as I sat at the bar with Richard. Camille already knew from the trial he was not the sweet, loyal husband he portrayed to the outside world. In fact, he was just the opposite. He'd fathered a child with his housekeeper. And that evening in the Falconer's Arms, I had discovered more about his wandering hands.

"What about your mum, Richard?" I'd asked him. "I always liked her; she was a lovely lady. And you have a sister if I remember correctly?"

"Me mam died about ten years ago, and me sister's married; nice bloke, couple of kiddies, all grown up now though. They moved to Sheffield. You probably know me and Sarah have two girls. Nicola lives in Brixton, of all places, but they have a nice little house, and Jen lives in Derby. Jen's got a little girl, Emily, cute little thing she is, and Nicola has two boys: Josh, who's six, and Will, who's four. Them boys is quite a handful, but they do love a bit of footy, so whenever we're in London, we take 'em to the local park, have 'em running about, buy 'em an ice cream, and once we've worn 'em out, we take 'em home and give 'em back to their mam and dad. I have to say being a grandad's the best; you have all the fun, then when you've had enough, you give 'em back." He'd laughed at the well-used cliche as if he'd thought of it.

"How about you Peg? I heard you was a solicitor. How's that going for you? Nice little gig in London, our Sarah tells me."

I remembered thinking to myself at the time that it would sound a bit pretentious to try and correct Richard. He didn't need to know I was actually a barrister, besides which he probably wouldn't know the difference.

"Yes, that's right. I've been working at a law firm in London for years, but I enjoy it. Mind you, I think the time is coming to consider retirement. We're all on the wrong side of twenty-nine, aren't we? There are so many young people *coming into the profession that I feel rather antiquated. How about you? Are you ready to hang up your calculator?"*

"I've got a couple more years to go 'cos I need to collect a full pension, but it can't come quick enough for me," he responded.

Looking at his glass, I asked, *"How's the beer? Does it come from your brewery?"*

"Yeah, it does, actually, but you know, they just don't make it the way they did in the old days back when it used to be Bass Ale. The brewery was taken over by some American company." He frowned as though such a turn of events signaled the imminent collapse of British society.

"So what about you, Peg? I heard you married Chris from up at the 'Big House,' but didn't he die a few years back?"

"Yes, I did marry him, and yes, sadly, he did die. It seems he got bitten by something when we were in the jungle in South America. And before you ask, no, I didn't marry again. Once was quite enough. Talking about people from the past, can I ask you about the kids we knew growing up? How about Catherine Stratton? She lived down the road in that large Tudor-style house opposite the wood, and what about Kevin? He lived just down from us. Do you ever see either of them?"

"Dunno much about Catherine, although I remember the house she lived in coming up for sale a few years back. They was asking a bloody fortune for it. As for Kevin, he still lives in that same house. You probably knew he'd married Colleen O'Brien from the council *estate. She were a couple of years*

younger than us but went to our school. Anyway, turns out they had to get married as Kevin got her up the duff, stupid bugger. Still, you can't blame him; she were a bit of a knockout."

At the time, I remember hearing him mutter to himself: *"She still is, considering."* Considering what, I now wondered.

"Yes, I remember Colleen. She used to come up to London to stay with her brother. After Harry moved to London, he, Chris, and I became really good friends, and the four of us would meet up. She and Kevin must have been married for quite a few years now, so it must have worked out okay for them."

I remember glancing at Richard and seeing him fidget on his stool and look quite uncomfortable, as if something I'd said had unnerved him. I wondered what. I wish Aunty Bridget were still alive; I bet she would have known all about it. When I went up to Lower Naughton for her funeral, so many intriguing questions surfaced, and there would have been no better source of information than my beloved aunt.

"Did you hear the council houses come up for sale?" asked Richard, who had calmed down again. *"They were offered to the families what lived in 'em. You remember when Maggie Thatcher were Prime Minister? Well, she comes up with the idea that everyone should own their own house, so she put loads of 'em up for sale, all up and down the country. Me mam bought our house, too good an opportunity to miss. They were pretty cheap, too, good interest rates, and Mam*

had a little bit of money put by. That's how come Kevin could afford to buy his house."

I'd burst out laughing. Now, thinking back, I realize it had been a bit rude, but I'd had a couple of glasses of wine by then.

"What's so bloody funny about that," Richard had said, looking a bit put out.

"Sorry, I was just thinking that I hoped the houses had been updated by the time they went up for sale. They badly needed an indoor toilet; otherwise, I couldn't imagine anyone buying them if you still had to go outside to the loo."

Richard realized why I was amused, and we both laughed heartily at the thought of suffering the indignities of those damnable outside toilets.

"Bloody hell, yes, they were updated. Full bathroom with a flushing toilet and hot and cold running water." He'd laughed. "They even have central heating."

"Oh my God, Richard, do you remember getting up in the middle of the night because you needed to pee so badly and having to go outside when it had been snowing? There I would be in my nighty and slippers, running downstairs in the dark, absolutely freezing cold, unlocking the back door, running through the snow, and trying to open the toilet door, which, of all the most ridiculous things, opened outwards. Imagine a six-year-old girl trying to pull it open against the weight of the snow because the wind had blown the snow up against the door."

"Know what you mean, Peg. I used to open the back door, take a look at the snow, and think, 'fuck that, I'm not going out in that lot,' and I'd pee from the doorway into the snow, hoping that it would keep snowing and cover it up." He'd said, still laughing.

"Anyways, the council moved us out in the late Sixties and did a number on the houses. They made the small bedroom into a bathroom; it meant the houses only had two bedrooms, but it were fine for me and me mam, as me sister had moved out by then. And thank God they added central heating. The outside lav was knocked down, the sewer were sealed up, concrete was poured over, and some cheap tile put on top. I suppose the idea was it would make a small patio, but to be honest, now and then, you can still get a whiff of something that I'm pretty sure comes up from the sewer. Me mam used to put pots of plants out there to try and disguise what used to be there, but you always knew, deep down, where that smell come from. Another glass of wine, Peg?" I nodded. *"Hey Jake, same again, mate."*

When the drinks arrived, I'd thanked Jake, the barman, and thanked Richard, *"Cheers."*

We chatted for a while longer until I'd realized how late it was, *"I should head upstairs, Rich. I'm worn out from the drive up here this morning."*

"Oh, come on, Peg, the night's still young. At least let me buy you a nightcap, a brandy, or somethin'. You'll sleep better."

Shuddering, I remember Richard suddenly leaning forward and putting his hand on my knee. I'd recoiled at his beer breath in my face. Instinctively, I'd pulled my head back.

"What on earth do you think you're doing?"

"Come on, Peg. You must be lonely, a widow for so many years. You know I've always fancied you from when you was a teenager and came to stay with our Sarah. I used to follow the two of you around. Of course, I couldn't say anything at the time, but I never forgot about you."

Could he possibly have imagined that his beer belly and boozy breath would be an inducement to seduction?

"For goodness sake, Richard, don't be ridiculous. What about Sarah? You've been happily married for years."

"Yeah, she's been a good wife and an amazing mam to the girls, but I've always had this thing for you, Peg. I give up hope there when I heard from me mam that you'd married another bloke from the village. That's when I started dating our Sarah."

I'd stood up to leave, *"Well, I can guarantee this: nothing is going to happen between you and me, Richard. To be honest, I have no room for men in my life."*

His not-so-subtle retort had sounded almost venomous, *"Well, that explains a lot!"*

Then that bombshell, she remembered.

"Thinking about it, I don't remember you ever having a boyfriend. In fact, I actually wondered if you did prefer girls.

Except there was that thing that happened between you and Sarah's dad."

What the hell! Where had that suddenly come from?

"I remember you staying with Sarah during the summer holidays when we was all in college. Had a thing for 'er dad, did you? Sarah's mum threw you out of the house, didn't she? You come running to me, wanting my help. I told you to bugger off. I saw you crying in Harry's car, and then you disappeared."

What exactly had he meant by that? I hadn't gone to anybody. I'd gone straight back home to my rooms in Oxford. Plus, at that time, I'd never been in Harry's car.

Richard continued, *"Sarah knew nothing about it 'cos years later, I asked her quite casual like, and she didn't know what I was on about — told me not to be so bloody stupid. How do you think she'd feel if she knew you'd been seducing her dad, eh Peg? Got you pregnant, did he? Had an abortion, did ya? Oh, I can't wait to tell our Sarah it was all true. Of course, if you play your cards right tonight, she'll never know. It'll just stay our little secret. So, I bet we can come to some kind of arrangement, don't you reckon? If you know what's good for you, maybe you'd better start being nice to me."*

"You're disgusting." I'd spat at him in anger.

I remember sliding unsteadily off my barstool, summoning all my fortitude, and storming off towards the stairs, desperately praying that he hadn't followed me. I remember walking up the stairs, gripping the banister.

Having had a little more to drink than usual, I felt a bit shaky, although it may not have just been the drink; it was probably more to do with Richard and what he was implying. How did he know all that? Okay, some of it may have been lucky guesswork, but the fact he knew about the abortion worried me. I'd staggered along the corridor feeling quite nauseous, which wasn't helped by the colour of the walls, a green that matched the colour of the sick room back in my high school. When I reached my room, I'd unlocked the door and, once inside, carefully re-locked it behind me. I remember putting a chair up against the door handle. After getting ready for bed, I lay back against the pillow when a thought had popped into my head; I could almost visualize how the chain of gossip had flowed through the village. Colleen knew what had happened, and I could imagine her telling her husband, Kevin, about the abortion. And I bet that over a few beers, Kevin had told Richard, and goodness only knows who else. I remember panicking and shouting, "Fuck, Fuck, Fuck!". Goodness knows what the people in the next room must have thought.

The next morning, as I was leaving the hotel for the funeral, I saw Richard leaning on the bridge. As soon as he saw me, he'd wandered over to me.

"About last night," he'd said. Hoping he was going to apologize, I'd smiled and responded, *"What about last night? Nothing happened. All forgotten."*

"Not exactly what I was thinking. You owe me, but I think we can come to some arrangement."

'Holy shit,' I remember thinking.

236

"You know, you're right, Richard. I do owe you a debt of gratitude for keeping my secret all these years. Obviously, we need to be careful about how we do this, as Sarah mustn't know. Give me your mobile number, and I'll text you with a place we can meet."

"See that you do." Smiling, he gave me his mobile number and casually walked away.

Troubled by the memories of that bizarre evening with Richard Slater and exhausted from the long day with Camille, I groaned, 'AAAAAGH!' and took a large gulp of wine.

I decided the next time I saw Camille, I would tell her about what had transpired with Richard to see what she'd make of it.

In some ways, the project to find the actual murderers had developed a life of its own. It was like an ever-widening treasure hunt. Who knew what further intriguing surprises would pop up out of the woodwork?

Part 3

Chapter 11

It was only a few days after Camille and I had our field trip to Lower Naughton that Sarah rang. Though it had been several weeks since the trial ended, I was surprised to hear from her quite so soon. It's rare to have any contact with a client after a trial is over unless they need your services again. But this was a completely different situation; we were friends, after all, or at least acquaintances. Sarah suggested meeting for lunch to thank me for the successful defence I'd mounted. Nicola had invited her mother to stay with her and her family in Brixton for a few days, and if I was available, we could meet up. The phone call was quite a coincidence as I had planned on inviting her to stay with me after an appropriate amount of time had elapsed. So I agreed without hesitation: "Of course, that would be lovely." We arranged to meet the following Wednesday.

Camille and I were still working on our evermore fascinating amateur detective project, so I needed to be careful what I said to Sarah, especially as Camille was still convinced of her guilt.

When the day rolled around, I spent a while choosing something appropriate to wear. It was forecast to be a hot day, so I decided on a summer frock in cream silk covered in pale blue flowers. I paired it with tan leather sandals with a wedge heel that would be comfortable to walk in — a hot London pavement could be seriously unforgiving. I pulled my hair up in my usual chignon and applied a little mascara, pink blush, and my signature Chanel Rouge lipstick. I looked at Rocco for approval, but he just turned his back and headed out of the room, unimpressed as always. I then headed out the front door and drove to the train station.

Knowing the train times like the back of my hand and still having an active train pass, I walked straight onto the platform, and five minutes later, the train arrived. I settled into a seat in the First-Class compartment; after all those years of traveling up and down to London, I knew better than to rely on luck to find a seat back in second class, and at my age, I had no intention of standing for forty-five minutes. At Victoria, I grabbed a taxi and had the driver take me to Locanda Locatelli, an Italian restaurant just off Portman Square. Sarah was already there, and we greeted each other with a warm hug.

"My dear friend, you look so much better than when I last saw you at the end of the trial," I said truthfully. Sarah had dyed her hair back to its original ash blonde; it had gone quite grey while she was in prison, and she'd had it cut in a flattering bob. Her makeup had been applied very subtly, so it appeared at first glance that she wasn't wearing any. On closer look, there was a hint of grey eye shadow and navy mascara highlighting her eyes, her lipstick was a pretty cerise, and she wore a gorgeous pale blue linen dress that, if I'm honest, would have looked better on me. Sarah, too, was wearing sandals but in pale grey suede.

Laughing, she said, "Oh, Peggy, I should jolly well hope so."

'Peggy,' seriously? She's still calling me 'Peggy'? as I feigned a smile.

We ordered drinks: gin and tonic for me and a glass of Pinot Grigio for Sarah, which she asked for with a glass of ice. Really! I tried hard not to grimace.

"How does it feel to be back home, my dear? And how is your dog — Malcolm, right? I bet he was pleased to see you."

"It's really strange. I was only at the house for a day to pick up some clothes, then I went to stay with Jennifer. She didn't want me staying in the house by myself. I was so grateful. I really wasn't ready to live in that house without Rich. She had kindly taken Malcolm while I was in prison, and it did me the world of good to see him. I took him for lots of walks in the Dales, near her house, and to be honest with you, I talked to him. I hope you can understand that. I'm sure you talk to your cat when nobody's around — or do you think I'm completely crazy?"

"Of course I don't think you're crazy, don't be silly. And yes, I do talk to Rocco — sometimes, he even answers me! So, how's that for sounding crazy? When did you come down to Nicola's?"

"I drove down yesterday. I know I will have to go back to my house at some point, but it won't be easy — too many memories of Rich. I wasn't even looking forward to going to stay with Nicky. I mean, my last memory of that house is of Rich laying there dying on her living room floor. Nicky told me the other day that she and Keith are looking to move for

240

the same reason. Anyway, I'm putting on a brave face and trying to enjoy it. Even seeing the boys has been difficult. Will and Josh are lovely, but I have so many memories of taking them to the park to play football with Rich."

The waiter returned with our drinks, and we ordered lunch. Sarah promptly put three ice cubes into her wine, three, seriously! I then toasted her freedom. Once the food arrived and we started eating, we reminisced about the old days in Lower Naughton. I tried to cheer Sarah up, as she was clearly suffering from losing her mother and husband, and I thought talking about 'the good old days' might help. I flagged down the waiter and asked him for two more glasses of Pinot Grigio.

I was curious about the German-Browns and Nawerton Manor, so asked Sarah what she knew.

"I assume Patrick moved into the family house after his parents passed away?"

"Yes, I heard Lady Celia was devastated when Chris died. I suppose none of us expects our children to die before we do. I heard that she became quite a recluse. After she and Lord Percy passed, Patrick moved back to run the estate, but he never had any real interest in village life. He and his wife Poppy have four children, but they go to a private school in Rugby and don't interact with anyone in the village." Sarah said disappointedly.

"What a shame. I assume they don't have the garden party anymore, then. It used to be quite a fun day out, and it brought the village together. I can still see Lady Celia pottering about in her wellies and deerstalker hat, the earpieces flapping around her cheeks. I never saw Lord Percy, probably beneath him to mix with the riff-raff. He was such a snob. My mum went every year. She loved it. She'd be all dressed up: full makeup, hair in a French pleat, and glued in place with a gallon of hair spray. A new summer dress that she'd made especially for the occasion. She'd try and drag my dad there, but he would rather have walked over hot coals than be seen up at the 'Big House.' He stayed home with his beer, watching football on the television. Being a union man, he maintained a simmering anger or resentment toward landlords and factory owners. I do remember seeing you at the fête with your mum, though. She was usually chatting with Lady Celia. As the M.P.'s wife, didn't she present some prize for the best something or other one year, or maybe it was your dad? I just remember standing with my mum, looking up at the däis, and your parents up there with Lady Celia."

"Yes, my dad used to hand out some of the prizes. I agree. It is a shame they don't hold it anymore. It was a lovely day out."

We continued chatting while we enjoyed our lunch, which I have to say was really good. The trial seemed to have put our friendship on a different level. At last, after so many years, I felt Sarah was treating me as her equal. All those ridiculous but nonetheless tangible class distinctions had fallen by the wayside. Of course, that could be because Sarah thought she owed me, but I like to think it was more than that.

"Sarah, now I've retired and have so much time on my hands, I wondered if you would like to come and stay with me down in Surrey for a few days if you're not too busy with school? It would give you another reason to escape from the family house."

Sarah looked at me with a smile of genuine gratitude.

"I would absolutely love to. What a treat. I haven't been anywhere since the trial, apart from seeing Nicola and Jennifer."

"Wonderful. Once you're back home and can look at your calendar, give me a ring, and we'll arrange a date."

I then signaled to the waiter to bring the bill. When he returned, I reached out, but Sarah knocked my hand away and shook her head.

"No, absolutely not. After all you've done for me, this is my treat," she insisted.

Once she'd paid, we stood up, gathered our bags, and walked outside.

"I should find a taxi and head off to the station. I have an appointment at the eye doctor in Reigate later this afternoon," I explained to Sarah.

"Yes, I need to leave, too. I'm meeting Nicky. I promised her we would check out a new exhibition at the Victoria and Albert. I've so enjoyed lunch, and I think I've relaxed for the first time since the trial. I promise I will give you a ring about coming for a visit," she said earnestly.

We quickly hugged as I spotted a taxi, and I left Sarah on the pavement, waving goodbye.

I didn't really have an appointment; I just needed an excuse to leave. I'd never been the most social of people, and although we'd had a nice lunch, I was ready to return to the quiet of my home. As my late husband, Chris, used to say: 'Leave on a high. Enough is enough, darling, isn't it?'

Rocco was at the door to welcome me home with a loud purr as he rubbed around my legs. Much as I liked to think that he was pleased to see me, I have to admit it was more than likely a not-so-subtle hint that he would like some food. So, after kicking off my sandals, dumping my bag on the chair in the hall, and putting the kettle on for tea, I opened a tin of pungent-smelling tuna cat food and scooped some into his bowl. Once I'd made my tea, I took it over to the window seat in the kitchen, opened the window, lit a cigarette, and opened the post. The first letter was from Amanda; she'd sent me a copy of Sarah's parent's marriage certificate.

Later that evening, I sat out on the back patio in the setting sun with a cigarette and a large glass of wine in hand. I decided to review the latest draft of my book. I put my feet up on the chair opposite and flicked through the pages of the manuscript. It was coming along nicely, and I smiled as I took a long drag on my cigarette and blew a plume of smoke into the warm evening air. The only thing left was to plot out the details of the final chapter, and the anticipation sent a chill of excitement running down my spine. Once the sun had set, I went inside and started planning for Sarah's visit. I jotted down a rough itinerary on a piece of paper in the kitchen as I finished the last of my wine.

Chapter 12

Three weeks later, I was in the kitchen, preparing what I hoped would be a nice, light evening meal. I'd made a caramelized onion tart, and to accompany it, I was planning on making a tomato, pea, and mint salad using homegrown tomatoes and fresh mint from the kitchen garden. I heard a car pull up on the gravel driveway and opened the front door as a taxi drove away. Sarah was standing there with her suitcase in her hand, smiling shyly.

"Come in, come in. Good journey?" I hugged her briefly as a welcome after she put down her suitcase in the hall.

"Yes, not bad. For once, British Rail trains were on time," she laughed.

"Good, good. How are you? It is so lovely to see you. I'm so pleased you decided to come and stay." I said truthfully. "I'll show you to your room," I started up the stairs. "Hopefully, you'll be comfortable. It has an en-suite if you want to freshen up. In the meantime, I'll go back downstairs and put the kettle on. I'm sure after that journey, you're ready for a cup of tea."

"Oh, Peggy," she looked around at the wood-paneled hallway. "It's lovely to see you too, and what a wonderful house. Hopefully, you'll give me the Cook's Tour a bit later. And yes, I am gasping for a cup of tea." She followed me upstairs, attempting, as best she could, not to bang the polished oak banister with her suitcase.

After a few minutes, Sarah found me in the kitchen making the tea.

"As it's such a nice afternoon, shall we have tea in the garden?" I asked, "I need to pick some tomatoes and mint to go into the salad for dinner." Sarah nodded with a quiet sigh of contentment that confirmed how relaxed she'd quickly become in my company.

As we walked outside, Sarah spotted Rocco lying in his favourite spot on the low wall at the edge of the patio, fast asleep in the sun, as befitted a cat of his ripe old age.

"Ah, so this is Rocco. What a beautiful cat. May I stroke him?"

"Of course, he likes people, and he loves having a fuss made of him."

She walked over and tickled him behind his ears, which always made him happy. Recognizing that a token show of activity might now be required, he stood up and stretched, arching his back. He lazily turned around, looked at Sarah, and then lay back down, licking his paw before washing behind his ears and settling down to continue his nap. The contented rumble of his purring was audible from where I was putting the tray down on the wrought-iron table in the shade of the crab-apple tree.

"Would you mind terribly if I have a cigarette? I know it offends many people, but I do enjoy one with my tea, and as we are outside, I hope you won't mind."

To my surprise, Sarah replied: "Of course not. I'm so glad you smoke because so do I, though I'm always wary of putting people's backs up when I do. My daughters are so angry with me for doing it, lecturing me on the dangers, which, of course, I know only too well, especially in light of my mother's lung cancer."

We sat quietly, drinking our tea and savouring our cigarettes, safe in the knowledge that we were kindred spirits in our addiction.

"Are you back home now in Lower Naughton?" I asked, breaking the silence.

"Yes, I moved back home nearly two weeks ago. It felt awkward at Nicky's house, plus I needed to take the plunge and go back to real life, such as it is. To be honest, it's not been particularly pleasant since I returned. I have basically been shunned by everyone: friends, parents of kids at the school, and even the Women's Institute. You would think I'd been found guilty. But I suppose they think there's no smoke without fire and assume there must be some reason I was accused in the first place. Besides, the police have no other suspects, so I assume I'm still Number One in their eyes."

I attempted to show some pity, but I was more concerned about watching Rocco, who was rolling dangerously close to the edge of the wall, oblivious to his imminent peril as he stretched in the evening sun.

"I am sorry, Sarah. I had no idea. Much as I love living in a village, there is something about village life and its small-minded parochial attitudes that is so alien to life in a large city. With such unpleasant reactions from everyone in the village, do you think you'll stay there? Have you thought about moving somewhere else? After all, your daughters don't live there anymore, and, like me, you're at an age where retirement is an obvious option, so I shouldn't think there is anything to keep you there."

Sarah seemed slightly taken aback at my indifference to her current situation, although she knew I could sometimes be unempathetic. "Yes, I have actually been thinking about it, but I don't know if I've the confidence to make such a significant change. I miss Rich terribly, and the thought of moving all by myself and starting again somewhere new is quite daunting. I accept it's something I should consider after what's happened, but as you know, I have lived in that village all my life. I have relationships with people who live there, or at least I used to. So many of the villagers came through my school, and I've watched them grow up. Some of the older folks knew my parents, and I know many women through the Women's Institute. But, there again, they all seem to be treating me differently now. I haven't been back to the school yet as I'm still on a leave of absence, so I don't know how the other teachers will react to me. I've heard the substitute Headteacher has settled in and is well-liked, which is a bit concerning. Will I even have a job anymore? I went to church last Sunday, and that was really difficult. Apart from not having my mum with me, which was quite upsetting, in the past, I would always chat with the other members of the congregation after the service. But now, they all seemed to magically find someone else to talk to, doing their best to avoid looking at me. Of course, the vicar was friendly. He asked me how I was and kindly offered his time if I needed someone to talk to. He's a lovely man, very genuine. He seems to understand that although I didn't do anything, and I was found innocent, there will always be this little bit of doubt hanging over me as far as the rest of the village is concerned."

Sarah's voice trembled a little as she fought back her tears and looked off into the distance while taking a long drag on her cigarette in an attempt to pull herself together.

"I suppose if I am going to move, I should also start looking to see what's out there job-wise unless I decide to take the retirement option. Updating my CV would be a good place to start. I have a lot of experience, and I used to have a good reputation as an educator until this happened, so hopefully, I can still obtain some good references. And surely, my current position as headmistress would work in my favour too."

I nodded, I hoped, encouragingly. "Have you thought about where you'd like to live?"

"Well, I do love Devon, and living near the sea is rather appealing. Rich and I spent so many happy times on holiday down there when we were first married." I understood the appeal of being by the sea but not in England, somewhere around the Mediterranean, where it was a bit warmer, maybe.

We sat for a while, sipping our tea and enjoying our cigarettes, silently contemplating the unfairness of the world on that perfect afternoon. Unlike Camille, I had never

250

doubted Sarah's innocence, but the accusation alone had effectively and unfairly changed the course of the poor woman's life. I stubbed out my cigarette in the blue glass ashtray on the table and thought it might improve Sarah's mood if we discussed the next day's plans.

"I wondered if tomorrow you'd fancy heading out to a local scenic spot for a gentle stroll, and maybe we could find somewhere for lunch. Nothing too energetic, just so you can see a little of the local area?"

"Oh yes, that sounds like a wonderful idea. I don't know this area at all. We usually went to Spain for our family holidays, and the odd weekends when we went away meant driving north to the Lake District. So it will be lovely to see somewhere new."

"Excellent, I'm sure you'll enjoy it, and it's meant to be a lovely day again tomorrow. Now, I have a few bits to finish off for dinner, so shall I give you a quick tour of the rest of the house, and then we can crack open a bottle of wine and have some supper?"

We stood up and put our cups and saucers on the tray, which I carried back indoors. After showing Sarah the rest of the house, I left her to unpack and went back outside to pick tomatoes for the salad. Sarah wandered out a bit later and found me cutting some mint, admiring the garden as she walked around.

"I love your garden. Do you do it all yourself? I found mine was quite overgrown when I was released from prison. It's daunting to think I no longer have Rich to do the big jobs

251

like mowing the grass and trimming hedges, and I have to do it all myself."

She wiped her eyes with her handkerchief.

"It's so true when people say you take your loved ones for granted when you see them all the time. I still expect to see him sitting in his favourite armchair. The house feels so big now. It was bad enough when the girls left to go to university, and we suffered from empty nest syndrome, but we thought at least we would have each other around for a few more years."

I took Sarah's arm in a gesture of comfort, and we went back inside so I could finish making the dinner. I fetched a bottle of pinot grigio from the fridge, having stocked up on a few bottles the day before, remembering Sarah ordering it at our last lunch together. I poured two large glasses, and we toasted to each other's health and to absent friends, and then I continued putting together the finishing touches for our meal.

I planned to have dinner al fresco at the small dining table in the corner of the patio, as it was such a gloriously warm evening. Something I believed must be savored in the unpredictability of dreary England. We carried out the tart and salad, the plates, glasses, cutlery, and, of course, the remainder of the bottle of wine, although laughing, we agreed one wouldn't be enough.

Since that first phone call when Nicola asked me to represent her mother, Sarah's dilemma had been the focus of all our conversations, but as we ate, the focus turned to me. We chatted easily as old friends do, and Sarah began asking me about my life and what I had in mind now that I'd retired.

"Well, I admit that I'm dabbling in writing. I have always wanted to write a book. There are so many stories from my days in court, so maybe a mystery based on one of those. I've been taking a writing course to help in formatting a novel. I don't have many friends as I'm basically quite shy away from court, but we have known each other for so many years that I feel very comfortable talking to you, Sarah. More so than anyone else I've known. Although I appear to have a lot of confidence and friends to chat with, there are some things I prefer to keep to myself. I think it has a lot to do with how I was treated as a child. As you may remember, my Mum and Dad didn't go to university. It wasn't that they were ignorant or stupid, it just wasn't expected back when they were young unless they were wealthy or planning on becoming a doctor or a lawyer. So, it was a bit of a shock for them when I did well in school and announced that I wanted to go to university. I received no encouragement from them — more of a 'just who do you think you are?' attitude. I suppose their concern was where the money was going to come from. I think they had expected me to go straight to work once I left school so I could contribute to the household finances, but I ignored them and went to uni anyway. I managed to obtain a student loan, and with a part-time job at Sainsbury's, I was able to support myself." I sipped my wine, feeling comfortable and relaxed:

"So there I was, at Oxford, working on a degree that Mum and Dad thought was a complete waste of time and money. Then I met Chris, and funnily enough, their opinions changed; they were thrilled to bits when I married him, especially Mum. They still weren't interested in what I was studying; they were just relieved I'd found someone who could look after me, and Mum was thrilled to bits, as you can imagine when she found out who it was." I laughed, and Sarah smiled. "They couldn't fathom that I would ever be earning enough money to take care of myself. It was beyond my mum's imagination to envision the life of a successful London barrister, but she could undoubtedly imagine me living in the Big House in Lower Naughton.

"In her mind, she could see herself visiting me when the garden parties and flower shows were being held and possibly even handing out the prizes. But I was determined to become a lawyer in my own right, not beholden to someone because of who or what they were. I didn't want to be seen as just some woman who had married well and been handed a job because of who I knew, not what I knew. God forbid it had anything to do with the sheer hard work I'd put in. Did I have a chip on my shoulder? Damn right, I did!"

Sarah looked slightly uncomfortable at my forthright comments, and I noticed her take a large sip of her wine, but I was on a roll and continued.

"Anyway, my life seemed to be going well. I graduated with honours, had my dream job, and was on my way to becoming a successful lawyer. I was happily married, albeit there was a slight problem in my lack of desire for children, but then my life turned upside down; I lost Chris, followed by dear Harry. I was devastated twice over. Until then, I'd felt passion, love, and excitement about life, but it had all been snatched away from me. That was when I decided never to allow myself to become close to anyone again. Losing my husband was one of the hardest things I've ever faced. But losing Harry was unimaginable. He'd been such a wonderful friend. I felt so close to him, and he was so supportive when Chris died. We had such fun times together. It's funny, isn't it, how people make certain assumptions about you based on your public persona without knowing who you really are. I'd stand up in court, defending all sorts, from the dregs of society to the most innocuous souls, appearing to be such a self-confident and sympathetic individual, so surely, that's how I must really be. If only they knew!"

I was getting a bit riled up now, maybe from the pinot grigio or the excitement of having someone I felt able to unburden myself to. I took a couple of sips of my wine and some deep breaths. I really needed to calm down.

"Oh my God, Peggy, I had no idea you felt like that," commented Sarah. "You're right about your public persona. You do appear to have so much self-confidence. You come across as someone who is very self-assured. You leave no one in any doubt that you are highly qualified. You have such an incredible reputation."

I smiled. I was never one to shy away from a compliment, and I liked that Sarah had taken the bait. I picked up the empty bottle of wine, went into the kitchen for another bottle, and refilled our glasses. I raised my glass:

"Now that I have that off my chest, a toast — cheers, here's to a new beginning for the two of us."

"Cheers, Peggy. To good friends."

We clinked our glasses, and we both took a hearty swig. In my wine haze, I felt I needed to explain something to Sarah:

"Sarah, I feel I owe you an apology for something I brought up when I questioned Colleen Ryan at the trial. You obviously had no idea about Richard and Colleen's affair and the subsequent baby, and I'm so sorry you had to find out like that. I needed to prove you were innocent or at least that there was an element of doubt about your guilt. I needed the jury to see your reaction when it was announced that Richard was Tiffany's father. The only way I could see to do that was to find someone who could have had a reason to be angry enough to have killed him. I had my suspicions about Tiffany's biological father when I saw her photograph in the papers after the accident. Aunty Bridget sent me a copy of the local newspaper. The little girl's jet-black hair was the same as Richard's, and there was something about her eyes. It was blindingly obvious that Colleen had been seeing somebody else as she and Kevin were both redheads, so I was pretty much convinced that she had given birth to Richard's baby.

"Once the trial started and I looked for clues to prove someone else may have murdered Richard, I spoke to Kevin. He told me he had been suspicious about the little girl not looking like the rest of the family right from when she was born and admitted to me that he had previously taken a DNA paternity test. Although the result confirmed Kevin's suspicions were correct, that he was not Tiffany's father, he had no proof she was Richard's. So Kevin chose to keep the result of the test to himself and to bring Tiffany up as his own. What I didn't know was the prosecution also had a DNA paternity test done using some of the evidence that had been collected, and that was how Mr. Gryfidd-Jones was able to reveal the news that Kevin was not Tiffany's father.

"In the meantime, I decided to see if my suspicions were correct that Richard was Tiffany's father. Using some DNA that had been stored after Tiffany's accident and some DNA from the evidence collected from Richard's murder, I sent them off for testing. And, as we now know, Richard was Tiffany's father, although from what Colleen stated in the trial, Richard never knew or most probably didn't care anyway. But poor Colleen, she was so frightened that Kevin would leave her. Fortunately, he had already guessed who the father was and was willing to adopt little Tiffany as his own. I have to say that Kevin is one of the nicest and kindest men. And so understanding. So I felt terrible implying that he'd killed Richard. I discussed my plan to infer that he could be the murderer as I was sure he wouldn't have killed Richard and convinced him that he would never be accused of the murder.

"For a start, I doubt he would have known which poison to use, even though I was able to imply that he knew about poisons from his job on the farm. I just needed to put the idea in the jury's minds there was a possibility that Kevin might kill his friend if he thought he had been messing around with his wife and had fathered a baby with her. All I had to do was inject some degree of doubt that maybe you weren't the only person who wanted Richard dead — that's all I needed. Kevin was a true friend to you, Sarah, allowing me to cast doubt on his character in our effort to secure your acquittal. Colleen was understandably upset with me, but once Kevin explained to her that he had always known Tiffany wasn't his and that he had forgiven her, she was fine about it. Truth be told, she admitted to me later that it was a relief to have it all out in the open, as she'd hated keeping it a secret from him. I cannot believe you never suspected this."

Sarah had remained quiet throughout all this, but eventually, she smiled. "No, I may have been naïve, but I had absolutely no idea about Colleen. Of course I understand why you did what you did in court, and it was a shock to me and the girls knowing Rich had fathered little Tiffany. To be honest, I did suspect he played around, but I had no idea who the woman was. Poor Kevin. And that poor little girl, I've always wondered who ran her over and if it was deliberate. God, I hope not. It doesn't bear thinking about, does it."

The evening was turning cool, so, on that somber note, I suggested we head inside. Sarah agreed, and we cleared away the detritus from dinner. Walking into the sitting room, I went over to the drinks cabinet.

"Would you like another glass of wine or something stronger? We don't have to drive anywhere, so we can enjoy whatever we fancy. I'm going to have a whiskey. I have a very smooth, eighteen-year-old Glenfiddich. I also have a port, brandy, or sherry. What do you fancy?"

Sarah finally decided on a Courvoisier. I poured the drinks, and we settled in for the rest of the evening. I sat in my regular armchair and put my feet on the ottoman. Sarah sat opposite on the sofa with Rocco, curled up contentedly at the other end. He opened one eye, looked up at his new-found friend, and, deciding she wouldn't disturb him, went back to sleep.

I started rambling again, seemingly unable to control the inane chatter that flowed without the filter of sobriety. I felt comfortable with Sarah as I was no longer trying to impress her the way I had when we were younger. It felt strange that the research Camille and I had done meant I probably knew more about Sarah's family background than she did. They certainly weren't what they claimed to be: fine, upstanding members of the community. Not at all: her mother was from a family of criminals, and her father was a rapist. My parents may have been dirt poor, but as far as I know, they were good, honest people.

We spent the rest of the evening laughing and reliving the past. Like the time we'd gone up to London as teenagers to see Carnaby Street, and I'd found the cutest mini-skirt. Unfortunately, I had no money back then, so I could never have afforded to buy it, and so, in a fit of bravado, foolishness, desperation, whatever, I stole it. Luckily, I wasn't caught. Sarah, whose parents were relatively wealthy, could have bought it and couldn't understand why I would risk being caught and going to jail for stealing a skirt. She had no idea what it was like for me. My mum made my clothes or bought them at the annual jumble sale. Whereas Sarah's mum bought all her pretty dresses and school clothes. She had no idea what it was like for me, but even so, what on earth was I thinking? For years afterward, I would wake in the middle of the night in a cold sweat. I still have the skirt; it's hanging at the back of my wardrobe to remind me how stupid I'd been, and besides, it is adorable: brown suede with pink and purple appliqued flowers.

We sat quietly, sipping our drinks before I spoke again, "I think we've had enough to drink that I feel comfortable telling you a couple of secrets. Actually, it's more of a mea culpa." Sarah looked surprised but nodded, kicked off her shoes, pulled her feet up under her on the sofa, and settled in expectantly to listen.

"Ok, so if you're sitting comfortably, then I'll begin. Secret number one: Do you remember when we were young, and your mother accused me of stealing something from your house? Well, I hate to admit it, but your mum was right. Remember when we were six or seven, and I still lived in Lower Naughton? Occasionally, I'd come over to your house to play. One of those times, I did steal something."

Sarah looked shocked, but I ignored her and continued:

"I used to think you were so lucky because you had lots of toys. It's silly now when I think about it, but back then, I was jealous of you, pure and simple. Do you remember that beautiful doll's house you had? Each room had the most delicate furniture that, of course, you wouldn't let me touch. Your precious doll's house had a tiny, beautiful, hand-made wooden rocking chair in one of the bedrooms, and I remember you being so upset because it went missing. Your mum accused me of taking it, and of course, I used my

260

time-honoured trick and burst into tears and swore it wasn't me. I was pretty good at putting on the waterworks when I needed to, as you've no doubt noticed. Anyway, I told her I would never steal anything from you — you were my best friend in the whole world.

"Well, actually, I had taken it, and she knew it. She threatened to ring the police if you remember, then she telephoned my dad and told him to come and fetch me. When he arrived, your mum said something had gone missing, and although she couldn't prove it was me, she thought it would be better if I left, and she never wanted me in her house again. When we were outside, I lied to my dad and said I hadn't taken anything and that your mother was a mean old woman, but I'm pretty sure he didn't believe me. Of course, I was crying buckets and saying it wasn't fair that I was always blamed, but you know what, he never told me off because there was just a slight element of doubt. And, as you now know from your experience in court, an element of doubt can work every time. As for lying, I learned to lie when I was quite little — it worked every time."

Sarah shook her head and took another sip of her drink, looking a little stunned at my admission of guilt in the mysterious affair of the missing rocking chair. But she said nothing, and her silence encouraged me to keep going:

"Secret number two: I stole something else. Do you recall I came to stay when we were teenagers, and your mum lost a piece of jewellery? At some point during that visit, I was upstairs alone, and I couldn't resist looking around your parent's bedroom. Under the window, there used to be a

261

dressing table with your mum's makeup and jewelry box. I opened the jewelry box and had a look inside. There, among the necklaces and rings, I found a pair of the most exquisite sapphire earrings. I had no idea they were real sapphires; they just looked gorgeous. They were yellow gold with a sapphire teardrop. It was too tempting. I just wanted to take something. Your mother always looked down on my family, probably because we'd lived in a council house. I even overheard her calling me 'common' to your father. She always made it quite plain she didn't like me and didn't trust me. So call it revenge. An earring was something small I could take, and naively, I assumed your mother wouldn't notice. I thought I was being clever because if I took both of them, it would be pretty obvious somebody had stolen them. So I just took one earring, hoping your mother would assume she had misplaced it. Did your mum ever suspect it had been stolen, or did she think she'd lost it?"

"Peggy, whatever were you thinking? Yes, she did think it had been stolen, and she was pretty sure it was you, but she couldn't prove it. You're right. She never trusted you. Having said that, I don't know why you thought my mum didn't like you. For goodness' sake, Mum never liked *any* of my friends, well, except perhaps Catherine, but everyone liked *her*."

Sarah took another sip, actually more of a nervous gulp of her brandy.

"I still have your little rocking chair. It used to sit on my desk in chambers. I brought it home when I retired. It's in the den on one of the shelves. Of course, you can have it back, and I still have the earring. I can't give it back to your mother, but

I will give it to you. Do you still have the other one? I'm sorry to have unburdened myself to you like this, but it's bothered me all these years. I know it was stupid to steal those things, but I was just a kid and so envious of you. You and your family had everything, and we had nothing. At least, that's how it looked to me. I always felt I wasn't good enough, as I was repeatedly told by my mother, so I just acted the way people expected me to."

Sarah looked across at me, then, taking a deep breath, put her feet on the carpet and sat up straight. She did not look happy.

"Frankly, Peggy, I have to say, I'm in shock. I can't believe you stole those things from my mother and me, especially that earring. That pair was particularly meaningful to Mum. It was a gift from my dad on their tenth wedding anniversary. I don't think she ever admitted she'd 'lost' one of them; she always made an excuse not to wear them, saying they didn't match her outfit, but she told me how angry she was about it. As for the toy rocking chair, I don't even remember it, but I'm sure at the time I was upset. You really didn't like my mother, did you? What about Richard? Did you like him?"

"What a strange question, Sarah. No, I admit I didn't like your mother, but I always liked Richard, well, until I found out about Colleen and the baby. But I still didn't dislike him per se." I stated matter-of-factly.

"I'm sorry, but I'm finding it hard to believe you could be quite so jealous of me. Yes, I was lucky in many ways, but nobody else, as far as I know, resented me the way you did.

Back to Richard? Were you jealous of me because I had him?"

"Well, I liked him, but not like that. So, no, I wasn't jealous. What a strange question." I leaned back in my chair and chuckled to myself. I could tell Sarah was struggling to process this new information, but she finally appeared to reconcile her thoughts and smiled.

"This is ridiculous. Mum and Richard are dead, and I owe you a lot more than the price of a doll's rocking chair and an earring after your brilliant performance in court. But, as you still have the earring, I *would* love to have it back. You're right, I do have the other one. I inherited all my mum's jewellery when she died."

I decided that was more than enough for one night. It was nearly eleven o'clock. I told Sarah I would fetch the earring and suggested we go to bed. I popped into the den and retrieved the toy rocking chair and then went upstairs and found the earring in my jewellery box and gave them back to Sarah. At first, she said I could keep the rocking chair, but I insisted she give it to her granddaughter, Emily. We wished each other a good night and went into our rooms. Later, sitting up in bed, I thought about what Sarah had asked about Richard. She knew I couldn't stand her mother, but asking if I was jealous of her marrying Richard was very odd. I wonder what she meant by that.

I also wondered what Camille would think of my plans to go off into the wilds of Surrey with a woman she was convinced was a murderer. I smiled to myself as Rocco curled up at the foot of the bed, and we drifted off to sleep.

Chapter 13

Rocco woke me at seven when he jumped on the bed and started tapping my arm in his inimitable style. He was far more effective than any alarm clock I'd ever owned. I tickled the top of his head and around his chin before he leaped down as I flung off the comforter. I walked across the room to the window and pulled back the heavy, jacquard curtains. The sun was shining. It was going to be a beautiful day. I pulled on my dressing gown and slippers and sauntered downstairs to put the kettle on for tea. I fed Rocco while I waited for the kettle to boil. He'd followed me downstairs and had been rubbing around my legs as a hint that he was hungry. I heard Sarah come downstairs and into the kitchen just as I was reaching for the mugs.

"Good morning. Did you sleep well? I assume you'd like tea?" I asked her, holding up the mugs.

"Yes, I did, thank you, and yes, please, I'd love a cup of tea. That bed is so comfortable I had to force myself to get up," Sarah replied as she rubbed the sleep from the corner of her eye.

"I have cereals, croissants, and a berry compote with Greek yoghurt for breakfast. Once we're dressed, I'll set it up in the breakfast nook. The newspaper should be here soon. It looks like it will be a nice day for our walk." I said as I poured the steaming water from the kettle into the two mugs.

"A croissant would be lovely. Do you mind if I step outside with my tea? I'm dying for a cigarette," Sarah asked, without any sign of discomfort about what had transpired the previous evening.

"Absolutely, go ahead. I'll join you. I usually have one with my first cup of tea, too. Terrible habit isn't it? But it's so difficult to give up when you've smoked as long as I have. I think I was fourteen when I had my first one. It was menthol and made me dizzy, but I was determined to keep up with everyone else. It seemed everyone smoked back then, didn't they? The biggest mistake I ever made. How about you? When did you start?"

"I didn't start until I began dating Rich. He was a smoker, and I think I wanted to impress him, so I took it up, too. The ridiculous things we do to impress other people," she said quietly. "I'm sure back then, we didn't know about it causing cancer, and besides, as you said, everyone smoked. I do think now I might try to give it up. The girls have their little ones, and they forbid me from smoking when I'm around them. Neither of them has ever been a smoker, which makes me feel desperately uncomfortable when I light up. Rich didn't care what they thought. He just expected them to put up with it. He used to say, 'It is what it is, and they're making a fuss about nothing.'"

There was a slight early morning chill in the air as we sat on the patio, enjoying our cigarettes and tea. Our conversation was friendly and unsubstantial, like that of the closest of friends. After finishing our tea and cigarettes, we headed back upstairs to pull on some clothes ready for our day out. I decided jeans and a short-sleeved shirt with walking shoes

266

seemed the sensible way to go. I also put on a thin blue nylon rain jacket with a hood and pulled my hair up into a bun. After putting on some mascara and a coral lipstick, I picked up my bag and walked back downstairs, humming lightly.

Sarah came down as I was putting the croissants into a basket and making a pot of coffee. She was also wearing trousers with a pretty short-sleeved sweater, and she had a jacket with her, which I assumed she had brought, thinking it could be cool in the park despite the sunny weather. The newspaper dropped through the letterbox, and I fetched it, passing it to Sarah to read the headlines while I put bowls, plates, and cutlery on the breakfast table. Sarah sat down and took a croissant from the basket as she read out some of the news.

Once breakfast was over, I picked up my phone and found a map to show her where we were going. I thought Sarah might be interested to see where it was. I grabbed two small Thermos flasks from the back of the cupboard, one blue and one brown, then made another pot of coffee for our elevenses. Finally, I found a packet of Walker's shortbread and put everything neatly into my backpack. I noticed Sarah watching me quizzically.

"Elevenses," I explained, "we may be glad of this when we're wandering over the Downs,"

"I thought there was a café in the car park?" Sarah asked.

"Yes, there is, but who knows where we'll be when we fancy a break. Besides, I thought we'd end up at the cafe for lunch. A thermos each of coffee and a biscuit will keep us going until then." Sarah raised her eyebrows and nodded in agreement as she stood up and cleared the table.

After we'd loaded the dishwasher, I took an anorak from the stand in the hall and followed Sarah out of the front door, locking it behind me. We then piled into the car and set off toward Reigate. I'd been to Gatton Park several times, so I knew the route, and we chatted about the park as I drove around the country lanes.

"The park is a lovely mixture of woodlands and open parkland designed by Capability Brown, and capable he certainly was. I hope you are as impressed with it as I am." I proclaimed.

Sarah responded, "I'm sure I will be. From your description, it sounds like the perfect place to wander around and lose yourself in the scenery. It will be so relaxing. I'm really looking forward to seeing it."

There were at least half a dozen other cars in the car park, but nobody seemed to be about. They must have arrived early — probably joggers out for an early morning run before work. As it was still a bit nippy, I put on the anorak, slung the backpack on, and we set off at a nice, steady pace, following a well-worn path through the open fields. Strolling down one of the pathways, we stopped briefly to admire the sweeping views over the hills in the distance, and Sarah took some photos on her phone. My plan was to head toward the wooded area because, at this time of the year, the forest floor would be covered with a carpet of bluebells.

As we walked toward the deserted woods, I felt compelled to spill yet another secret:

"I never told you this, Sarah, but a couple of years ago, I needed to visit Lower Naughton. I didn't tell anyone I was going, not even Aunty Bridget. It wasn't intended to be a fun visit — I was there on a mission. I had barely seen anyone from the village in over thirty years, so I was reasonably sure I wouldn't be recognized. I booked a rental car for the drive and requested a satnav for the journey. Although at home, I'd looked at a map to familiarize myself with the route. All I had to do was drive through London, which I figured would be the worst part, merge onto the M1 and stay on it until I reached Derby, then cut across to Burton and down to Lower Naughton."

I looked over at Sarah, who was busy taking photos of the scenery on her mobile. She wasn't really listening to my seemingly uninteresting tale. Despite her lack of interest, I continued as I knew she would soon appreciate my story as it was far more compelling than the view, as spectacular as it was.

"The day before the trip, I took my car in for a service and ordered an Uber to take me back home. The following morning, I was up early and had another Uber take me to Gatwick Airport. But instead of going into the airport, I took the shuttle to the Hertz rental office. The girl at the counter was texting someone and barely registered I was there as I explained that I'd ordered a specific car. I'd requested an automatic. I'd learned to drive with a regular stick shift, but these days, there is so much traffic on the roads the last thing I need to do is think about changing gear, especially on hills. Oh, and my other request was that it needed to be a Prius. A red Prius. I've always liked red."

That grabbed Sarah's attention. With a quick intake of breath, she whipped her head around to look at me. "A red Prius? When did you say you went back to Lower Naughton?"

With this latest revelation, Sarah was now looking at me with, I noticed, concern in her eyes.

"Hmm, oh, a little while ago. I admit I thought it was quite a coincidence when I found out you had the same car. But there again, a Prius does make sense these days. We really should all be driving more fuel-efficient cars. We must consider the future generations, don't you think?" Sarah stood frozen in place.

I looked at my watch. It was a quarter to twelve.

"My goodness, the time has flown; we should have had our elevenses half an hour ago. Let's keep following the path a bit further into the woods." I pointed to a densely wooded area at the bottom of the hill. "I'm hoping the bluebells will be out at this time of the year. And there are a few benches just inside where we can sit down."

I put my hand on Sarah's shoulder and guided her down the hill. As I had predicted, there were thousands of bluebells, their violet colour carpeting the ground under the trees as far as the eye could see. Sarah looked impressed, but I sensed a deep unease was building in her.

"Breathtaking," she gasped.

"There is a legend that says, if you hear a bluebell ring, you will be visited by a bad fairy and will die not long afterward?" I said with a chuckle.

"Good Lord, I hope not," Sarah attempted to laugh.

We walked a bit further. My hand pressed into Sarah's back, gently pushing her along. Finding a bench, I gestured for us to sit down, opened the backpack, and gave Sarah the blue flask, keeping the brown flask for myself. I passed Sarah a shortbread, pulled out one for myself, and sipped my coffee. Sarah looked apprehensively down at her thermos and back at me. I smiled and nodded, encouraging her to drink.

She had a sip and asked, "So, back to this secret trip. What happened once you arrived in Lower Naughton?"

"Oh, I sorted out my little problem. I just needed to see an old acquaintance about something that happened years ago that had affected my dear Harry. As soon as I ran my errand, I headed back to the M1 and on to Gatwick, dropped off the hire car, and had an Uber take me to the garage where my car had been serviced, then drove home. Mission accomplished.

Sarah didn't say anything. I looked over at her. "Are you feeling alright? You've gone very quiet."

"I do feel a bit woozy, but I'll be fine. You said it was a secret trip to Lower Naughton. Is this another of your admissions about something else you did?" I could see she was attempting to put on a brave face but was swaying a little

271

on the seat. Sweat was beading on her forehead despite the cool, dappled shade from the trees.

"You're probably a bit dehydrated. Have another drink of your coffee, and then we'll walk a bit further and see if we can find a shadier spot."

Sarah sipped her coffee and then handed me her thermos, which I promptly packed away along with my thermos and the shortbread.

"Let me take your arm and help you up," I offered with an insincere kindness as Sarah swayed slightly. We walked slowly across the path and further into the woods. After a few minutes, Sarah started to sag; her legs buckled from under her, and she collapsed to the ground among the bluebells, her twisted body incongruous with the beauty of the flowers. Fortunately, we were close to a large tree, and with a bit of maneuvering, I was able to pull her over and wedge her up against it. I then sat down nearby, pulled the blue thermos back out of my backpack, and tossed it at Sarah, who was unable to catch it. It hit her in the stomach with a dull thud before rolling onto the ground. I found a perverse satisfaction in my old friend's weakness, and I continued with my story:

"Now, where was I? Oh yes, I had dropped off the hire car and just arrived back home. I omitted to tell you why I went to Lower Naughton, although I have a feeling you might have guessed by now. I'm convinced my decision to kill your mother would be considered a justifiable homicide. I'd despised that woman since I was a child. Accusing me of stealing and threatening to ring the police just because

272

some piece of doll's furniture was missing — I was a small child, for God's sake. But that wasn't the only reason I wanted to kill her. Do you remember talking about your mother's past and who her friends were? Well, after some rigorous research, I can tell you exactly who she was and the kind of people she knew. Let me take you back in time.

"I don't know if you ever knew this, but when he was in his early twenties, my dear friend Harry O'Brien was severely beaten by a couple of thugs who suddenly turned up in the village. Harry told Chris and me all about it when we had dinner with him just after he'd moved up to London. Apparently, he was coming out of the Post Office when these brutes set on him and attacked him. They beat him so severely that he was in hospital for a week. We asked him if he recognized them, but he said he had no idea who they were, that he'd never seen them before that day. The police interviewed Mrs. Layton, you remember her, she used to run the Post Office, anyway, she said she'd never seen them before either. And yet, these lads knew exactly who Harry was — they even called him by his name, well that and a lot of other things; fag, pansy, you know, the usual unpleasant stuff. But the worst thing was they told him they knew he was a paedophile and was known for molesting little boys. Harry was stunned. He couldn't believe anyone would think that of him."

Sara started to moan, and tears rolled down her face. She looked at me with a mix of hatred and fear, but I remained entirely unmoved. I picked a bluebell and began to pluck the petals from its stamen, then carried on with my story.

"I expect you'd like to know *how* I murdered your mother. When I went to pick up the rental car, it was exactly what I had ordered: a red Prius, just like yours. As you probably know from experience, when you request a rental car, it's unusual to be given exactly what you ask for. The times I've ordered an automatic only to find it's a stick shift, and I end up arguing with the manager until they give me what I wanted. I bet you're wondering why I chose a car that was identical to yours. Well, I could hardly have driven my own car to your mother's house because if someone had seen it and taken down the number plate, it would have been traced back to me. So I thought, what if I made it look as though you had visited your mother that morning? It would have been simple for you to deny it, and I assumed you'd have an alibi. No one could possibly suspect you of killing your own mother. Boy, was I wrong. You ended up being the only suspect. You probably don't believe me, but I honestly didn't intend for you to be accused of your mother's murder, so that's why I took your case. I actually felt a little guilty — but I was soon over it.

"I rang your mother the week before I planned on going to Lower Naughton and arranged to visit her. I explained who I was and that I wanted to surprise you for your birthday. Fortunately, I'd kept a list of all the kids from school with their birthdays, phone numbers, and addresses. I had a feeling it might come in handy one day. In any case, we agreed that I would pop in for five minutes so that I could drop off a present. I told her I was staying with my aunt, but I asked her not to tell anyone, especially not you. It was to be our little secret.

274

"Fortunately, it was a cold day, so I was able to wear a jacket with a hood that I kept pulled over my head as I drove up to her house. I parked on the driveway as I needed anyone passing by to assume it was you. Your mum let me in, and I put the parcel containing an empty box, ostensibly your birthday gift, onto the hall table. She invited me into the sitting room, my first time in there, by the way, and we had a nice little chat. She asked me about my job and said how proud she was of me and that she always knew I would make something of myself — lying bitch. She was actually quite friendly, asked if I would like a coffee, and apologized that she didn't have any milk, but she was waiting for you to go to the village shop to pick some up. She was pretty pissed at you for taking so long. I thanked her and told her I'd already had coffee.

"She asked about my work, seeming genuinely interested. When she asked if I ever had any important clients, anyone she would have heard of, I regaled her with the details of a couple of my juicier cases. One involved a Member of Parliament and a prostitute, which she remembered reading about in the newspapers. I embellished the story a bit by adding that a minor member of the Royal family had also been implicated. She wanted to know which one, but I told her I was sworn to secrecy. She actually seemed to enjoy hearing my stories. I'm guessing that, at the next meeting of the Women's Institute, she would have given a talk on how she knew a famous London barrister whose client was protecting a member of the royal family. It was a shame she wouldn't have the opportunity to give her talk — maybe I could have attended the meeting as the honoured guest. What do you think? I do hope you're paying attention, dear.

"I also told your mother about another fascinating case involving an East End gang, specifically, one particularly unpleasant character whose job it was to carry out the hits. She asked what he'd done and how many people he'd killed, so I described in pretty gruesome detail how he'd carried out two or three spectacularly appalling crimes. I added that he'd killed a little girl seemingly intentionally by running her over and implied that she might actually have known the man. The little girl was Tiffany Ryan, of course. Your mum looked at me and wanted to know what I was suggesting. I told her he'd been seen in the village that day. She seemed confused by what that had to do with her until I told her I'd found out the murderous thug was her cousin. I asked her if she was impressed with all my research on her family. To my surprise, she admitted he was her cousin, but she was quite upset at what I said and vehemently denied that he'd run her over on purpose — she swore it was an accident. 'The little girl ran in front of the car. It wasn't her cousin's fault.' I told her that witnesses had seen an accomplice on the opposite side of the road calling for the little girl to come over, shouting that he had something to show her. As she ran across the road, a car drove over the bridge and smashed into her. The accomplice jumped into the car, and they sped off. Surely, your mother's cousin would have stayed with the little girl if it had been an accident. Your mother turned deathly white as I detailed the sequence of events — I could tell she was starting to panic. She didn't know that all this was supposition on my part, but her reaction confirmed that my intuition had been correct about the events on that day."

I glanced down at Sarah to see the fear in her eyes that was almost palpable. Her mouth had fallen open as she attempted to speak, but her efforts were unintelligible. I smiled at her, patted her shoulder, and continued with my story:

"By the way, Sarah dear, you told me your mother had no other relatives, so were you lying to me, or did you really not know? I'm sorry if I seem to be rambling, but you're not adding much to this conversation, are you? No matter. Your mother callously planned the accident that killed little Tiffany Ryan — she actually arranged the cold-blooded murder of an innocent child. And how do I know all this? Well, it turns out that although the car had been bought and sold several times after the accident, the original owner was your mother's cousin. It was a brand new black BMW SUV that he'd purchased just two weeks before the accident and sold two days after. I think we can assume your mum's cousin ran over little Tiffany under instruction from your psychopathic mother.

"I asked your mum why she had a three-year-old child killed. To my amazement, she answered quite casually and with her typical coldness that she had to protect the family's good name. I asked her what on earth she was talking about, and she calmly said, 'Wasn't it obvious? The child was the spitting image of her father, and her father was not the man who lived with that slutty charwoman.'

"I told her I didn't know what Tiffany looked like. With an unpleasant sneer, she told me the whole Ryan clan were typical Irish redheads, while Tiffany had jet-black hair like her dad — her philandering son-in-law, Richard. So Sarah,

277

while you were in your pathetic naivety, your mother had guessed all about Richard's sordid seduction of Colleen and decided to take matters into her own hands. She couldn't have the village whispering that your husband was playing around with Colleen. What would they think? So, in her deranged mind, the simplest thing to do was to have her cousin take care of the situation.

"In my humble opinion, your despicable mother deserved to die. To be more concerned with her family's reputation than a little girl's life — what sort of woman would do that to a child?"

Sarah had gone quiet. She no longer had the strength to move or speak. I paid her no attention, relishing the odyssey I was recounting.

"I told your mother I needed to use her toilet and went upstairs and into the bathroom. Locking the door, I put on a pair of rubber gloves with gardening gloves over the top of them, a thin, plastic coverall over my clothes, and finally, pulled paper booties over my shoes. Entering your mother's bedroom, I deliberately started banging about. I knocked over a lamp, hoping she would come upstairs to see what the noise was, which, of course, she did. She walked into the bedroom, took one look at me, and wanted to know what the hell I was doing and why I was dressed like that. 'You know you can't prove I had that child killed; otherwise, you'd have gone to the police.' she sneered.

"I agreed with her. I couldn't prove any of it in a court of law, so I had to take care of it myself, just like she had with poor little Tiffany. She looked at me maliciously and

278

threatened to ring the police. When she reached for the phone, I knocked it out of her hand. I asked her if she honestly thought the police would believe her story that I was going to kill her when all I'd done was drop off a birthday present for my friend. They would see her as some poor, confused old lady.

"I admitted to your mother that Tiffany wasn't the only reason I was there. I wanted to know why she hated my dear friend Harry. She looked bewildered. I reminded her that although it was many years ago, he had been severely beaten for what seemed like no reason other than he was gay. I explained to your mum that after Harry was attacked and Mrs. Layton was looking after him, one of her customers in the Post Office had witnessed what had happened and remembered hearing cockney accents and seeing a couple of men in black running to a car parked down by the brook. The Cockney accent was a bit of a giveaway. The other giveaway was when Harry heard one of the men call the other 'Paul.' I asked her if Paul was the name of the creep who'd taken you out and tried to rape you? Your mother had arranged for Harry to be attacked by some friends of hers from her seedy past. Your dad was right; your mum heralded from a bunch of criminals and low-lifes from the East End. Anyway, I told her that I couldn't reconcile in my head why she would hate Harry that much when she didn't know him.

"Then I told her that after countless hours of research, I found out she had a younger brother, Wilfred. You probably didn't know about that, did you? Anyway, your mother had been playing with little Wilfred on the street outside their house when a man grabbed the boy and ran off with him. The police questioned your mum and some of the other kids they were playing with. They described the kidnapper as having red hair, an accent like the priest at the local Catholic church, an Irish man, and he was in his early twenties. A man who matched that description was already known to the police: an Irish dockworker named Harry O'Mara. The police found the little boy's body under Tower Bridge, where it had washed up. The postmortem revealed that from the trauma to his little body, he had been physically and sexually abused and strangled. The decomposition showed that he had been in the water for a few days. The assumption was that he had been thrown into the Thames after the abuse. O'Mara was never found, and it was assumed he'd escaped on a boat back to Ireland. I expect you've worked out what your mother was thinking when she saw Harry O'Brien in the village, a man with a strong resemblance to the one she remembered who'd murdered her brother. The Irish accent and red hair, and around the same age as the killer would have been at the time, and finally, the huge coincidence of the name, Harry. And despite the fact it was decades later, she couldn't accept that the two Harrys had nothing to do with each other."

Sarah, by now wooly-mouthed, mumbled something that sounded like 'Mum.' I ignored her.

"The guilt your mother must have been carrying around with her all those years, blaming herself for not looking after her little brother, must have been eating into her. Even so, blaming Harry and taking it out on him was unacceptable. I asked your mum why she thought Harry was the same man. Logically, it made no sense. O'Mara would have been in his sixties by then. Believe it or not, Sarah, your mother blatantly admitted she was aware of that, but she knew Harry was a homosexual, and she was convinced all homosexuals played around with little boys — she felt it was her duty to prevent it from happening again. She acknowledged quite openly that she'd paid those thugs to actually *kill* him, not just beat him up, which they would have succeeded in doing if Mrs. Layton hadn't come running out of the Post Office. Your mother was a psychopath, Sarah, and it was revealing itself in the most terrible way.

"I asked her why she'd said such dreadful things about Harry, and she became defensive, vowing she didn't know what I was talking about. She told me she'd heard stories about him that would make my hair curl. At that point, I'm afraid I completely lost my temper, I couldn't make her understand that homosexuality and paedophilia were completely different phenomena. I grew more angry and started shouting at her, but she just turned away and headed toward the door. I grabbed her arm and swung her around as I pulled the knife out of my overall pocket. She screamed when she saw it. I shouted at her to shut up, but she kept screaming. I grabbed her hair, pulled her head back, and slit her throat. Just like that. By then, I was so enraged with that wicked bitch that I continued stabbing her. I'm afraid I made a bit of a mess in there. I am sorry that you had to be the one to find her."

I looked at Sarah. She was so white her skin seemed nearly pearlescent. Grinning, I tilted her head around to face me.

281

"Are you ok, Sarah, my dear? Don't worry. It *was* quick — she didn't suffer *too much*.

"I'm sure you understand that I needed to be extremely careful in removing all traces of my presence in your mother's house. So, before I left the room, I took off the booties, the coveralls, and the gardening gloves as they were covered in your mother's blood. I rolled them around the knife and put the incriminating evidence in a plastic bag I had ready in my pocket. I'd planned it well, you see. I hope you're impressed. I kept the rubber gloves on. Making a spur-of-the-moment decision, I took your mum's handbag to make it look like a burglary that had gone wrong. In the hall, I grabbed the fake birthday present from the table, slammed the front door shut, got into the car, and backed out onto the road. Unfortunately, the damn postman spotted the car, and assuming it was you, he waved. Unusually for me, I panicked and stuck my foot hard onto the accelerator to get away as fast as possible. It turns out it was the best thing I could have done, as his response when I asked him about it during the trial was that he wasn't one hundred percent sure it was your car, and it certainly wasn't your style of driving, and so he couldn't swear, under oath, it was you. It's ironic when you think about it, as he looked at me when he said that. Anyway, his answer gave the jury that small degree of doubt that you had been at your mum's house any earlier than you said."

I leaned back onto my elbows as a sense of pride for my last successful court case swept over me. Then I sat back upright.

"Now, back to Harry. I hope you're still paying attention. Did you know that your mother was actually pleased when she found out that he was in the Admiral Duncan the night that bomb went off? And then, all those weeks later, when Harry couldn't face the future any longer because of his hideous injuries, Aunty Bridget told me your mother was positively delighted when she heard he'd killed himself. Apparently, your mother was in the hairdressers when she heard the news, and her only comment to Aunty Bridget was, 'Good riddance, filthy pervert. You know he molested little boys, don't you?'

"Aunty Bridget was beside herself. She told her that she was no longer welcome in the salon. So now you know why I wanted that bitch dead. Of course, I could have saved myself a lot of trouble had I known she was dying of lung cancer, but still, it gave me a lot of satisfaction doing it."

Sarah, struggling to remain conscious, threw up a thick brown sludge onto her shoulder. It ran slowly down onto her jumper.

I'd not planned on her vomiting. I needed her to drink more coffee in case she recovered enough to find her phone and ring for help, although I seriously doubted she'd have the strength. Anyway, it would probably be best to let her sit for a moment or two before suggesting she have another sip of her coffee. In the meantime, I needed to find her phone. The handbag was lying on the ground on the other side of her.

"Would you like me to pass you your handbag so you can find a tissue?" I suggested, ignoring Sarah's obvious incapacitation and her pathetic, gurgled answer. I leaned across, trying to ignore the vomit, and picked up the bag. She tried to stop me, but in her drugged state, she wasn't strong enough, and I brushed her feeble hand away. Opening the bag, I found a tissue, which I tossed casually into her lap, and rummaging around a little deeper, I eventually found her phone.

"I'll take your mobile, shall I? You won't be needing it, will you?" I callously joked.

"While we are on the subject of your parents, just one more little anecdote about your lovely family, and this time it concerns your father. I'm sure you remember me staying with you over the summer holidays when we were at uni that first year. You and your mother had gone out one evening, and I had dinner at Aunty Bridget's house. I walked back to your house and let myself in. Your father appeared and asked how my evening was and invited me to join him in the garden for a glass of something. It was the most he'd ever spoken to me, and so, not wanting to appear rude, I agreed. I think I had a gin and something. I can't remember what we talked about, but it doesn't matter. After the second drink, I excused myself and went to bed feeling a little woozy. I had changed into my nightdress and was curled up under the covers when the bedroom door opened, and your father came in."

Sarah was writhing around, trying to stand up, but she didn't have the strength. She kept shaking her head.

"You need to hear this, Sarah. Your dad may not have paid much attention to you, but let me tell you, he certainly paid a lot of attention to me. Foreplay he was not good at. I almost felt sorry for your poor mother. He tried to kiss me, but I turned my head away; I didn't want his tongue down my throat. Then he pushed back the bedclothes, and when he pulled up my nighty, I started screaming and crying, but your lovely daddy stuck his disgusting dick inside me. Grunting, he rammed himself as far into me as he could over and over, and eventually, he came. Having satisfied himself, he stood up, zipped up his trousers, and left the room. He never spoke to me again. I'm sure you heard all the rumours at the time that I was pregnant and had an abortion, and yes, it was true, and now you know who it was and how it happened — your dad raped me. And by the way, when I heard he'd died in a car accident, I have to admit, I was thrilled; he deserved it, the rotten bastard. I just hope his death was slow and incredibly painful, and he rots in hell."

Sarah gradually slid sideways and now sprawled inelegantly among the bluebells on the forest floor, vomit crusting on the shoulder of her pretty sweater. Tears rolled down her face as she twitched in agony from the poison coursing through her bloodstream.

"So, now, my dear Sarah, as this is a day of confessions, would you like to know how I murdered your beloved husband?"

Chapter 14

"A couple of months after your mother died, I came back to the village for my aunt's funeral, and I stayed at the Falconers. If you remember, we had lunch together at the café by the shop. Anyway, the evening I arrived, I was walking out of the hotel restaurant, having just finished dinner, when I spotted Richard in the bar. I wandered over to him, and we started chatting. It started out innocently enough. We reminisced about the old days when we were children and lived next door to each other. Did he tell you he'd seen me? I assume he did. He bought me a glass of wine. I told him I couldn't believe he'd married you, 'batting out of your league, weren't you,' I remember saying, teasing him. When I asked him how he got on with your mother, he'd laughed, he'd said she was okay with him, but there were times when he could have throttled her for how she treated you. Wasn't that sweet?

"We talked about the other children from the old days. Richard said how lucky Kevin was to have married Colleen. He said how pretty she was, quite a catch. He said he didn't know her very well, which we now know was bullshit — he knew her extremely well — quite intimately, in fact, didn't he? A bit of a lad, your husband, huh? He never mentioned the baby, so I still don't know if he knew he was the father."

Sarah made a choking sound. I wondered if I was upsetting her by talking about Richard and Colleen. Not that I cared. I suggested Sarah have a last sip of her coffee, but she shook her head. Unfortunately for Sarah, I couldn't take 'no' for an answer as I needed her to drink all the coffee for the poison to be effective. I brought the cup up to Sarah's blue-tinged lips, pushed her head back, and poured it into her mouth; most of it went in, and the rest went down her chin and dribbled onto her pretty sweater. Sarah started coughing and spluttering, the coffee spraying everywhere, some onto my arm, which I brushed off in disgust. I stood up and put the lid back on the now-empty thermos, then tossed it on the ground next to Sarah. I would have plenty of time to tidy things up once I'd finished recounting my past deeds with my latest victim.

"Come on, Sarah, you need to stay awake. Pay attention, dear. I want you to hear the rest of my story so you understand that none of this was my fault. Your deranged mother arranged to have my dear Harry attacked by those thugs she'd hired. And you must agree that she deserved what was coming to her for having that poor little girl killed. As for Richard, that was his own fault. You don't threaten me and assume I won't exact some sort of revenge.

"Let me go back to that evening in the bar. It was getting late. I was tired from the journey, and I'd had a few drinks. I told Richard I was going upstairs to bed. Your lovely husband decided otherwise. He offered to buy me a nightcap, which I refused. The last thing I needed was another drink, but then he put his hand on my knee and said, 'I know what you need. You haven't had a man for so long, let me remind you how good it feels.' He slid his hand further up my leg and under my skirt. I tried to push his hand away, but as you know, he was very strong. How did you put up with that creep for so many years?"

287

I was interrupted by a sob and realized Sarah was crying, not silent tears from the pain of the poison but hysterical sobs. Looking down, I smiled at Sarah's blotchy face; her mascara had run, and tears were streaming down her cheeks, mixing with the coffee that had dribbled out of her mouth and the snot oozing out of her nose. Sarah tried to lift the tissue up to her face to wipe her eyes but couldn't summon the strength. I saw no sense in trying to clean her up now, and besides, I needed to finish my confession while she was still conscious enough to witness it.

"I pushed Richard's hand off my leg and called the bartender over to ask for the bill, and at the same time, I stood up. Richard stood up, too. I asked him where he thought he was going. 'With you, sweetheart, we're going upstairs.' Oh no, we're not. Fortunately, the bartender realized what was happening and came out from behind the bar and told Richard in no uncertain terms that he was drunk and to get the hell out of his bar or he'd ring the police. After thanking him, I hurried up the stairs and back to my room."

"No, he's not like that." Sarah garbled, drooling as she attempted to deny her husband's failings.

"Well, bless your heart, Sarah. I hate to disappoint you, but actually, yes, he was like that. In fact, the following morning, when I was leaving the pub to walk to the café and meet you for lunch, I spotted Richard heading toward me over the bridge. I pretended I hadn't seen him and started walking in the opposite direction as fast as possible. He was the last person I wanted to see. But he was determined to catch me up. 'Trying to avoid me, are you?' he shouted. 'Well, bad luck. Next time, you won't be so lucky. There won't be a bartender around to protect you. You owe me, sweetheart, so you might as well give in. You know you want to, really.' I said nothing and kept walking. 'Your little secret is about to become public unless you give me what I want.'

"I admit I was curious to find out what your Richard thought he knew, so I turned around and asked him. He said he knew about me and your father. As you can imagine, I was horrified. I hadn't even told Harry and Colleen who it was, but they must have guessed — it was fairly obvious. But I was surprised they had told somebody else. Anyway, he was adamant he knew I'd had an affair with your father when I was at uni that had ended with me having an abortion. I told him not to be ridiculous, but he continued on that he remembered me coming to stay with you during the summer break. He'd heard about the abortion from Colleen — part of their illicit pillow talk, I assume. What I don't understand is if everyone else in the village knew about your dad and me, how come you didn't? Or did you?"

Sarah let out an animalistic grunt that, under better circumstances, would probably have been a sob.

"As you can imagine, I needed to deal with this, and the only thing I could think of was to kill Richard, and that's why I arranged to meet you both for lunch in London. I honestly didn't care whether I saw either of you again, but I needed you to think of us as friends so you wouldn't suspect anything. I agreed to meet Richard at a hotel later that day, implying I was ready to submit to his sexual demands. He planned on inventing some excuse for not going back to Nicola's house with you — maybe a story about having a beer with an old friend, whatever. The thing was, I needed to convince him he would be meeting me so he could fuck me, which he'd told me he'd wanted to do since we were teenagers. Did you know he only married you because he couldn't have me? I know; I was as surprised as you must be, knowing you were actually second best. I guess if you are council house trash like Richard and I both were, then like attracts like. Anyway, I wasn't too concerned about agreeing to this so-called date as I was sure Richard would be dead by then. It's such a shame it never happened. I would have been quite interested to experience his love-making skills. I was looking forward to a few hours of tawdry passion with the love of *your* life," NOT!

"So now you know everything. Your dear Richard was trying to blackmail me into having sex with him. He threatened to ruin my career even though I told him he was talking rubbish. But truth be told, he knew enough to have made it difficult for me, and I couldn't risk it coming out and ruining my reputation. I'm sure you understand why you're the only person who could appreciate why I did what I did."

Thank goodness the prosecution never found out about any of this. Had Hywell known that Sarah's dad had raped me and Richard was blackmailing me over it, I certainly wouldn't have been allowed anywhere near the trial except as a witness.

"Hopefully, you're beginning to understand my motives. I don't let anyone take advantage of me or the people I care about. I will exact my revenge at some point, even if it is years later. Remember the old adage, 'Revenge is a dish best served cold.'

"Now, I expect you would love to know how I killed your sweet husband. We had that lovely lunch, if you remember, at that cute little café in St Christopher's Place. I made the reservation for a table outside quite deliberately. I had a delightful meal of scallops while you and Richard had halibut fish and chips. I had my usual glass of Sauvignon Blanc, and if memory serves, you had the same. Richard, I know, had a lager."

"How?" she struggled to ask, sounding as if her tongue was swollen to twice its normal size.

"Well, it was pretty easy, really. I picked that restaurant for its location. I don't know if you recall, but I told you both that you needed to see the public toilet in the middle of the square because it had won awards for being the most beautiful in the city. We ordered our meals, and when the waiter brought us our drinks, I suggested you both walk over to look at the lovely loo. Meanwhile, the food arrived, and I sprinkled the poison onto Richard's fish and chips. Minutes later, you both returned to your seats, and the first thing Richard did was generously sprinkle salt over his chips. Actually, Thallium Sulphate is tasteless, so even if Richard hadn't seasoned his food, he wouldn't have tasted it. We parted company after a very pleasant couple of hours, and at that point, all was well, just as I'd planned. When you rang me about an hour after you'd arrived back at your daughter's house to ask if I was feeling ill because Richard was in a bad way, I feigned surprise and told you that I felt fine. All I could think to say was maybe it was food poisoning, and I'm sure he'd feel better later. But of course, he didn't, did he — he died — poor soul.

"As I knew it would, the postmortem revealed Richard was poisoned with Thallium Sulphate. I really am so sorry you were initially blamed for his death — I hadn't planned on you being arrested for *either* of the murders. It didn't occur to me that you'd be suspected of killing your own mother and husband. Nobody was more shocked than me when Nicola rang to ask for my help. But at least you now know who the murderer really was. In case you are wondering how I managed to acquire the Thallium Sulphate, it was simple. It was at a trial I worked on years ago. I defended a young woman accused of poisoning her boyfriend after discovering he was seeing someone else. Thallium Sulphate was the poison she used. In the pretense of doing some research for the trial, I kept some and saved it for just such an occasion. In fact, I put some in your coffee at home before we left this morning and added more to your flask of coffee just to make sure you'd taken enough. Now, just relax. It will all be over soon. And, just to show you what a nice person I am, I'll stay with you for as long as it takes. Much as I despise you and your family, I don't want you to die alone."

Chapter 15

It could be maybe another hour until the poison worked its fatal magic, so I poured myself another cup of coffee and helped myself to another shortbread biscuit.

As I drank my coffee, I thought about the old Sunday school in Lower Naughton and decided to kill some time during Sarah's last painful moments. I figured Sarah might as well hear my final confession, not that I was expecting any absolution.

"Do you remember when we lived in Lower Naughton, we used to go to Sunday school at the church? The teacher was a very strict old lady, but once a year, she'd arrive with a basket filled with bonfire toffee. It was the most delicious toffee I'd ever tasted; very dark and very sticky, almost a burnt flavour and rock hard."

There was a groan of agony from Sarah — I wondered if she remembered the taste of that bonfire toffee, or maybe she was letting me know she was still clinging on by a thread! Maybe she was in severe pain. Whatever, I didn't really care as I carried on with my story:

"Anyway, every Palm Sunday, that basket would be full of palm crosses supposedly sent from the Holy Land. It was certainly possible as there weren't many palm trees in England. I still have mine, as I'd put it into an old bible belonging to my grandmother. I do hope I'm not boring you, Sarah. Anyway, one Palm Sunday had particular meaning for me as it fell on my birthday. I was seven, I think, and I wore my new grey suit with its pleated skirt that Mum bought me for the occasion. I was so proud of that suit. Mum had bought it new from a shop, not second-hand from a jumble sale. Every year on Palm Sunday, the Sunday school children were invited to join in the church service and were expected to hand out palm leaves to the members of the congregation. I was so proud standing in the procession in my new suit, thinking how pretty I looked. We walked down the aisles handing out the palm leaves, everyone smiling at us and thanking us. Do you remember? Ugh, what a bunch of superstitious idiots. Anyway, your Richard stood next to me and, like a typical boy, kept pinching my arm, trying to make me shout. I managed to stay quiet until we were outside, and then I kicked him in the shins as hard as possible. He yelled and told the teacher I'd hurt him, big baby. I was told off, of course, which was unfair as he'd started it, but it was okay. It was worth it."

Sarah writhed about in apparent agony, but I ignored her and continued.

"I remember leaving the church by myself, walking past the Falconer's Arms and across the bridge. Richard came racing past me and shoved me into the side of the bridge, scraping my leg and making it bleed. It was his payback for the shin-kicking I'd given him. As I ambled alongside the brook, Alan, the blacksmith's son, came running across the road from the forge, shouting my name. I waited for him to catch me up, and we walked along together. He asked if I knew my leg was bleeding and offered to wipe the blood off. When he pulled out the filthiest handkerchief I'd ever seen, I quickly told him I was fine, that my mum would clean my leg and

294

put a bandage on when I got home. He then opened up the handkerchief and showed me a little pile of brown stuff. He'd stolen some of his dad's pipe tobacco. He boasted that he often went down to the wood by himself, sat by the brook, and had a smoke. He would roll a cigarette with cigarette papers and matches he had stashed in a hole in a tree trunk. He asked me if I'd ever smoked a cigarette, and I said, 'Absolutely not. It's disgusting.' He could tell I wasn't too impressed, so he re-wrapped the handkerchief and shoved it back into his pocket.

"Then he asked me if I knew about the baby rabbits in the woods and if I'd like to see some. Of course I said I would, but I didn't have much time. I needed to be home for my dinner, or I'd be in trouble. He told me not to worry; it would only take five minutes. We walked into the woods, me being very careful where I walked so as not to dirty my white shoes and socks. We kept walking and walking deeper into the wood and further away from the road, getting closer and closer to the brook. Starting to panic, I asked him how much longer it would be and suggested that maybe I could see the rabbits another day. I knew my mum would be annoyed as the dinner would be ready, and it would be my fault if it was spoiled, not that there was much to spoil with my mum's cooking — it was pretty awful. Are you keeping up with me, Sarah?

I glanced at Sarah's grotesquely sprawled body, pleased to see she was still breathing. I wanted her to hear the end of the story.

"A hollowed-out log was on the ground at Alan's feet, so I assumed the rabbits were in there. He told me to kneel down so I could see them properly. As I did, he pushed me over onto my back amid the leaves and ferns and straddled me. I started to scream, and he yelled at me to stop. He pulled the dirty handkerchief with the tobacco out of his pocket and tried to shove it into my mouth, but I bit his hand as hard as I could. Then he put his hand up my skirt. I remember wriggling, trying to move away from him, but he had me pinned down. Flailing about, my hand felt something hard, and realizing it was a rock, I grabbed it and, as hard as I could, smashed it into the side of his head. He fell backward, and I managed to push him off. I spat the handkerchief out of my mouth and stood up, then turned to look at him. He wasn't moving. Blood was slowly oozing down his face and over his eye while he lay there. I just stared at him. It was pretty gruesome, but I was mesmerized. I remember wondering if he was dead. I was seven. I'd never seen a dead body before, but instead of being frightened, I felt the opposite; I was completely calm. In fact, it was quite exhilarating looking at his body, seeing all that blood. To think, I'd done that. My heart was pounding, but for the first time in my short life, I was totally in control of a situation. But what to do with Alan's body? I'd seen lots of cowboy programs on the television; you remember them: the Lone Ranger, Laramie, and Bonanza. They would always dig a hole to bury a dead body and then cover it with rocks. Well, there was no way I'd be able to dig a hole big enough, and there weren't enough rocks about to cover him up. Then I had an idea; the brook was just there. Maybe I could drag him across the ground to the bank and push him in. I naively thought he would just float away downstream to the sea and be gone — no one would ever know what had happened to him. So that's what I did. I grabbed him underneath his arms and started to tug with all the strength my little body had, and eventually, I maneuvered him over to the edge of the water and rolled him in. There was an almighty splash as he landed among the reeds, facing me with his eyes open. It should have been frightening for a seven-year-old girl, but on the contrary, I was fascinated. I sat down beside him with my legs crossed and just stared at him, spellbound. Then I calmly leaned forward and pushed his head under the water, stood up, and walked away.

"But, just before I reached the edge of the wood, I heard what sounded like a twig cracking as if someone had stood on it. What if someone had seen me or heard the splash? I began to panic and started running. At one point, I tripped on a branch and was convinced I could hear something behind me. I was terrified someone was following me. I scrambled back to my feet and started running again, hoping whoever it was wouldn't catch me. Eventually, I reached the road and realized I was at the back of the farm. I saw a hole in the hedge and wriggled through, my little suit jacket catching on the brambles. By that point, I didn't care. I just wanted to go home. All the calm and control I'd felt earlier was gone. I was crying; I was so frightened. I started running across the fields, and out of nowhere appeared that bloody farmer with his shotgun aimed straight at me. He yelled at me to get off his property as he raised the gun into the air and fired two shots. I kept running, sobbing with relief when I reached the farmyard. I ran over the cobbles, slipping on them as they were damp, and my little white shoes had no grip and on through the gate, which, thank goodness, was open as the farmer still hadn't had it fixed. I ran across the road, gasping for breath, down the hill to our house, through our front gate, slamming it shut after me, my heart pounding as I ran up our garden path and in the back door. I was safe.

"It's a strange feeling when you kill someone. I always assumed that you'd feel sad, frightened, or disgusted, and maybe it would even make you physically sick — but I felt none of those things; perhaps you need a conscience. I have now killed four people. You will make five. There's a strange emotion you feel, somewhere between the pleasure of the physical act and the fascination with the body afterward, especially the eyes when they look at you just before death, registering confusion, surprise, or, in the case of your mother, pure hatred. Of course, the way I killed Richard deprived me of that pleasure, but just knowing he'd suffered compensated for that. Besides, all my victims richly deserved what happened to them, don't you think, Sarah?"

Sarah moaned weakly. I was up and pacing now, basking in the glory of my successes, mercilessly crushing the tiny purple flowers under my feet. I suppose it's how I destroyed anything or anyone who stood in my way.

"Oh, and in case you're wondering, yes, I did kill Chris. When we were first together, life was so much fun. He was easy to fall in love with, tall and handsome, and wealthy; what was not to love? I couldn't believe he had fallen in love with me. Ok, we did share a history of growing up in the same village and going to the same school, and even though I lived in a council house with no running hot water, and he lived in a mansion, we still shared a love of the arts, going to the theater and museums. Life was perfect. But then he married me, and that's when it all went to hell. His attitude toward me changed. He felt he owned me, probably a bit like how your father felt when he married your mother, taking her out of the slums and making her his trophy wife. She and I were the same. We now owed these men everything. Whatever they wanted, we were expected to provide, and in my case, it was a child. Chris began making demands on my life — how I was to give up work and produce a baby — well, think again, matey. No man was going to tell me what to do. I loved my work, and no baby was going to mess with my plans. When I told him I was not willing to give up my career, I was given an ultimatum: either produce a baby, or he would divorce me. I couldn't let that happen. A divorce when I was just starting, especially from a member of a family whose patriarch was a member of the House of Lords, would destroy my reputation. Oh yes, I could become a divorce lawyer, but that was not in my plans. I wanted to be a criminal barrister, a QC. I wanted everyone to admire me, to look up to me, to be intimidated by me. I didn't want a baby getting in my way, and so my only option was to get rid of him. I simply arranged for him to have a tragic accident.

"It was the easiest of murders. When Chris asked me if I'd like to go on a trip to the Amazon, he gave me the perfect opportunity to kill him. I simply injected cyanide into the granola bar I put into his backpack, and then once he'd died, I had him cremated, no post-mortem, no review of how he died. I just let everyone assume he'd accidentally ingested something poisonous on his exploration in the Amazon rainforest. Chris was always tasting things, claiming he knew

299

what everything was. Nobody questioned how he'd died when I returned home alone. The poor grieving widow. Haha!

"Now, your father's death was an accident, nothing to do with me, although he did deserve to die. I would have derived a lot of pleasure arranging for that to happen, and I had even started to think of the different ways I could bring Mr. Weston to a painful end, but fate took a hand there. Bloody drunk driver, taking away my opportunity for revenge.

"As for you, well, you are my confidante, my muse, and my priest. If I still believed in all that crap from the church, this would be my confessional. Forgive me, Sarah, for I have sinned!" I started laughing again, "I was dying to tell my story to someone. And I chose you — posh, pretty, pathetic Sarah. Watching you at the trial, I knew you would be the perfect choice. How I used to admire you in school, and now look at you. Covered in your own sick, crying, and blubbering. What a pathetic sight."

Reaching across, I put my fingers up to Sarah's neck to feel her pulse. It was very weak. It wouldn't be too long, so now was as good a time as any to clear away any evidence that I'd been there with her. Picking up Sarah's mobile with my handkerchief, I opened it and took out the battery and the SIM card. I threw them and the phone as far as I could into the wood. Taking a spare set of car keys from my pocket, I slipped them into the pocket of Sarah's jacket. If questioned by anyone, I intended to tell them that Sarah had seemed a bit upset about her husband and asked if she could borrow my car to go for a drive. Not realizing how disturbed she was, I readily agreed.

From the backpack, I retrieved the suicide note I'd composed and laid it in Sarah's lap. I had addressed the envelope to Nicola Smith and Jennifer Forbes but had not put an address. Not having children of my own and not being particularly empathetic, I'd had to dig deep to imagine how someone would feel if they were suicidal. I tried my best in the letter to explain what I thought would have been Sarah's reasons for not wanting to be in this world anymore:

My dearest Nicola and Jennifer,

First, let me say how deeply sorry I am to be leaving you both like this. You mean the world to me, but I am finding it so hard to keep going by myself. I know you will be fine. You have your own families now, loving husbands, and the most amazing children I would have loved to have watched grow up.

You have probably realized that your dad and I were having some serious problems. It wasn't just the drinking. Even before the trial, I'd suspected he'd had an affair, although I didn't know who the woman was. I was shocked when I learned it was Colleen, and he had fathered a child with her. I was absolutely heartbroken. Your father truly was the love of my life, but clearly, he did not feel the same about me.

I thought once the trial was over, I would feel nothing but relief. Everyone would know I was innocent, and I could move on with my life. But it didn't work out like that. I can tell from the way the people in the village are avoiding me; they still suspect I killed your dad and grandma. After what he did to me, it would have been difficult to convince them otherwise. Although there were times I wished your dad was dead, please, believe me, I did not kill him.

301

I love you both so much and wish only the best for you.

Much love

Mum

I had typed the letter on an old typewriter I'd picked up at a charity shop in Farnborough and subsequently dumped in a skip in Brighton. Copying Sarah's handwriting was easy for the simple three-word closing, as I had numerous documents with her signature from the trial. After practicing multiple times, I'd signed the letter with a blue ballpoint pen similar to the one I'd seen Sarah using.

After wiping the flask that had contained the coffee with a disinfectant wipe to erase any of my fingerprints, I put it in Sarah's hand so that it only had her prints on it, then put it on the floor beside her as if she'd dropped it. She had drunk all the coffee I had laced with Thallium Sulphate, the same poison I'd used when I murdered Richard. A nice little touch, I thought. It added an air of doubt that maybe Sarah had actually murdered her husband. I put the other flask I'd been drinking from into my backpack, along with my beige anorak.

I pulled the hood of the blue jacket up over my head and strapped on the backpack.

Bending down, I felt once more for a pulse and found none.

Murder — an act quite easy!

I took a last look around to make sure I hadn't left anything incriminating and that no one had seen me, stood up, and walked out of the woods towards the car park. Checking no one was about, I hurried to my car, unlocked the boot, and took out my fold-up bicycle. I slammed the boot shut and, after unfolding the bike, pushed it across the cobbled stones of the car park and pedalled out onto the road towards Reigate.

THE END

Epilogue

Hywell and Camille pulled into the driveway of Margaret German-Brown's imposing Victorian house on a particularly dark and dismal English day. Camille hadn't noticed the eeriness of the place when she had visited before, but under the gray canopy, the house appeared to loom over them as they approached. They walked up to the policeman standing in front of the door and told him they had been called, as Camille had been identified as Margaret's executor. The policeman had been expecting them and introduced himself as Sergeant Whitbread, then pushed open the front door, letting them into the house.

Having made a promise to care for Rocco in the event something happened to Margaret, Hywell, and Camille went looking for the cat. They walked down the dark hallway and up the creaking stairs. Turning right at the top, they walked into the master bedroom, where a pair of blue-striped pajamas were folded neatly on the bottom of the skillfully made bed with its hospital corners. Margaret's cat, Rocco, was curled up on one of the pillows. As they entered, Rocco stretched and arched his back and hopped casually off the bed. He slinked past Camille and rubbed himself against Hywell's leg as he left the room. Camille spotted a picture frame on the bedside table. The photo was of a bride and groom, and another person she assumed was the best man. The three of them were grinning from ear to ear.

"Hywell, look at this. It must be Margaret on her wedding day. She promised to show this to me the last time I saw her," Camille said as she picked up the photo. Turning it over, she read the handwritten note.

"'Mr. & Mrs. Christopher German-Brown and Harry O'Brien, the best bridesmaid a girl could wish for. On the happiest day of my life, 16/06/1980.'Hywell peered at the photo over Camille's shoulder.

"That wouldn't have been long before I met her." He said as he turned and walked out of the bedroom.

The next room appeared to be the guest bedroom. Spotting a suitcase in the corner, Camille put it onto the bed and opened it. The only items inside were a tiny wooden rocking chair and a sapphire earring.

"I wonder where these come from?" said Camille as she picked up the items.

"No idea, my dear, and I guess we'll never know."

The final room at the end of the hall was Margaret's study. Camille approached the desk and spotted a manuscript lying open to the last page. Leaning down to read what was on it, she suddenly gasped so loudly that Hywell jumped back into a bookshelf. The cat, who had been observing them from one of the shelves, screeched at Hywell's disturbance and ran out of the room. Rubbing the back of his head, Hywell asked: "What, what is it? What have you found?"

He walked over to Camille, her face pale and her mouth wide open, and looked down at what she was reading:

'Reaching across, I put my fingers up to Sarah's neck to feel her pulse. It was very weak. It wasn't going to be too long. I decided it was as good a time as any to clear away any evidence that I had been there with her.'

"Good heavens, Camille, you don't think Sarah is actually dead, and Margaret killed her? We need to read the whole thing. I bet it explains everything."

In his best courtroom voice, Hywell read out the rest of the last page:

"Bending down, I felt once more for a pulse and found none.

Murder — an act quite easy.

"I took a last look around to make sure I hadn't left anything incriminating and that no one had seen me, stood up, and walked out of the woods towards the carpark. Checking that no one was about, I hurried to my car, unlocked the boot, and took out my fold-up bicycle. I slammed the boot shut and, after unfolding the bike, pushed it across the cobbled stones of the carpark and pedalled out onto the road towards Reigate.

THE END"

Hywell looked at Camille, "Yet the ultimate irony of her closing paragraph is that despite all Margaret's intricate planning and apparent foresight, what she should have written was:

306

'I pedalled out onto the road towards Reigate, but unfortunately, I didn't see the black BMW SUV come around the corner.

THE END"

Acknowledgments

Many years ago, a revered old friend suggested I write a novel. He was convinced I had a story in me somewhere. And now I have brought his kind words to fruition in this tale. So, thank you, Craig Murray.

Over the course of those pandemic years, I wrote and re-wrote and re-wrote some more, passing each iteration to my sister Gill in New Zealand, who enthusiastically read each version, giving me enough positive feedback that I continued sitting at my laptop typing away.

Knowing absolutely nothing about the British legal system and how a trial is conducted, I am so grateful to another friend, Andrew James. His knowledge and expertise were invaluable.

I must fondly mention Dan Staley, who had the unenviable task of being brutally honest in recommending a significant edit that, although it appeared quite ruthless when he first suggested it, was essential in making the story tighter.

Another dear friend, Karin Gist, I am so grateful to. Her insights and experience in the art of storytelling were an immeasurable blessing when it came to constructing the personalities of each of my characters.

One of the most important people in my life and my chief collaborator on my intrepid journey into the hitherto unknown world of story writing was my daughter, Sophie

Ludlow. Although she is now living and working in Australia, she still found the time to spend many hours editing and suggesting beautiful prose where there was previously none.

And finally, there is John, my husband of so many glorious years, who has spent almost as many hours as me, reading, re-reading, mopping up my tears of frustration, making me cups of tea, and encouraging me to keep going until the book was completed.

I owe you all a huge debt of gratitude for your encouragement and expertise. Thank you all so very, very much.

About the Author

An Act Quite Easy is Isabel Herridge's first novel. During the Covid lockdown, she finally decided to put pen to paper and write a story that for several years had been festering in the back of her mind. And so, with much encouragement from her husband, this is the result.

Brought up in a small village in England Isabel now lives in California with her husband John and their cat Boheme.

Made in the USA
Las Vegas, NV
29 January 2024

85054256R00184